Small Hours

Small Hours

Jennifer Kitses

GRAND CENTRAL
PUBLISHING

New York   Boston

Copyright © 2017 by Jennifer Kitses
Cover design by Brian Lemus
Cover copyright © 2017 by Hachette Book Group, Inc.

Grand Central Publishing
Hachette Book Group
1290 Avenue of the Americas
New York, NY 10104
grandcentralpublishing.com
twitter.com/grandcentralpub

First Edition: June 2017

Grand Central Publishing is a division of Hachette Book Group, Inc. The Grand Central Publishing name and logo is a trademark of Hachette Book Group, Inc.

The publisher is not responsible for websites (or their content) that are not owned by the publisher.

Library of Congress Cataloging-in-Publication Data

Names: Kitses, Jennifer, author.
Title: Small hours / Jennifer Kitses.
Description: New York : Grand Central Publishing, 2017.
Identifiers: LCCN 2017002992| ISBN 9781455598526 (hardback) | ISBN 9781478915843 (audio download) | ISBN 9781455598496 (ebook)
Subjects: LCSH: Spouses—Fiction. | Family secrets—Fiction. | Domestic fiction. | BISAC: FICTION / Family Life. | FICTION / Contemporary Women. | FICTION / Literary.
Classification: LCC PS3611.I8795 S63 2017 | DDC 813/.6—dc23
LC record available at https://lccn.loc.gov/2017002992

Printed in the United States of America

LSC-C

10 9 8 7 6 5 4 3 2 1

For John

Small Hours

CHAPTER ONE

TOM, 6:20 A.M.

They wanted to go to the playground. No, Tom told them, it was way too early for that, and besides, he wanted to show them something beautiful. Something they'd never seen before.

Tom's daughters, standing beside him on the porch, gave him skeptical looks.

Sophie had been up since five. She found him on the couch, where he'd spent the night staring at the TV until he'd finally—seconds ago, it seemed—drifted off to sleep. Jolting awake, Tom had opened his eyes as her soft, damp hand landed on his face.

"Daddy," she'd said. "Wake up and play."

Minutes later, Ilona was running down the stairs, asking for paper and overturning a basket of crayons. The girls were three years old and had been up before dawn every day that week. Today, Tom decided, he would make the best of it. While Helen got a chance to recover from her late nights and deadlines, he would take their daughters out for a little adventure. So he made a quick breakfast. Got the girls dressed, crouching down to squeeze twin sets of feet into miniature sneakers. Bundled them in an extra layer, in case there was a breeze coming off the water. Before ushering them out the door, he left a note on the kitchen table: *Taking the girls out! Back soon.*

And they were off. Next door, at Karl and Jackie's house, a purple light glowed in the basement, where Jackie's son, Nick, was probably listening to music and getting stoned. (*Lucky Nick.*) In the driveway, illuminated by a security light, was the old Chevy Nova that belonged to Nick's girlfriend. There was a crumpled takeout bag in the passenger seat and a pack of cigarettes on the dashboard.

Tom had once had a '73 Nova. He'd loved that car.

Of course, that was a lifetime ago. He unlocked the second-hand Ford Taurus wagon he'd bought when they moved out here. The girls climbed into the back. As he buckled them into their car seats, he gave them his brightest, most enthusiastic smile.

"Ready?" he said. "We'd better hurry! We don't want to miss it."

His daughters stared out at the dark sky and said nothing.

There would be just enough time for them to get to the creek before they'd have to turn around and come back, so Tom could drop off the girls at home and then catch the 7:13 train to the city. He had to be in the newsroom by nine o'clock and not a minute later.

But he wasn't going to let that bother him right now. He was glad they were doing this, that he'd motivated himself. When he and Helen had first left the city for Devon, it was the kind of idea they'd talked about all the time. But the special excursions usually got pushed off, as the hours raced by in a blur. Not today. Today he would claim some freedom from all the ticking clocks. Before he dealt with his commute and work—and the anxieties that snuck up on him late at night, his thoughts spiraling until he was too exhausted to go up to the bedroom—he would enjoy this time with his daughters.

Sophie and Ilona chattered away as he started to drive, finally struck by the novelty of being out so early. Up ahead, they could see headlights from commuters heading for the train station. After the morning rush, Tom knew, that avenue would be almost deserted.

Out of habit, as he curved down Crescent Street, he scanned the yard of a rambling old mansion. The house's former owner, a filmmaker desperate to return to Brooklyn, had struggled to find a buyer before she sold it that May at "a huge fucking loss." Four months later, the couple who'd bought it still hadn't moved in and were said to be having second thoughts. A hot summer with lots of rain had left the once-manicured yard overgrown and thick with weeds. Some of the neighbors complained, but Tom couldn't help admiring the sunflowers that stood fourteen feet high, their bobble heads swaying, and the rosebushes that had grown to the size of small trees.

In the chaos of the filmmaker's move, her little white dog, Cotton Ball, had run off, and Tom had offered to keep an eye out for it. Even after all these months, he refused to believe it was hopeless.

Ilona shrieked in the back. A stray cat was emerging from the tall grass.

"Daddy!" she said. "That cat has four legs!"

Tom was sure she'd seen four-legged cats before, but for the first time, she'd recognized the difference from their own, a rescue from a vet in Queens that had come with the name Pussyface.

"It's okay," Tom said. "Most cats have four legs." And so did Pussyface, until she fell from their bathroom window days after the move. That weekend, Helen had replaced every screen, even the ones that weren't old and warped.

The drive to the river was lined with ranch houses and modest colonials like their own, until it shifted, at Main Street, into a mile-long strip of nineteenth-century storefronts. At first, Tom hadn't been all that excited about Devon. Helen, nostalgic for the tree-lined streets and quiet roads of her hometown outside of Boston, had brought all the enthusiasm. There was the river to the west, the creek to the east. "You can see mountains," she'd said. And though parts of the town had a blighted, postindustrial look, she'd encouraged him to see the beauty of the old structures, like the graceful but dilapidated yellow-brick building that he and the girls were passing now.

He stopped at a light. From the backseat came cries of excitement. On the other side of Main Street, between a gas station and the Key Food, a chain-link fence enclosed a small, half-finished playground.

"There!" Ilona twisted in her seat, trying to get a better look. "Go to the playground!"

Sophie didn't seem so sure. "That where we going?"

They'd never taken the girls to that playground. Helen preferred the one behind the middle school, where there were trees and sprinklers. Though no matter where they took the girls, they often felt out of place, even after two years here. He was forty-two and Helen had just turned forty. In Devon, unlike their old Queens neighborhood, he seldom saw middle-aged men wearing baby carriers or weathered moms chasing after toddlers, calling out for little Caspar and Django, Theo and Cleo, Eero and Oona and Esmé. Here in Devon were the names of Tom's childhood. His daughters' preschool had a Mike, a Dave, and two Jessicas. He'd even made the acquaintance of a little Tom and a little Helen.

Ilona gave a soft kick to the back of his seat.

"Playground now!"

He looked at the playground. It was just a fenced-in lot with a jungle gym and a pair of benches separated by a thin-limbed tree. Not a bad place, really, though it looked so abandoned it was hard to imagine kids playing there.

A woman came out from the gas station next to the playground. She began sweeping the sidewalk, though the breeze was working against her. Her broom made soft brushing sounds against the pavement. At this hour, on this dark stretch of Main, there were no other sounds.

Even on a weekday afternoon, Devon was a town where you could walk down a street and hear only your own footsteps. Sometimes, Helen told him, she saw the same few faces all day long, at the bakery and market and preschool. That didn't bother her. But nothing in Tom's childhood, in a working-class neighborhood in Philadelphia, had prepared him for streets so achingly quiet that he would brace himself, on alert for a scraping of shoes or a squealing of tires to break the silence.

Two years ago, they'd celebrated their good luck. Here was a place with potential, where they could afford a home. *"That should have told us something,"* Helen said later. In the Hudson Valley, but farther out than most commuters were willing to manage—ninety-five minutes to Grand Central. A former mill town, now an exurb, as their real estate agent had put it. Plans were in the works for the vacant warehouses. Some of those buildings were nothing but brick shells with shattered plate-glass windows, open to the sky and shot through with tree branches. But the developers were going to do *something* with them.

On their first trip out here, he'd browsed in the used bookstore; Helen wandered along the little street of art galleries. There was a dive bar, a nice bar, and a vegetarian restaurant. Even the stores that sold bespoke denim and artisanal fennel products had seemed like a good sign. "There are things to buy," Helen joked. "People will come!" Many of those businesses were gone now. *But we'll always have the dive bar,* Tom would tell Helen, and smile.

Most days, he could believe that their gamble would pay off, that he and Helen hadn't made a huge mistake. He hoped he was right, because they couldn't afford to get out. Not now, at least. They'd stretched themselves far too thin for their down payment, buying at the height of the market, right before it tanked. And then came those months when he was out of a job and desperate to find another. Even now that he was at the newswire and Helen was doing contract work for her old boss, they had no room for error. An unexpected bill or a single missed paycheck would send them into a tailspin.

Helen blamed herself, he knew. She'd fallen for the house and the town. But hearing her talk about it—how Devon might look in just a few years, with the way things *keep going up*, as everyone liked to tell them—he had fallen for it too.

He'd owed her that, at least. And so he would tell her, *We had big hopes and bad timing. That's all.*

A horn blared. Two sharp blasts, followed by an outraged, prolonged *honk* that made Tom jump in his seat.

"Drive, Daddy!" the girls yelled. "Drive!"

The horn blasted again behind him. He blinked at the green light.

"Daddy!"

He drove. After he swerved past a trashcan left in the street, he glanced in the mirror at the driver behind him. She was a square-jawed blonde with three kids jostling in the back. When he stopped at the next light, she pulled alongside him, pausing to glare at him before racing away on Commercial Street.

Tom passed a hand over his eyes.

"Daddy's sleeping," Sophie said.

"No, honey. I'm awake." He smiled at her over his shoulder. "Almost there."

He turned his attention back to the street, focused now and determined to stay that way for the duration of their daybreak mission.

It had become a problem lately.

Not even lately—ever since the girls had been born. And others were beginning to notice. One moment, he would be absorbed in his day, his thoughts clear as he carried out his tasks at home or at work, and an instant later he would find himself distracted by the simplest of things. It could be anything: an old man scratching a lottery ticket. A passenger on the train whistling softly out of tune. A woman sweeping against the wind.

The next thing he knew, he would be zoned out. Hypnotized. And he would slip away. Nothing, none of his problems—not even his failures—could reach him.

It never lasted long. All at once, everything would come rushing back. And he would realize he wasn't slipping away, exactly. He was sinking. But for those few moments he was outside of time, outside of himself. It was a way he hadn't felt in many years. Since he was a kid, maybe.

But like a kid, he was losing things. The twenty-dollar bill that Helen's mom had given him, during her last visit, to buy the girls some drawing paper. His credit card. His wedding ring. (Helen hadn't noticed yet, and he hadn't told her.) There were also the small mistakes, the lapses of judgment. Like the ticket he'd gotten earlier that week for parking too close to a fire hydrant. And then losing that ticket on his way home from the train station.

So he was making mistakes and couldn't afford them. If he'd learned anything these last few years, it was that the slightest misstep could screw up everything. But the more he tried to concentrate, the more he wanted to drift.

Like last night, when he was supposed to be setting up the

morning coffee but instead was staring out the window at the neighbors' backyards. Butch, who lived two doors down, had just come out of his garage. He spent most of his days in there, when he wasn't working on his meticulously landscaped garden.

Butch was glowering up at the sky in his muscle T-shirt and basketball shorts. But something about the set of his shoulders, the almost-proud look on his face, made Tom think it had been a good day. That Butch was getting somewhere, wherever that was.

Tom wanted to believe that. He was rooting for him, his vaguely hostile, barely civil neighbor.

"Are you okay?" Helen said. "What are you looking at?"

He hadn't realized she'd come into the kitchen. It must have looked like he was staring at his reflection in the window.

"Nothing," he said. "I'm fine. Maybe I need more sleep. But I'm fine."

Farther down Main, they drove past minimarts, a New Age shop, and a former warehouse that had been divided into retail spaces, with signs for imaginary wine bars and upscale clothing stores. So far, only two storefronts had been rented: to a pet-supplies shop and a Laundromat, both *Coming Soon!*

After a few last blocks, they came to the old railroad station, out of use for decades. Tom pulled over. There was no sidewalk here, just a strip of grass that bordered the street. A few paces away, past the rusted tracks, was the brush- and tree-covered slope that led down to the creek.

"Here we are," Tom said. He could hear the rushing of the water. "And just in time."

He got out and released the girls from their car seats, eager to get them to the water before the sunrise. But Sophie bent down to press her hands against the tracks. Ilona stomped in the wood chips and weeds, filling her shoes with dirt. As Tom waited for them, he was struck by how green everything was, even now—the vines and grass and even the water. Though tomorrow was the first day of fall, there wasn't a hint of leaves changing. The air was soft and damp.

About twenty feet north of where they stood, the creek dropped sharply and came crashing over the rocks.

"That's a waterfall," Tom said. "You've never seen one before. Want to get a better look?"

When they'd come up for the closing on the house, he and Helen had climbed down the three crumbling steps to sit on the concrete platform at the edge of the falls, surrounded by all of that green. They'd gazed across the water at the brick warehouses and graffiti-covered foundry and the peak of Mount Cavan in the distance. Recently Helen had started coming back on her own. Sometimes she would spend an entire weekend afternoon wandering around the empty buildings. Taking photographs, painting watercolors. "Relax," she told him. "I'm not doing anything crazy."

They'd never come back together or taken the girls to the creek. But if Sophie and Ilona thought this was something special, they gave no indication. Light was beginning to hit the water, turning its smooth surface before the falls a deep bottle green.

"See the sky?" Tom said. "The pink and yellow? That's the sunrise."

He'd imagined doing this all summer long—taking his daughters out to see the sunrise over the water. As he led them closer to the falls, he pointed out the purple and yellow wild-flowers and the shallow pool at the creek's edge that was covered with tiny, lime-green leaves. But they just wanted to stop and pull up weeds. He found a flat patch of grass and swept away rocks and twigs so that the girls could plop down on either side of him. He stretched, his bones creaking, while they sat with the perfect posture of little children. Sophie had blue eyes and sandy hair, like him; Ilona was long and lean, with dark eyes and hair, like her mother. Together they looked down at the bricks and slabs of slate that lined the banks of the creek. They could walk right down there if they wanted to, pick their way through the wet reeds and muddy puddles to the rocks at the water's edge.

And if he were alone, maybe he would.

The sky brightened. As the water turned from green to gold, Tom was reminded of how lucky he was, and he told himself that it would all work out. He could almost picture a time when at least some parts of his life were simpler, when he didn't feel pulled in so many directions. If only he could figure out how to get there.

His phone buzzed. Sophie and Ilona scrambled onto his lap, wanting to talk to Mommy.

"It's only a text." He reached into his pocket. "Not a call."

They sank back, disappointed. At three years old, they already knew the difference.

Stop by at lunch? Important.

His daughters were watching him. Until the phone disappeared, nothing else would interest them.

Sure, he texted back. A moment later, he added, *Everything OK?*

Everything's great.

"What Mommy say?" Sophie asked.

"Not Mommy." He put a hand on her back. "Just work."

Tom deleted the messages. The girls stared at him, their faces taking on almost identical looks of curiosity. He felt his pulse accelerating under their gaze. He needed to distract them.

"See that?" He pointed south, where the creek passed under East Street. "That bridge goes over the water."

"Want to see the bridge!"

He had to get them home. But for the first time his daughters looked excited to be there. He was determined to make this a happy memory for them somehow.

"All right." Tom pulled himself up from the grass. They would have to move fast. "We'll take a very quick look. Hold my hand."

He led them back over the tracks and down the strip of grass. At the bridge, they watched the water course over the rocks. They crossed the narrow street to see the southern view, where the creek cut between wooded banks, opening up as it approached the old mills.

Here Sophie and Ilona began to squirm and twist, straining to get closer to the guardrails. Ilona, who was prone to sudden movements, was putting all of her strength into wrestling free from his grasp.

"Time to go," he said, his anxiety rising.

Sophie turned immediately and tried to tug him down the sidewalk. Ilona made a last protest, a lunge toward the guardrails that sucked the air out of Tom's chest. She managed to get herself between two of the rails, her head and shoulders suspended over the water. Holding tight, his heart racing, he maneuvered her back beside him.

Ilona never missed a chance to flirt with danger, and it terrified him. It was what he'd seen in Helen lately, with her solitary painting trips in desolate areas. That summer, she'd also started running in the early hours of night, leaving a little later each time. Unlike him, she didn't read the crime reports in the local paper. "I *like* running after the sun's gone down," she told him. "I'll be fine." She'd never been a worrier, but now she seemed immune to fear. At times he wondered whether she was testing her own limits or testing his.

Tom was leading his daughters back up East Street to the car when Ilona came to a halt.

"Potty!" she said.

Before Tom could tighten his grip on her hand, she slipped away and ran through an open gate to an empty lot behind a warehouse. She stopped in a stretch of gravel that served as a parking lot and shimmied back and forth, pushing her pants down to her ankles.

Fortunately, there was no one in sight. Beyond the gravel, the lot was overgrown with weeds and brush. Tom hurried after her, towing Sophie behind him.

"Okay," he said. It was too late to stop her. "Just make it fast."

He checked the time. If this took any longer, he would miss his train. Lights were coming on in the warehouse windows. On the other side of the lot was an old shack, so neglected it was hard to believe it was still standing. Tom glanced at the heap of scrap metal and junk not far from where they stood, an unsteady pile of broken chairs, an old plastic tub, what looked like a tricycle. Why had he dragged the girls out here? If he weren't counting the seconds until Ilona pulled up her pants, trying not to let the tension show on his face, he might have laughed at himself for bringing his daughters to this place.

While he was checking his phone again, Sophie darted from his side. She was heading for the shattered glass—it looked like someone had intentionally smashed a large mirror—that was strewn across the gravel a short distance away. In a voice so loud he hardly recognized it as his own, Tom shouted at her.

"No! Don't touch that!"

He caught her by the arm. Sophie burst into tears and whirled to face him. Had she ever been afraid of *him* before? But he couldn't wonder about that, because now Ilona had noticed the junk pile. Sticking out from the splintered wood and jagged metal was an old toy stroller. She ran for it.

Pulling Sophie with him, he raced for Ilona. His phone buzzed with another message. *The train!* he thought. *I am going to miss the train.* Around him, the tears were in full force: frightened from Sophie, hot and angry from Ilona as he steered her away from the stroller. Tom looked up. A man in work boots and dust-covered jeans had stopped outside the gate and was watching him. Watching him struggle with his crying daughters in a lot behind a warehouse. With a hard look of appraisal that said he saw Tom for what he was—an interloper from the city who couldn't control his own kids—the man shook his head and walked on.

Tom led his daughters to the car. If they remembered anything from this morning, he realized, it wouldn't be the sunrise or the waterfall. It would be these moments: how he'd scared them, how they'd cried as he hauled them to the street. And though he told himself it was a small thing, that there would be so many times to make it up to them, his heart sank.

Sophie's tears were unstoppable. Ilona managed to belt out a few words between furious sobs.

"Don't *want* to be here!" she cried out. "Want to go *home*!"

He had been sinking for years now, really. One of these days, he would go under.

CHAPTER TWO

HELEN, 8:30 A.M.

*J*ab, *hook, kick.*

This was the best point of the workout, when her muscles were sore but not yet stinging, and energy flowed through her—*out* of her—each time her fists and feet connected with the heavy bag. Helen breathed hard, no longer bothered by the smell of sweat and disinfectant that hit her as soon as she entered Joe's gym.

Sick kick. Knee to groin.

Joe was across the room, working with the real fighters: the young guy with cornrows, the older tattooed guy, and the South Asian girl who had massive, built-up shoulders and kept her hair shaved on the sides, the rest tied in a short ponytail. Helen didn't know their names or what they did when they weren't training. She'd only crossed paths once with any of them outside the gym—that time she saw the girl at the Key Food, talking on her cell in a soft, airy voice that seemed left over from some previous life. Helen had turned down the produce aisle, slipping away before she could be seen.

She worked on a move Joe had taught her last week—*yank*

the attacker's head down, then raise your knee in a kick—until her arms burned and her knees ached. She wiped her arm across her forehead and ran through the series again.

Last winter, she'd seen a flyer on Main Street: INTENSE CARDIO, 5:30 A.M., ROOSEVELT GYM. The next morning, she dragged herself out of bed. "Who knows?" she told Tom. "Maybe I'll meet some people." She went over to the high school, only to find herself in a class with people she already knew—by sight, at least—from all the usual places: the playground, the school drop-offs, the organic bakery where everyone got their coffee. There was the mom who'd house-trained her chickens, which laid eggs on the couch and in the laundry basket. There was the man who spoke to his two-year-old daughter only in French, and to everyone else in a vaguely European accent, though it turned out he'd been born and raised in Michigan. And there was the pair of earnest young journalists who drove a great distance to their NPR jobs and who'd been introduced to her, more than once, as the town's "public radio power couple."

Helen didn't really mind any of those people; she even liked the radio couple. But all of them, and many others, liked to bring their kids to the class, despite the early hour. The babies would sleep in their convertible car seats, but the toddlers and bigger kids would spend the hour spiraling around the gym, chasing and shoving and tackling each other, until they collapsed, hungry and on the verge of meltdowns. During the floor exercises, she had to stay on guard against the four-year-old who liked to steal his dad's weights and let them drop near other people's mats. She spent most of her day with her own children. She needed time to herself—time when she could burn off energy.

After a few weeks, she told Joe she was dropping out. "I've always been a runner," she said. "Maybe I'm not cut out for group classes." He'd looked her over, thought about it, and gave her the address of his own gym.

Now, as often as she could, she'd drop the girls off at preschool and then head over to his one-room studio, reachable by an exterior stairwell behind a storefront on Main. In the group class, Joe had radiated warmth, with a positivity that seemed well intentioned but somehow *off*. In his gym, he seemed like a different person. Here, he was quiet and intense, though the way he interacted with everyone—his deliberate speech, his long silences—made her think this was no less of a performance. Even after all the time she'd spent in the gym these last few months, she knew almost nothing about him, and he knew almost nothing about her. But there were days, like today, when she thought they understood each other.

Joe came up to her on his way back from the cooler.

"You're doing it wrong," he said.

Helen looked at him in the mirror. He was dressed in heavy sweatpants and the knit cap he'd worn all summer. He lifted her right arm.

"Look," he said. "You took the skin off."

She had been working on a left punch, followed by a right elbow. He showed her how to hit the bag without skinning herself, then moved on to the guy with the cornrows.

She had a few minutes left. She did her push-ups and stretches and went back to the bag for a last round of punches and kicks, knowing she would pay for that later. She could feel it already, in her knees and her shins. But it felt so good to push herself, to see how far she could go. To exert a decisive force.

Joe was watching her. He gave her what, for him, passed as a smile.

"Better," he said. "Keep breathing."

Helen caught a glimpse of her face in the mirror and remembered what the cashier in the organic bakery had said last year.

"You all right?" the girl had asked, with a smile too caring to be genuine. "Sorry, you just look so *angry*. Like you want to hit somebody."

Helen had walked out and never gone back. She hadn't always looked angry, she thought as she punched the bag.

The call came on her cell as she parked in front of her house.

"I hate to do this to you," Ryan said, his voice muffled. "But Lou is breathing down my neck. It's about that wrap deck for Mega Crux."

Helen checked her watch. By this time of the morning, she was usually in her home office, hard at work designing visuals for marketing campaigns to sell products with names like Iron Fuel, Molten Rage, and Jacked 'n Loaded.

She'd worked on Mega Crux last night, returning to her computer right after the girls went to bed, but around midnight had decided to give her eyes a break, knowing she would work faster—and better—in the morning. She was still feeling the effects of the all-nighter she'd pulled on Wednesday, churning out revisions to a different assignment, only to find out the next morning that the project had been killed. (It wasn't the first time something like that had happened. She'd lost track of how many late-night and weekend hours she'd spent on projects only to get an email the next day: *Sorry. Guess we should have called you.*) She hadn't complained. How could she, when so many other graphic designers were desperately clinging to their jobs?

"It's almost done," she said. "Seriously. You'll have it in an hour."

"Ugh," Ryan said. "This is the worst." He dropped his voice to a whisper. "Lou just got a call from the client, and they're changing everything. There's new art, new slides, and now they're sending us a video. And Lou needs to see it before he leaves tonight, because he wants to show it tomorrow morning at that conference in Pittsburgh."

"*Tomorrow* morning?" She couldn't even keep track of how many assignments she'd pushed off, promising everyone that she'd get to their projects today, *no worries*, so she could spend yesterday working on the presentation for Lou. "That's Saturday. He said he needed it by Monday."

"He's seeing the client. They've got a new campaign." Ryan sighed into the phone. "I'm so sorry. For both of us! I'm doing eleven mock-ups. I'll never get out of here."

In the background, she could hear Radio Jello, the late '70s/early '80s Internet radio station that Ryan liked. Back when they'd shared an office, they'd close the door and turn up the volume on particularly stressful days.

Her phone buzzed. A text from the preschool. *Reminder: No dance class today. Please be on time for pickup at noon.*

She squeezed her keys in her hand to stop herself from cursing out loud. Dance class was only forty-five minutes, but she had been counting on it. Lately, even her daughters' scheduling changes were always sneaking up on her.

"Okay," she said, her voice calm. "What time does Lou need to see Mega Crux?"

"I'd show him something by four." Ryan exhaled. "If not earlier! Check your email. It's all in there."

Helen got out of her car. As she headed for her house, ready to plant herself at her desk and start pushing pixels, the door opened at Karl and Jackie's. Jackie burst onto the porch with her coffee and cigarettes, caught sight of Helen, and turned on a bright smile.

"Karl's in his studio," Jackie called to her. "He said you would come by." She breezed over to her car in the driveway between their houses, popped the trunk, and put in a shopping bag filled with books. Jackie worked part-time as a teacher's aide at the middle school and was always taking in donations. She blew out a puff of air, lifting her brown-going-gray bangs off her forehead, and circled around to the driver's side. Before getting in, she looked at Helen. "You coming down with something? You're all flushed."

Helen touched her face. Her skin was hot.

"I'm fine," she said. "Just getting back from the gym."

Jackie laughed, though with a sharpness that took Helen by surprise.

"Of course you are. Anyway, he's up there. Now don't forget to let him pay you!"

She was off before Helen could respond, honking her horn as she reversed out of the driveway.

Pay you. Helen had felt bad about that ever since she'd offered to design the cover for Karl's album. He'd been out of work for years. But when she tried to protest, Karl had laughed. "Our house is paid off. Our kids are grown. You're doing me a favor."

Helen let herself into Karl and Jackie's house. She could steal a few minutes—five minutes, tops—before she went home and tackled the latest changes. She stepped over the piles of shoes and flip-flops near the door and entered the clutter of the living room. Their home was a smaller, cozier version of the house she'd grown up in: wavy glass in the windows, hardwood floors that creaked with every footstep, furniture handed down from thrifty ancestors who'd never known the pleasure of flopping onto a couch or into a bed. But while her childhood home in Massachusetts had been spacious and spare, Karl and Jackie's was crammed with knickknacks and photos, including a framed *TIME* magazine cover, hung over the mantel, of a soot-faced American soldier staring out at an Iraqi battle zone. Helen and Jackie didn't talk politics. The one time the subject had come up, Jackie told her, "Look, I'm no *birther*. I believe that Obama was born in Hawaii. I just don't think Hawaii really counts as part of America."

Helen's phone buzzed, and before heading upstairs to find Karl, she checked the emails that had already come in. According to her contract, she could work whenever she wanted—no one cared, as long as she met her deadlines. On paper, it came out to three-quarters of the time she used to spend in the office, for half the pay. The extra hours she put in weren't part of the deal. Still, she was lucky to have the job, and it wasn't a bad gig. Back when she was starting out, she'd worked as an illustrator, freelancing for newspapers and designing book covers for small presses. But those jobs didn't pay much, so she took on Web and video projects. After years of floating between temporary gigs, she'd jumped at the offer of a full-time job: marketing and promotions for a media conglomerate best known for its lad mags.

Her title was art director and she did everything: animated videos, online sweepstakes, print ads. She obscured nipples and retouched "elephant flaps" on photos of models' underarms—the folds of skin that, in real life, allowed people to move their arms. In recent years, the company had put more money into its fitness brands, selling training DVDs, vitamin supplements, and protein shakes. The Jacked 'n Loaded manager was so happy with her work that he'd signed her up for a free year of Jacked *RE*loaded, delivered to her door.

She did her best with every assignment; she was promoted and worked even harder. When she got pregnant and was ordered by her doctor to get more rest, she'd taken a break from work for the first time in years. She'd spent those weeks getting the place ready for the girls—and Tom had helped her, ordering and assembling everything they needed. He was always working, at home or in the office, and when he wasn't working he was often distracted. It made sense, she supposed, with all the changes that were on the way back then, though that didn't explain why he was still so distracted now.

A few months after their daughters were born, as her maternity leave ended and she was getting ready to go back to the office—scrambling to hire a sitter, wondering if management would possibly consider a more flexible schedule or at least fewer late nights—she got a call from Lou, her boss.

"Wait...wait...I just gotta hit send." Lou pounded on his keyboard. "Helen! Swing by tomorrow. I figured out a way to make this work for you."

The next day, she took the subway to the office, excited to be back on the busy streets, hopeful about what Lou might offer. He knew how many hours she put in, that he could always count on her to get the work done. She sat in his office, letting her cup of coffee cool in her hands while he gave her the news.

"By the end of this week, half of these people will be out the door," he said. "But I stepped in to save a job for you."

He wanted her to work on contract and off-site, for a lot less money. At first, as he urged her to take it, she couldn't even register her shock or disappointment. All she could do was look back at him, calm, professional, revealing nothing.

"Sorry, Helen," Lou said. "I know it sucks."

She managed a smile.

"It totally sucks," she said. "But thanks. I'm sure it wasn't easy."

"I know you, Helen. You're like me—you've *got* to work. You'd go crazy if you had any free time on your hands."

"Well. I'm glad I won't have to find out."

She got up, put on her coat, and said maybe it was for the best. After all, she'd been hoping for a way to spend more time with her daughters.

"See," Lou said. "That's what I like about you." He clapped her on the back as he walked her to the door. "You don't let the turkeys get you down."

Back outside, she drifted along the Midtown streets, jostled by the crowds. At Grand Central, as she approached a stairwell that led down to the subway platform, a huge guy shoved past her. His bicep plowed into her shoulder, almost knocking her off her feet.

Helen stared after him, immobilized by a sudden fury. It

was like nothing she'd ever felt before, immediate in its intensity. As if it had been simmering for years. The guy who'd shoved her was stuck just a few steps below on the stairwell. There was nowhere he could go—there were too many people packed onto the stairs, marching shoulder to shoulder. Like a slow-motion stampede. Helen looked at him and thought of how much damage she could do if she pushed him. She imagined him falling down. Getting trampled, getting hurt. Maybe badly hurt. She pictured herself making that push, just enough to send him toppling forward, and then slipping away into the crowds. Hearing the shouts and screams and curses but not sticking around to witness the fallout.

That was three years ago. She'd never said anything to Tom about that moment of anger. Or about any of the ones that followed. They became part of an ever-widening category of what she kept to herself.

Like her little acts of rebellion. Stealing a few minutes away from her desk to drop by Karl's house. Through the door to the basement she could hear Nick, Jackie's son from her first marriage, and Monica, his girlfriend. They were laughing. A patchouli smell floated up the stairwell.

Helen put her phone away. She knew she should just turn around and go home—she didn't really have any time to spare, or steal—but the morning sun was coming through the wavy glass, and the patchouli was taking her back to high school. She could almost see the kids heading to the woods behind the parking lot, leaving a trail of smoke behind them.

The door to Karl's studio was open. He sat in front of his computer, headphones on, eyes closed, nodding to a slow beat.

She knocked three times before he heard her.

"Hey there, Helen." He slid his headphones onto his shoulders. "Come on in."

It was a small room, just big enough for the old kitchen table that he used as a desk and a beat-up couch that until recently had lived in the basement. The walls were bare except for a few snapshots, including one of Karl's adult children (like Jackie, he had an ex) and one of himself as a teenager, singing in a garage band, his feathered hair down to his shoulders, a slimmer, narrower version of himself. Helen took her usual spot on the couch, beneath the poster for the band he was in now, a bunch of middle-aged guys who played classic rock covers at Trax twice a month, with some grunge thrown in to satisfy the band's slightly younger members.

Last Sunday, when Jackie had invited Helen and Tom over for burgers and beer, Karl told them about something new he'd been working on, an album of his own music. He played a few tracks while Sophie and Ilona raided Nick's old toys in the basement. Helen was surprised—it was the sort of downtempo electronica she listened to while she worked. The spacey beats helped her concentrate. "It's great," she told him, then added, "You need someone to design the cover?"

He'd called last night, asking if she wanted to stop by and pick up a copy. Now he spun around in his seat and gave her a disc.

"Let me know what you think," he said. "I'm not sure about the fifth track. You'll see what I mean." There was a hint of a smile in his eyes. "You sure you have time to work on this?"

"Sure," Helen said. "As long as you're not in a rush."

"No reason to hurry." He opened his arms wide. "I've got plenty of time."

Until a few years ago, Karl had an IT job at a telecom across the river. Except for a short stretch at a record store and the occasional shift at the secondhand guitar shop on Main Street, he'd been out of work ever since.

"Are you still looking?" Helen asked. "For a new job, I mean."

She wouldn't normally ask such an abrupt personal question, but she felt comfortable with Karl. Over the past couple of years, his studio had become a second home to her, a refuge from the pressures and frustrations of her own desk.

"*Still* looking?" Karl said. "I can't say I've ever looked." He leaned back in his chair. "I've got three-quarters of my pension and the health insurance. What I earn at the guitar store's good enough for pocket money."

"That's a pretty good deal," she said. "For getting laid off."

"Oh, I wasn't laid off. I was fired. Jackie never told you?"

In all the time they'd spent together, the subject had never come up.

"What happened?" she asked.

He laughed, ran a hand through his hair.

"I locked my boss in a supply closet. Not for too long. The janitor had him out of there in forty-five minutes."

She gave him a steady look.

"You're not kidding."

"Nope," Karl said. "He was crazy, horrible to work for. Shit rolls downhill—that was his philosophy. He liked us to feel that every day could be our last. Anyway, he'd been hounding me all day, nagging about productivity and expenses. He sort of lost it when I asked for a box of staples. Said this would be my last pack, ever, and that if I wanted anything else, I'd have to go out and buy it myself. Finally he went into the closet to get the stupid staples, and I shut the door behind him and took the keys." He gave her a somewhat regretful shrug. "Once I'd thought of it, it was hard to resist."

Helen knew that feeling. How many times had she come close to crossing a line since that incident in the subway station? If she ever decided to tell anyone, it would be Karl. He wouldn't judge her, and might even understand.

"What did you do?" she asked. "After you shut the door?"

"Well, I was hungry. I'd been working all day without a break. So I hit the vending machine. Combos and a Fanta."

Helen smiled. She pictured Karl's boss, spinning around in the sudden dark to rattle the doorknob.

"Did he try to get out?"

"He slammed against the door for a while," Karl said. "Called me every name he could think of. He knew I was there. And you'd be surprised how many people walked by. A few of them more than once. I'd tossed the keys on a desk beside the door, in plain sight. And this was at the end of the day, when the whole staff was heading out, one after another. No one did a thing." Karl grinned, remembering. "That made it worth it. Watching their faces as they kept moving, pretending not to hear him shouting in there, pounding on the door. I think the janitor would've left him in there, too, if I hadn't been there to witness it."

Downstairs, the front door slammed. Nick and Monica were heading out, probably to their classes at the community college.

"And you didn't get in trouble for that?" Helen said. "I mean, besides losing the job."

"Not really. He threatened to press charges, but in the end I think he was too embarrassed. Jackie read me the riot act—said I'd have to sign up for anger-management classes or see a therapist, in case we got sued or something. So I did. It wasn't bad. I mean, everyone could use a few hours with a shrink." Karl's screen had gone blank behind him. He tapped his keyboard. "And I was lucky. I had a great union lawyer. So now I can kick back, work on my music, work at the guitar store when they want me. It's not bad at all."

Helen saw him in a new light. Here was someone who'd crossed the line and had no regrets. Her whole life, she'd never veered off course, never strayed from the path. A step too far, and she might not find her way back. But where had a life of the straight and narrow taken her?

Her email gave another buzz, and she checked the time on her phone. She'd stayed longer than she'd planned. The stress must have shown on her face, because Karl was studying her.

"I hope I didn't freak you out," he said.

"Not at all. But I should go." She got up. His studio was so much like her own office, a tiny room where she worked alone all day. "Though I *am* wondering why you have a toy AK-47."

"That's a water gun," he said. "Nick got it for me. For the squirrels."

She knew all about the squirrel problem. The gray squirrels had tried to chew through the screen of her office window. They liked to leap from the nearest branch to her windowsill, their nails clicking and scratching as they made their way to the roof, a sound that made Pussyface hiss at the ceiling.

Karl picked up the water gun. It was a camouflage model, motorized and loaded. He aimed it out the window.

"Check out the range on this thing," he said. "I managed to hit one in Butch's birdbath yesterday."

She joined Karl at the window. There weren't any squirrels out, so he aimed down the length of his yard, hitting an azalea bush and sending a shower of pink petals to the grass.

"Can I try it?"

"Sure."

He gave it to her. Helen saw a branch shake on the nearest tree. She pulled the trigger and sent a squirrel running down the branch. The squirrel stopped, sat up on its hind legs, and stared at her. She fired again.

"Take *that*, you fucker."

Karl laughed.

"Yeah. I had a feeling you'd be into it." He opened his closet. "You want my old one? Not as much power, but it does the trick."

"I can borrow it?"

"It's yours. Let me fill it up for you."

He came back with it. They kneeled side by side at the window.

"I see one."

"Look, he's got a nut. You want him?"

"Got him."

Helen aimed, and the squirrel scurried down the tree, nut in mouth. She and Karl leaned out the window, firing their guns and drenching the nearest branches. They were still firing when Butch marched out of his garage and stared up at the trees, his eyes narrowed. They jumped away from the window before he could see them, laughing in the shadows.

CHAPTER THREE

TOM, 9:03 A.M.

Tom stood next to Mark in the company kitchen, a gleaming, open space stocked with bowls of free fruit and energy bars. In the sink sat the mug that they saw every morning, already stained with dark coffee rings, as if it had been left untouched for hours before its owner returned and drained it down a level. On its side, in neon letters, it read:

> Act like you're 20?
> Feel like you're 30?
> Look like you're 50?
> MUST BE 40!!!

"I bet he works the overnight," Mark said. "Otherwise we would've run into him by now."

"Not sure about that," Tom said. "The other day I saw it next to the toaster. An hour later, it was back in the sink, with a half inch of grounds floating in it."

Mark waited while a young woman from sales breezed in and fired up the Flavia. She stared right through him, as if unable to register his features—Mark was lanky and pale, with glasses slipping down his nose—while the machine steamed and hummed. Then she claimed her coffee and breezed out again, high heels clicking on the slick floor.

Mark watched her go, then turned back to Tom.

"I hate to ask," he said, "but did you badge in on time today? Because I just saw Tadpole, and he was heading for the newsroom with that look on his face. Like he's ready to bust some chops. Or chop some balls."

Everyone—even his assistant, when he was out of earshot—called the bureau chief *Tadpole*. His face was smooth and unlined and had a certain undeveloped quality, as if he hadn't yet come into his adult features. Though he was in his late thirties, maybe even his early forties, he looked so young that he could pass for an intern. He had short beige hair in a businessman's cut and pale blue eyes that never seemed to blink. Outside of his fits of rage, which were as frequent and intense as a toddler's, he seemed incapable of any emotion.

Tadpole kept track of every reporter's and editor's performance in elaborate spreadsheets that he analyzed at their quarterly reviews. "Somewhere, in some file, that guy has an algorithm for how long it should take me to piss," Mark once said. Thanks to the badging system, it was easy to track whether or not they came in on time—or, better, came in early and stayed late. In Tom's year and a half at the wire service, he had accumulated a less-than-satisfactory record in both of these categories.

But today he'd gotten lucky. Missed the 7:13 but caught the next train, an express. He'd made it to Midtown just before nine. Though he should have been at his desk by now.

"Minute to spare," Tom said. "A miracle."

"That's a relief." Mark picked up his *Journal*. "Because I'd hate to watch him tear you to pieces while I eat my cranberry muffin."

They left the kitchen and took the long route, the one that avoided Tadpole and the high-ranked editors, to their row in the far right corner of the newsroom. There were just three of them on the science team. Tom sat by the window, with its floor-to-ceiling view of Park Avenue, sixteen flights below. "Vertigo, and too much to look at," Mark had said when he ceded the desk to Tom; he now had the middle spot. Their boss, the global science editor, had the aisle seat. Rita's chair was spun around, its back to the blank computer screen, but she had probably been at work for hours. Her breakfast can of Coke, unopened but sweating, was in its usual spot beside her phone, along with the hard, dry roll that she would throw away, uneaten, at the end of the day.

Mark scrolled through the queue, claiming stories to edit. Tom placed his cell facedown beneath his computer monitor. The tone of the text he'd received that morning was bothering him. He kept checking his phone but there was nothing new.

"Hey," he said. "Do you think you could cover for me if I run out at lunch?"

Mark kept typing. He was one of those editors who could carry on a conversation while taking apart a story and rewriting it from top to bottom.

"You know I'll try."

"Thanks," Tom said. "I shouldn't be too long. I'll take our next Saturday shift."

"Well! I'll do my best. But I still can't promise anything."

Mark didn't ask why he needed to leave or where he would

go. He never had, in all the months he'd covered for Tom's escapes. He had a rare gift of knowing when to hold his questions.

"Which do you want?" Mark squinted at his screen. "Flying tree snakes? Latest strain of avian flu? Chlamydia in pigeons?"

Between them, they edited all of the science stories that went out on the wire. *It's the best of both worlds,* their boss liked to say. *A ton of work and no recognition.* The wire service was known for financial news, and science stories that were considered even slightly important were covered by the market or industry teams. Even weather stories were handled by general assignment or the commodities guys. Which often left Mark and Tom with features about animals or diseases or asteroids, the more ridiculous the better.

"Flying tree snakes," Tom said. "Do we have images?"

"Oh, plenty." Mark skimmed the queue again and let out a stream of curses. "I've got to swing by Charlie's desk. He's offloading his junk on us."

Tom was grateful to have a moment alone. Around him, the newsroom was whirring, the reporters typing at full speed, phones wedged between heads and necks. The energy was fresh and spirits were high, or at least holding level. If he rose a few inches from his seat, he could see the entire expanse of the newsroom. The men wore blue or white shirts, without exception; the women were polished, conservative, an army of smooth-haired, slim-hipped Banana Republicans. Tom did his best to look the part, though just a few years ago he would have never pictured himself in a place like this. At the front of the room, the top editors were sealed inside their glass-walled conference room, a fishbowl within a fishbowl. This meant that the team editors could breathe a little. Across the aisle, a real-estate editor was checking his horoscope. The finance team leader clipped his nails. In the row ahead of Tom, Vanessa, the news assistant, was fixing her lipstick in the mirror attached to her computer screen.

Tom sat down and opened the story on flying tree snakes. The images were even better than he'd imagined. He gave a quick look at the captions, fixed the headline, and moved on to the story itself, tightening the lede and anecdote, bringing up a quote, falling into the work's easy rhythm. It wasn't the worst way to lose himself. The buzz of the activity around him filled his ears, a constant hum that drowned out all other sound.

Five years ago: He and Helen were living on the top floor of a four-story walk-up in Long Island City, Queens. Outside, beyond their block of redbrick houses, avenues of warehouses and former factories stretched as far as they could see. But inside, sealed off from the noise and exhaust, there was only a muted rumble of trucks.

Helen sat across from him on the couch. She was ready to start trying, she said.

They'd talked about this before, in the abstract. He'd never objected, not really, but the longer the possibility floated around, the more he'd come to believe that they could have a nice life, even a great life, on their own. He was thirty-seven years old; she was thirty-five. She had her graphic design work and all the time she wanted to paint. He loved his editing job at the science magazine. They had a decent apartment and few expenses. Think of all that freedom! They could still do everything their friends with kids had given up. They could travel. They could order cheap takeout without consulting a budget spreadsheet. They could get drunk, stay out all night, sleep in, get laid.

And there was something else, something he had trouble admitting even to himself. Sure, he liked kids—everyone had always told him that he was great with kids—but the older he got, the more afraid he became of having children of his own. It wasn't just the loss of freedom that scared him, but all the *fear* that would fill the void. Fear for their safety, for their futures. That he would mess up their lives through his own shortcomings. Even that he would die young, like his father had, and leave Helen to cope on her own. Once children were born, there was no going back. Those fears would always be there, a relentless drumbeat he couldn't ignore.

As it turned out, he was right about that. He hadn't even known how right he was.

That afternoon, he'd looked at Helen on her side of the couch, waiting. He saw the hope in her eyes, a hope that was now wavering as he hesitated.

"I love you," he said, and meant it. He knew it wasn't an answer, exactly, but he imagined it was a way to ease into a longer talk. But her relief broke his heart—she thought it was what she'd wanted to hear. So he said nothing more, and she took on their new project with her usual diligence.

Within a few months, their lives were very different. Stresses, small as they seemed to him now, confronted him wherever he turned. At home, sex was scheduled but unproductive, and Helen was trying to remain stoic in the face of each month's disappointment. At the science magazine, there had been two rounds of layoffs, and he wanted to survive the third.

He put in long hours. During shipping week, he and Donna, the managing editor, were often the first ones in and the last ones out.

He didn't mind the late nights. Despite the looming layoffs, there was an energy in the office. Donna would pace the halls, cracking jokes, passing out beers. She stood six feet tall and had an athletic build and long, wild hair that she shoved over her shoulders. She was, as Tom's twenty-two-year-old intern informed him, a *star*. During the day, the young assistants and writers seemed to circle around her, always thinking of reasons to *shoot her an email* or *grab lunch*. He was one of Donna's first hires, and in their years of working together they'd become good friends.

Late one night, she stopped by his desk.

"You've been working hard, buster," she said. "You look like you could use a drink."

At the bar of a tourist restaurant near their Midtown office, they ordered rare steaks and shots of tequila. They traded stories about their earliest years in the city, the crazy nights they would never forget. With every round, his stresses lifted, and Donna would toss her dark hair over her shoulder and order another. Which came first—her hand on his arm or his hand on her leg? Tom already knew he wouldn't remember and for a moment didn't care. When had he last felt so free? Two hours later, they were in her Battery Park condo.

Their little affair never seemed real. The days passed in a haze. More than anything, it felt like getting addicted to a TV series and plowing through the episodes. Later, all he would recall were a few images: vivid flashes, blurry around the edges. The way she kicked off those boots, with heels that could take out an eye. And the glass walls of her apartment. How they'd sprawled on the floor and looked out at the skyline.

Four weeks later, it was over. They'd spent all the energy between them. He'd come close to ending it a few times, but then a night came when they agreed, without needing to talk much about it, not to leave together. The imaginary world vanished, and Tom emerged from the fog, claustrophobic and blinking and dazed. He'd never cheated before—not on Helen, not on any girlfriend, ever. Now that it was over, he felt relieved.

Late one day, about a month after it ended, Donna called him into her office.

"I'm pregnant," she said. "Crazy, right? I mean, I'm forty-four years old." Her voice was neutral, but her eyes looked shadowed. "I know, we used condoms, but we weren't always very careful. Not as careful as we should have been, clearly."

Tom remembered. There had been a couple of reckless moments. He felt a sudden hollowness in his chest.

"I'm going to take care of it," Donna said. "Let's forget about this. You don't have to do a thing."

For a moment he couldn't breathe. He didn't respond to Donna but didn't need to; he knew she could see the shock on his face. He left the office, reeling. If only he could fall into a deep sleep that would erase all memory of the last few hours— or, better, the last few months.

Two days later, the meaning of "take care of it" had changed.

"Look, it's not what I was planning," Donna told him. She placed a hand on her tight, flat stomach. "And I don't know if I can explain it, or want to. But I'm going to *do* this. On my own. I'm *happy* to do this on my own."

She would have the baby, she said, and raise it, and pay for all of its expenses. Alone. She had her own money, and her parents could help her, if needed. The baby's lineage would be their secret.

He looked at her, stunned. A pain surged inside him, and before he could stop himself, he told Donna that Helen was trying to get pregnant. Had been trying for almost a year. Donna looked at him, understanding.

"I'm sorry, Tom," she said. "I had no idea. Focus on Helen—that's what you need to do right now. I realize this puts you in a difficult place. But this is my decision and my responsibility. One thing hasn't changed: You should walk out that door and forget this ever happened. You're free."

But of course he wasn't free. He felt like he would never be free again. That evening, as he walked aimlessly along the city streets after work, he could think of nothing but Donna's baby, or the cluster of cells that might someday become a baby. Two days ago, none of this had seemed real—it was a terrible mistake, one that felt like a gut punch, but for better or worse it was a mistake that was soon going to be erased from everything except his and Donna's memories.

Now, though, there would be an actual *child* out there in the world. *His* child. Even if this child never knew about him. It was the strangest feeling. He realized, turning down yet another street, that this was exactly the sort of thing he would have wanted to talk over with Helen—she was the only person he could trust with the terror, the uncertainty, even the weirdness of it all. But it's not as if he could tell her now. Or could he? Did Helen need to know? Would she understand?

He felt a simultaneous need to hide and to run. But the more he thought about it, the more he realized he had to tell her. A child was too much to hide from her. And how was he supposed to *forget this ever happened*, when he and Donna worked together? Was he supposed to disappear when someone asked about the baby? Never look at any of her photos? On the walk home, he felt his steps weighed down with dread as he ran through the many ways this news would hurt Helen. But he owed her the truth. They would rebuild from here, somehow.

He climbed the stairs, reached for his keys, took a last breath. Helen would be home in an hour, and he would use that time to think over, once again, exactly what he planned to say. But when he opened the door, there she was, waiting for him on the couch with eyes that belonged in a dime-store painting. She looked mysterious and wounded and proud all at once. His heart skipped a beat; he stared back at her, queasy. Had she spoken to Donna somehow? What did she know?

"I didn't want to jinx it," Helen said. "But I've taken three tests. The sonogram's on Monday."

Without looking up, Tom sensed his boss approaching. She slid into the space next to Mark's empty chair. Her fingers rested on the edge of his desk.

"Tom Foster," she said.

He wondered if she always greeted him this way so that he would respond with her full name: "Rita Ravenbush."

He glanced up at her. Her reddish hair was held back in a low ponytail. Today, as always, she was dressed in a crisp white shirt and black jeans. No one understood how she got away with wearing jeans in the newsroom. At the end of the day, she would ride her motorcycle back to her high-rise in Newark. She was often the first to come in and the last to go, and she rarely discussed her life outside of work, where she was known for her loathing of errors.

Tom turned his attention back to his screen as Rita, her eyes shaded by pale sunglasses, started fussing with his desk. First, keeping a strict distance from his shoulder, she lined up the folders in the metal rack beside his phone. Next, she nudged his loose papers into a precise stack to the left of his keyboard. Finally, she focused on the problem that vexed her on a daily basis: what to do with his penholder, which was semicircular, designed to be placed against a cubicle wall. But the newsroom was open plan, without any walls or divisions between desks. If she pushed the penholder too close to the desk's edge—aligning it perfectly was the ideal—it might fall. In the end, she positioned it next to his computer monitor.

All of these moves were in addition to the adjustments she had made either late last night or early that morning. He could always tell she had been there, even if all she'd done was straighten up his desk drawer or fan out his pencils in a symmetrical pattern. (As far as he knew, she never bothered with Mark's desk, possibly because it was too far gone.) Her face became oddly peaceful as she untangled the cord of his phone.

Throughout all of this, Tom kept his eyes on the file he'd opened, a story about antibiotic-resistant, flesh-eating superbugs. The superbugs disturbed him, but not Rita. His acceptance of this morning ritual was, at least as he understood it, a key part of the unspoken agreement between them, their acknowledgment of how each could discreetly compensate for the other's flaws. He would let her indulge all of her OCD urges, without judgment. In return, she would pretend not to notice his late arrivals and early departures, his unexplained absences and long lunches in a newsroom in which everyone, from the news assistant to the editor in chief, ate at their desks.

Mark came back just as Rita was finishing with Tom's phone.

"Ms. Ravenbush," he said.

"Someone on the metro team filed a three-part series on the history of subway grating," she said to Mark. "Howard would like some help. You'll get the first part to him in twenty minutes?"

She headed for the printer, Coke in hand. The first time Tom and Mark went out for after-work drinks, Mark had told him all about his interest in their boss and his despair that this interest wasn't mutual.

"I think she almost smiled at me," Mark said. "Wonder what's going on with her today. You notice anything?"

"No. Not really."

"Of course not."

Mark sat at his desk, and Tom got to work. He had a new story on his screen, a Hong Kong feature on panda kindergartens, and nothing was going to tear him away.

———

Dick Maddox was doing his rounds. He was the top of the tops, second in command to the editor in chief, a former weightlifter who looked like he spent his spare time training for the Highland Games. He came down their row and landed a hand on Tom's chair. Tom could feel him leaning in, reading over his shoulder, and had to resist the urge to shift away.

Maddox gave Tom a friendly clap on the arm and swiveled to face Mark. He looked like he wanted to try some sort of physical contact with Rita but then thought better of it.

"Looking good, guys!" His voice boomed at the backs of their heads. "Liked that subway feature. A relentless assault of scintillating factoids! Keep 'em coming."

He gave Tom a last frat-boy punch and turned away, gripping the back of Rita's chair as he headed for the aisle. She whirled in her seat and glared at him.

Tom let out a breath, realizing that he'd been caught staring blindly at his computer screen. He checked the queue and opened the next story, a brief filed by a young reporter—the nephew of the global sales manager—whose tendency to cut and paste from Wikipedia had earned him the nickname *Control V*. Tom forced himself to concentrate. He couldn't let a plagiarized paragraph or a single error hit the wire. It was exactly the kind of task that he was likely to screw up today, working on just a few hours of sleep.

Tom finished the brief and sent it to the wire. The bottom of his screen blazed red with an urgent message from the Hong Kong bureau chief, who apparently never left the office.

WTF? Where's our panda feature?

The Hong Kong bureau chief was a screamer, and Tom knew from experience that it was never a good idea to engage him. But for a moment he felt like firing back a message of his own: *CHECK THE WIRE, ASSHOLE!* Then he realized he'd forgotten to include one of the news codes that should have appeared on the story, which was why the bureau chief hadn't seen it. Tom added the code and sent out the story again.

A second later, a new message appeared on his screen.

So you forgot the buro code. Same thing happened with our cyanide story last week.

Tom deleted the message before he was tempted to respond. He felt like he'd already run a marathon today—getting the girls home, then rushing to the train station, only to lock himself in place for the train ride itself, that long stretch of forced rest in which he had nothing to do but gaze at the scenery. It was usually his favorite time of the day, the one time when no one needed anything from him, when there wasn't anything he could do wrong. But instead of relaxing, that morning he'd spent the journey checking his phone, dreading what was waiting for him at the end of the line.

Another message, all caps and blinking. The Hong Kong bureau chief wasn't letting this go.

THAT WAS YOU, RIGHT? WHO FORGOT THE BURO CODE ON THE CYANIDE STORY?

Tom closed his eyes. At the science magazine, he'd been known as a good editor, hardworking and dependable, an easygoing guy who got along with everyone. Here, where eyes were constantly on him, where every achievement and failure was recorded and compared, he couldn't stop fucking up. Or pissing people off.

Tom opened his eyes and read the bureau chief's message again. Mark looked at him.

"What's the problem?"

Tom shook his head.

"Forgot a bureau code," he said. "It's fixed now."

Mark glanced at Tom's screen and read the message.

"You don't want to get into a pissing match with that guy," he said. "I suggest you stay in your little box. Let him stay in his little box." He smiled at his screen, editing as he spoke. "And then on Monday, we'll all move on to the next little box."

Tom could almost see the walls of his own little box. At times it seemed like he spent his days moving along a grid, trying to stay inside the lines as best as he could, determined not to mess up, not to let anyone down.

To stop himself from responding to the bureau chief, he read Donna's text again. *Everything's great,* she'd said. *For me,* that implied. *Not necessarily for you.*

He swiped over to his saved photos and looked at the picture he'd taken a month ago. It was a great shot, capturing the exact moment when a little girl finally managed to swing herself across the monkey bars. She'd made many attempts. Each time, she dropped to the rubber-matted ground, dried her palms on her leggings, and tried again, a look of intense concentration on her delicate features. Though her hands were raw and on the verge of blisters, she hadn't given up.

That was at an Upper West Side playground, and he'd wound up staying for almost an hour: hoisting her to the monkey bars for yet another try (*again!*); climbing the slides in his work clothes; even, at her request, folding himself onto one of the miniature cement hippos, then toppling over as she collapsed with laughter. Right as they were about to go, a slightly older boy appeared out of nowhere and, with a ferocious shout, tried to shove her under the sprinklers. She pressed her hands against the boy's chest and shoved back, landing him flat on his butt in a puddle.

The boy's mother, catching the end of this confrontation, turned to Tom and said, "You better watch out for that girl of yours. She's a bruiser."

She was shaking her head with dismay. But Tom couldn't hide his smile. Or his pride.

His little bruiser.

It was one of many moments that he wouldn't have given up for anything.

He remembered sitting in Donna's office. *I'm happy to do this on my own.* His involvement with her—and contribution to the problem, or situation, at hand—was over and done. He was free and clear. No responsibilities, no obligations. Donna had told him that many times.

But it hadn't worked out like that. And after three years, how could he walk away? Donna knew as well as he did how impossible that would be. But how did he go forward from here? He knew what was at stake. Who he could lose. Whenever he tried to get his head around it, the enormity of his mistakes threatened to overwhelm him completely. And he would feel himself slipping.

This time, he snapped out of it fast. Mark spun around in his seat.

"You gotta check out this video Charlie just sent me," Mark said. "It's about the guy who set a new world record for hammering nails with his forehead."

Tom pressed a button on his phone, and the photo disappeared. He should have erased it by now; he'd been telling himself that for days. He leaned back and gave a casual glance at Mark's screen. If anyone in his life sensed the pressure he was under, it was the guy who sat next to him forty-odd hours a week. But Mark had already turned back to his monitor, as if he hadn't noticed Tom's startled look or his hopeless attempt to hide it.

"Well," Mark said, and shuddered. "Maybe you shouldn't check out that video. Graphic ending. Still, he has that record." He was smiling now, his eyes on his screen. "Which is more than the rest of us can say."

———

"Tadpole."

Rita exhaled the warning, barely moving her lips.

A moment later, the bureau chief appeared between Mark's and Rita's desks, intruding just enough into Rita's space to brush against her file folders. Tom felt a twinge of sympathy, knowing how much time she would spend rearranging those folders later.

"How is it going, guys?" Tadpole said.

None of them answered. Tadpole glanced at their screens, his pale eyes registering nothing. Rita crossed her arms and leaned back in her seat, forcing Tadpole to move a few inches away from her desk. She flashed him a cold smile. He didn't seem to notice.

"So we're going to need some extra coverage this afternoon," he said. "We're down a pharma editor." He ran a hand through his almost colorless hair. It fell immediately back into place. "Joel's stepson was under that scaffolding that collapsed on Lexington this morning. So he's off to the hospital."

They stared at him.

"That's awful," Rita said. "Is he going to make it?"

"He's fine. He'll be back in the office tomorrow."

"I meant his stepson."

"Oh. I don't know." Tadpole peered at the story on Rita's screen, searching for errors, though he wouldn't find any. In her years at the wire, she'd never had to send out a correction on a story she'd edited. "At any rate, it's not a great time to be short staffed. As you can see, Sammy isn't happy."

Sammy, a slight, plain-featured man who wore wire-rim glasses and shapeless suits, was the editor in chief. Tom and Mark glanced over their monitors at the middle of the newsroom, where Sammy was standing with a recently hired reporter, delivering a series of withering complaints in a misleadingly pleasant voice. There was a brief silence as everyone watched the young man's face turn red and his eyes fill with tears. When the reporter was finally dismissed, he made a quick exit for the men's room. The newsroom returned to its usual hum.

"Anyway," Tadpole said. "So we're short. I told the pharma team they could route some stories to you. We'll be fine, right, guys?"

He rapped his knuckles on Rita's desk and headed back to the inner fishbowl.

Rita began to realign her folders. Mark answered his phone and started going over edits with a reporter in the London bureau. Tom stared at his screen, knowing that neither Rita nor Mark ever screwed up, no matter how preoccupied they seemed. He reached for his cell and sent Donna a text.

Busy day here. Could we do after work?

As always, the reply came instantly.

Can't. Booked. A moment later, his phone buzzed again. *Like I said. This is important.*

OK, he wrote. *But I can't stay long.*

Not a problem. Won't take long.

He deleted the messages and placed the phone facedown below his monitor.

He knew it was getting close to noon when Vanessa, the news assistant, returned to her desk with an enormous container of noodle soup. She sat in front of her computer, chopsticks poised, steam rising above her shoulders.

It seemed like only minutes had passed since she'd drifted by their row, asking if anyone wanted anything from the café. As soon as she left, taking careful strides in her heels and tight skirt, Mark had shot Tom a message.

Volatile. Watch out for that one.

Tom shrugged it off.

Harmless, he wrote back. *You're paranoid.*

Now she'd caught him looking at her, her eyes meeting his in the mirror attached to her computer screen. She held his gaze and gave him a private smile.

Tom glanced quickly away and stared at his own computer screen, vowing never to make that mistake again. He clicked through the last few stories he'd edited and checked for missing news codes. This was the perfect time to go without leaving Mark in too much of a bind. He looked around the newsroom, wondering if he could leave without being seen by Tadpole or the pharma team leader. If anyone tried to contact him while he was out, they would see that he'd left the newsroom; the badge system let everyone know when a staffer was checked out of the building. He wondered if he could breeze past the guards who manned the exits without swiping his badge. He'd never heard of anyone who'd even tried it.

He looked out his window. Across Park Avenue, he could see the open-plan floors of a bond-trading firm. He could even see their computer monitors, the same model as his own. In front of them, men in blue or white shirts were eating lunch at their desks.

His phone buzzed. *ETA?*

On my way.

He put his phone in his pocket and turned to Mark.

"So—"

"I said I'd try."

"Thanks," Tom said. "I'll be back as soon as I can. I owe you." He kept his voice low. "Call if you need me."

"By the time you'd get that call, it would be too late." Mark pushed his glasses up his nose. "But I'll try."

Mark was right, but Tom couldn't wait any longer. With a last glance at his screen, he got up from his seat, leaving his jacket on the back of his chair. Rita was on the phone, dealing with a possible update to a feature that had gone out two hours ago. Not one that he'd worked on, he was happy to see. She pretended not to notice as he passed by, never looking back as he headed through the newsroom and kitchen to the elevators and out the door.

CHAPTER FOUR

The girl behind the receptionist's desk stopped Helen before she could go down the stairs to the preschool classrooms.

"Ms. Nichols?" she said. "Helen? Did you get my message?" Her voice floated above the din. "About the bill?"

The receptionist, who was wearing headphones, said this loud enough to be heard by all the moms and dads and babysitters who were streaming through the hall. Helen could feel them slowing down for a beat, glancing over at her. She pretended not to notice. Two women formed a line behind her, wallets in hand.

"Yes," she said. "Sorry, I haven't had a chance to call you back. But we've already paid that bill."

The receptionist furrowed her brow at her computer screen.

"You paid *September's* bill. This is for October. We bill on the fifteenth for the following month."

"Okay," Helen said. "Then you can put it on the card you have on file."

"I tried that," the receptionist said. "It didn't go through."

She thought for a moment, then brightened. "Do you want to try splitting it with another credit card? Like we did last time?"

Helen glanced at the balance on the computer screen. She could have chosen the cheaper preschool, but she'd visited there, seen the bored looks on the young teachers' faces, the children running a little too wild as they engaged in minor acts of cruelty and violence. *This* preschool—small, progressive, and more expensive—had been one of their real estate agent's main selling points when she drove them around Devon. Helen wanted to set her daughters on the right path, and weren't these years the most important? And so she'd convinced Tom that she'd figured out a way to stagger the payments. He didn't know she was charging each month on a credit card—or cards, at this point.

"I'll come back with my checkbook at the end of the day," she told the receptionist. "Thanks for the reminder."

Before the girl could respond, Helen turned away and headed for the stairwell, knowing she wouldn't come back with her checkbook. Instead she would call and give the number of her other credit card, the new one she'd opened without telling Tom. She hoped to pay it off, somehow, before he ever found out.

Helen couldn't imagine her parents, well off but frugal New Englanders, ever charging a preschool bill, no matter what unexpected circumstances might have befallen them. Though, of course, none ever had. Their American Express card had been rarely used and promptly paid in full. Of all the financial mistakes she and Tom had made these last few years, this would have shocked her parents the most—that they'd maxed out a credit card.

That day three years ago, after Lou gave her the news about her job, she'd made her way home to Long Island City. She told herself, as she'd always been told, that everything would be fine. She would just keep working, as hard as she could. She could almost hear her parents' voices in her ears: *It will be fine.* It was more than a prediction; it was a matter of principle.

But in the days and months that followed, she seemed to get angry at so many things that had never bothered her before. Like the trucks that thundered through the neighborhood, waking the girls from their naps. And the gusts of street trash swirling on the sidewalks. Even the woman down the block who sat on her stoop all day, handing bags of Cheetos to her daughter while she talked on her cell phone. The man on the steps at Grand Central had been only the start. Some days the smallest incidents would trigger a burning in her stomach. It was like she'd waited her whole life to get angry.

She knew she'd never act on it, or even let her family see how she felt. But after months of silently seething—and then, one night, discovering that email—she was reminded of what Lou had said about her: She always felt better when she was busy, hard at work on a problem. Her problem seemed clear—she and her family had to start over somewhere new, leave their problems behind. So she got to work, looking up towns within commuting distance, reading articles about families that had left the city for the Hudson Valley. She admired photos of houses: unpretentious, slightly ramshackle places that resembled—just enough—those on the outskirts of Belham, her hometown in Massachusetts. There was a restored farmhouse with an old barn. A weathered cottage with a pitched roof and dark shutters. And, on a quiet, curving street, a century-old house, pale green and with a little front porch.

The prices were high, almost out of reach, but she wanted to believe it would all pay off in the long run. One night, she printed out the listings and presented her research to Tom.

"We'll be happy there," she said. She showed him a photo of the house in Devon. "I'm sure of it."

She'd wanted it so badly. She was determined, just this once, to get her own way. And she could see in his eyes what they both knew: He owed her this; he couldn't say no. But the cost turned out to be higher than she'd imagined. They spent everything they had on the house and the move. Then Tom lost his job and it was months before he found another. Their expenses had piled up fast: car troubles, home repairs, COBRA payments—and, right in the gap in their coverage before Tom's new insurance kicked in, a trip to the ER when Sophie came down with that mysterious infection. In just a few years, her family had wound up with exactly the kinds of money problems she'd hoped to avoid and that her parents had raised her to dread: always short on cash, shifting funds around to cover bills, deciding which utilities to pay.

And, worst of all, her anger was still there, growing hotter below the surface, sending up flares whenever she worked all night on a dead project or checked the balances on their credit cards. Tom, too preoccupied to deal with their finances, didn't realize that things were getting worse, not better—that every month, they slipped a little further behind.

Sophie and Ilona wanted to go to the playground. That was what they told her as soon as they saw her—their arms reaching, both of them hopping with excitement—a reaction that made her want to do anything to please them, until a moment later when the reality of her deadlines came crashing back. She'd hoped to walk the girls home, give them lunch, and usher them off to a long afternoon nap so she could get back to work. And they made a good start, leaving the school quickly, keeping up a decent pace on the first long street. But before she could stop them, they were racing down the sidewalk and up the path that led to the playground's rusted gate.

Helen pushed the stroller after them. She usually enjoyed the walk home, even if she wound up pushing an empty stroller while they explored the pavement and stumbled around her legs, turning a fifteen-minute walk into an hour-long saunter. But today their only focus was the playground. They chattered at the gate, telling her about the trip they'd taken that morning—how they'd wanted to go to a playground but Daddy wouldn't let them and then he yelled when Ilona went potty and Sophie wanted to play with the pretty glass.

"What playground?" Helen said. "What glass?"

They stared at her blankly. She would have to ask Tom about that later.

"Okay," she said. "Fifteen minutes. Then home."

Helen opened the gate. The playground was on an enclosed lot behind the middle school, a redbrick fortress whose rear windows were shaded against the sun. There was a jungle gym for the big kids and a smaller version for toddlers, both on a rubber-matted play area bordered by benches. To the right were the sprinklers, shut off for the season, and to the left was a fenced-in area with swings. A row of pigeons sat on the swing set's top beam.

For once, they had the place to themselves. Helen sat on a bench as Sophie and Ilona took off for the jungle gyms. She watched them climb up the spiral slide, slide down, and climb up again until she began to drift off, her eyes closing. She straightened her back and turned her face from the sun.

She could still hear Tom's voice in her head. Under pressure from one of the marketing managers, she'd been forced to spend part of her morning editing the Iron Fuel *Summer!* buzz reel, a three-minute video she'd turned in earlier that week. There hadn't been time to hire a voice-over actor, so late on Tuesday, after the girls were in bed, she'd recorded Tom reading the script. And though he was clearly exhausted, he'd recorded it three times, bringing all of his optimism—even enthusiasm— to every silly line. The marketing team had loved it. But this morning, they gave her a list of last-minute changes that had to be completed before eleven, and she lost an hour getting it back to them. (Only to then get a complaint from Lou: *Where's that wrap deck for Mega Crux? I'd thought we'd have something to look at by now.*)

As she made the edits, and listened to Tom say the same punchy phrases over and over, she was reminded of something that Donna, his old boss, had said at a work party years ago. "Tom's one of the good guys," she'd told Helen, throwing an arm around her shoulder. Donna was tipsy that night and throwing arms around everyone. "You know what I mean? He doesn't have to *try*. Not like us."

Why was that still bothering her? Was it what Donna saw in Tom? Or what Donna saw in *her* that others didn't recognize?

Helen was trying to figure that out when something made her jolt up in her seat. A moment later, the sounds fell into place, breaking the silence: a young girl's hard laugh, followed by a high-pitched scream.

They must have come in through the back gate. Two teenage girls, fourteen or maybe fifteen, shoving against each other as they came into view along the cement path. Smoking cigarettes, cutting school.

Helen remained still, cautious, watching. The teenage girls strolled through the playground and sat on a bench on the far side of the jungle gyms, slouching in the shade of a low-limbed tree. The smoke from their cigarettes was masked by the burning-rubber smell of the mats in the midday sun and swept away by the light breeze. One of the teenagers—the skinny girl, tall and wiry—was rummaging around in her backpack. Her blond friend sat with her arms crossed, folded in upon herself, as if hiding behind her hair and rounded shoulders. They kicked at the pavement beneath their bench, making scuffing sounds with their thick-soled boots. The skinny one said something, and the blond one laughed again, a hard bark that carried across the playground.

Helen had probably seen them before, or teenagers just like them, hanging out on Main Street at night or in the little parking lots behind the stores. They were just kids. She tried to picture her own daughters that age, swearing and smoking. *But not like that,* she told herself. She wouldn't let that happen. These teenagers looked tough, too hard for their years. The truth was she hadn't known kids like that when she was growing up. Even the kids who cut school, who smoked pot in the woods, they were nothing like that.

Sophie and Ilona emerged from the dark space below the jungle gym, where they had been absorbed in some private game. They looked at the teenagers. Helen watched, tensing, knowing she should probably just take her daughters and go. But they wouldn't understand having their promised playtime cut short. There would be protests, almost certainly a meltdown. Part of her wanted to teach Sophie and Ilona to stand their ground, to show them their mother wouldn't let herself get chased away by a couple of teenagers. (Twenty years from now, did she want her daughters to get shoved on the subway and not say a word? That was not a trait she planned to pass down.) Helen glanced at the teenagers on their bench. They'd come here for privacy, not to listen to toddlers shrieking. They wouldn't stay long.

Ilona approached the edge of the play area. Helen shifted her weight, ready to jump up and steer Ilona away if she went near the bench. Then Sophie ran for the swings; Ilona followed.

Helen was glad they'd moved closer to her. But she dreaded the idea of pushing them for the next ten minutes.

"Hungry?" she called to them.

They ran to her.

As Sophie and Ilona wandered in circles with their Ziploc bags of Cheerios, the teenagers began tossing their cigarettes, shoving their hoodies into their backpacks. Helen could hear them talking—"*Where* is *that shit?*" "*I don't know, wherever the fuck you put it*"—as they cleared out from the bench. They ran their hands over their hair and brushed dirt from their jeans. Helen was happy to see them go.

But they weren't leaving. They walked through the play area, their faces dull and blank, not looking in her direction, then veered left toward the swing set. They slumped onto the swings, their butts hanging over the backs of the seats. The skinny one took a bottle of what looked like vodka from her backpack. She took a long swig and handed it to her friend.

Helen glanced at her daughters. As soon as they finished their snacks, she would take them home.

She had a better view of the teenagers now. The skinny one sat with her arms hooked around the chains, her stomach concave beneath her stretchy shirt. She had the kind of bad skin you could see from a distance, teenage acne inflamed by a late-summer sunburn. Her hair was shiny and dark, and she wore it pulled back into a tight ponytail, exposing a high forehead and brows that had been tweezed into a set of mismatched commas. She pushed at the ground with her boots, moving the swing just enough to make the chains creak and groan.

"*Bitch!*" she yelled at her friend. She reached for the bottle. "Give it."

Her friend laughed, hard and loud. She was shorter but curvier, her body plush. Her belly rolled over the top of her jeans, and her chest strained against her T-shirt. An almost pretty girl, with a round face and that soft, blond hair. Every time her friend said something, she let out one of her barking laughs. Her shirt was riding up, and she tugged it down, first in the front and then in the back. Helen felt a little sorry for her. She looked like a girl who was often teased and had attached herself to a stronger girl to stay out of reach.

Sophie and Ilona were watching them. They took a few hesitant steps forward. There were two empty swings, and they wanted them. Sophie had almost reached the low fence that enclosed the swings. As she smiled at the older girls, she stuck her hand into her Cheerios bag and spilled its contents onto the ground. Realizing what she'd done, she balled her tiny fists in despair.

A pigeon left its perch at the top of the swings and swooped down. At first it was just one, pecking at the cereal near Sophie's feet while she watched, her eyes wide. By the time Helen reached her, there were four more, wings flapping as they moved in.

With Ilona beside her, Helen tried to lead Sophie away. But Sophie wouldn't budge. She seemed to wobble for a moment, teetering on the edge. Then she let out a shriek and burst into tears. She was flapping, too, her arms beating at her sides. Scared of the birds but also angry, she stomped one foot. The pigeons scampered back, flapped and cooed, and advanced again.

This cracked up the teenagers. They slid off their swings, flung their backpacks over their shoulders, and came around the fence.

"You got the right idea," the skinny one told Sophie. She stood a few feet away. "You just got to do it *harder*."

The skinny one stomped her boots. The birds backed away, necks jerking. She gave Sophie a proud smile.

"See?" she said. "Like that! Tell them to fuck off!"

Helen saw the girl glance at her, seeing if she would get a reaction. Helen ignored her. She spent every day dealing with difficult people; she wasn't going to let teenagers rattle her.

She looked at the blond girl, who stood a step behind her friend. Up close, Helen felt her sympathy for the girl evaporate. Her deep-set eyes, flat and cold, gave her a jaded look that went beyond the initial impression of toughness. She had a tattoo on her neck, a dark-blue amateurish attempt at a starfish. She would pass for twenty-one before she was out of high school and would look forty by the time she was twenty-five. Helen realized that this girl wasn't the one clinging to a friend; she was clearly the leader of the pair. The girl shifted her gaze toward Helen. It was a look that said she knew how shit worked and wasn't impressed.

The skinny girl made a last stomp at the pigeons. She was tall, almost as tall as Helen, and her eyes were glassy, probably from the vodka. She was still holding the bottle. She gave Sophie a conspiratorial wink, as if they were partners in crime.

"See what I mean?" the skinny girl said.

Sophie whirled away and pressed herself into Helen's legs.

Helen was sure that the skinny girl was trying to provoke her. At the same time, she could almost believe the girl was trying to help Sophie.

"Thanks," Helen told her with a forced smile. She reached a hand toward each of her daughters. "Let's go to the swings."

But Sophie spun around, yanking herself away.

"No! Don't *want* to go!"

Sophie was overloaded, her circuits crashing. Helen knew it would blow over in minutes if she could distract her. But the pigeons were coming back, which set off another wave of angry tears. The skinny girl glanced at Helen, one hand covering her mouth, showing fingernails that were gnawed to the quick, knuckles raw with bite marks. Then she turned back to Sophie.

"Come on," the skinny girl said. "You really gonna cry about some nasty-ass pigeons?" Her eyes cut sharply to Helen as she added with a smirk, "All they do is shit all over the place."

Helen could tell that the skinny girl was a little drunk and showing off for her friend, seeing how far she could push a fortysomething mom who'd found herself in territory she didn't really understand. But Helen felt strangely determined to dig in her heels. She stared back at the girl, feeling the full force of her own anger, the anger she'd fought so long to keep in check. For once she didn't try to hide it or bury it inside, and she was surprised by how good that felt. She wasn't going to let them push her, she realized. After so many years of yielding, she was rooted to the ground.

Maybe that showed on her face. Because when the blond girl stepped forward, holding out her pack of cigarettes, the skinny girl hesitated, her eyes on Helen. The blond girl followed her friend's gaze and responded with a cold smile.

"Suit yourself," she said. "Like I give a fuck."

She lit her cigarette and gave Helen that same smile, a stone-cold triumphant look. Helen felt heat rise in her spine, blood rush to her face. It was an instant surge of fury, threatening to explode. The blond girl saw it and smiled even more. She kept her eyes on Helen. It was a challenge. A dare.

Helen knew what she should do: sweep up her daughters, avoid confrontation. But she didn't want to back down. Not to these teenagers. Not today.

And they could see it, what she'd only just now seen in herself—that she *wanted* a fight. Maybe it was that simple: For three years, she had been looking for a fight, and now she had found one.

The blond girl took a long drag off her cigarette and exhaled a cloud of smoke that drifted over Sophie's head.

Helen felt acid rise in her chest. She let the words come out before she could stop herself—knowing, even as she spoke, that it was the wrong move, that she wouldn't win.

"Hey," she said, making no effort to hide her contempt. "I

don't care who you are or what you do. But get lost. Take your vodka and your cigarettes and *get lost*."

The blond girl shot her a look that belonged on a woman twice her age. She took a quick step forward and spat out each word.

"*Fuck you, bitch.*"

Now it was the skinny girl's turn to laugh. She passed the vodka to her friend. As the blond girl raised the bottle, Helen felt something inside her finally fracture. In one swift motion, she stepped forward, free of her daughters, and smacked the bottle from the blond girl's grasp, sending it shattering to the pavement in a spray of liquid and glass.

The teenagers stared at her. They knew what she saw in them, what she thought of them. She knew what her parents would say: *trash*. They were trash. Helen hated that word, hated the way it echoed in her ears, her parents' voices telling her this wasn't about the cigarettes or the liquor or the clothes. These teenagers might grow out of that, but they would still be trash.

For a moment Helen braced herself, her hand shaking. But the blond girl never even flinched. The girl's coolness in the face of violence unnerved Helen more than anything else. She couldn't look away.

Behind her, Sophie and Ilona burst into loud, frightened wails. It was enough to break the spell. Helen took her daughters by their hands and led them to the stroller while their screams mounted. She was walking too fast, almost dragging them. But they were too scared and confused to argue as she loaded them in.

"Time for lunch," she told them. "Let's go."

Her skin was slick, tingling as if electrified. Helen shoved the stroller through the open gate, then down the path that led to the street. As she neared the bottom of the slope, she heard a loud *clunk* on the asphalt nearby. She jumped. A fist-sized rock had landed about ten feet behind her.

She looked up. The teenage girls were watching from the top of the path. The skinny one had that hand over her mouth. The blond one just stared down at her.

Helen secured the stroller in place and picked up the rock. It felt hot in her hand. Without stopping to think, she slipped it into one of the stroller's many compartments, then pushed her daughters toward the street.

Moving fast, her grip tight, she wheeled the stroller up Osprey, the street that bordered the playground. It was lined with small, two-family houses with shared porches and tiny front lawns. On the porches were discarded living room furniture and toys: La-Z-Boys with duct-taped seats, kids' bikes with busted tires. The lawns were ragged with weeds or sunbaked patches of dust. It was her least favorite part of these walks home, the street she often went out of her way to avoid. The street glittered, its surface streaked with tar-covered cracks.

Now that she was a block away, she couldn't believe that she'd let those teenagers get under her skin. That she'd taken the bait. That she'd crossed a line. What if she'd hurt them with the broken glass? They were just kids.

She didn't really understand kids—what knowledge she had was limited to her own—and she knew almost nothing about teenagers. She hadn't related to them even when she was one herself: smart, serious, at her best on her own. By that age, she'd already absorbed the message that it was important to focus on goals, not dreams. (*The best goals are within reach,* her mother always said.) Her friends were studious rule followers, just like her, though when the kids who smoked pot in the woods would ask if she wanted to hang out, she sometimes surprised herself and went with them.

She wondered what those long-lost friends—though they were never really friends—would think of her now. That she'd wound up here, in a town whose dwindling prospects seemed to mirror her own. She saw her surroundings through their eyes: this run-down street, this sad little town.

She was still so angry that her legs trembled with every step. What if that rock had landed just right, and with just enough force? What if it had struck one of her daughters? She thought of all those news stories that Tom read as if compelled—as if, on some level, he believed that confronting tragedy offered some small protection against it. He would drift by her office while she was catching up on her work and talk about the article he'd just read. *Did you see the* Times? he'd said one night. *That story about...*

He left it there, hanging. He couldn't get his head around it, or make himself say the words.

The teenagers who shot the baby in the stroller, she'd answered. Yes. She'd seen it.

Tom wandered off, shaking his head. And she tried to shake the horror, to focus on the video that was due in the morning.

That was a year ago, maybe more. She'd read the story and hadn't forgotten the details. The two friends, a thirteen-year-old boy and a fourteen-year-old girl, had lived in a town in Vermont. They found a gun and shot a baby.

They didn't know why they'd done it, or so they'd told the cops. Didn't know and didn't seem to care, and it was this lack of intent and remorse that had struck Helen at the time. Now she wondered if those kids had been daring each other, caught in a game that each was determined to win. How could a child be capable of such violence? Could anyone, if pushed hard enough in a moment of fear or rage?

She was sweating. Her shirt stuck to her chest, her hair to her neck. She wanted to lift her hair, let the cool air hit her skin. But she kept her hands on the stroller and kept moving.

There was a laugh in the distance behind her.

She stopped and turned. They were there, on the street, watching her, waiting. Were they following her? She refused to believe it. Maybe they were just headed this way.

She began walking again but could hear the scuffing of the teenagers' boots on the asphalt.

So this is the game they want to play. Her throat went tight. She told herself to relax, breathe. They were just fucking with her. Because she was an easy target. Because they'd seen her snap.

At the end of the block, near the intersection with Linden, a woman in a pink sweat suit came out of her house. Without glancing down the street, she scooped up the circulars from her front steps, shook off the water, and went back inside, letting the door slam behind her. Helen thought of the times she'd taken stupid risks in the city: wandering down empty streets to take photographs, stumbling home late at night. *And here.* That was what Tom would say. She was taking risks in Devon, and he didn't like it. She thought of her evening runs through town. Growing up in Belham, she'd never worried, knowing that if she were in danger or hurt, she could knock on a door and someone would help her. Here, she realized, she couldn't count on that. Not on this street. That woman in the pink sweat suit might not open the door to a face she didn't know.

Helen's anger gave way to fear. Her hands clenched the stroller. Her legs ached with the urge to run.

Sophie had started crying. A series of muffled sobs had gained force quickly and was now a high-pitched, full-throttle tantrum. Ilona joined in, twisting in her seat, punching her fists. Sophie belted out a few words between bursts of tears. She was still upset about the Cheerios.

"It's *okay*!" Helen had meant to reassure her daughter, but her voice was sharp, and Sophie cried harder. "We have more at home!"

Helen paused to look behind her. The teenagers were walking faster, gaining ground. They came to a stop a few houses away and waited for her next move. She couldn't call the cops—that would take too long. And what exactly would she tell them? She couldn't prove anything, not even that they'd thrown the rock. What if they challenged her? *She* was the one who'd smashed the bottle, with her own daughters watching. With an increasing sense of dread, she realized that the police might not take her side.

Years ago, when she was just starting to go out on dates and long-distance runs, her father had taught her how to grip her keys in her right hand, the biggest key wedged between her first two fingers, its base secure against the heel of her palm. She should aim for the throat, he advised. One good thrust would puncture the windpipe.

"If that doesn't work, go for an eye," he said. "Don't be squeamish."

She wasn't squeamish. She would give them one last chance, but she wasn't going to let them threaten her or her daughters. Keys in hand, she locked the stroller in place and gave her daughters what she hoped might pass for a smile.

"Mommy will be right back," she said, looking from one set of streaming eyes to the other. "Everything's fine." She hoped the confidence in her voice would calm them, though she could hardly hear herself over the roaring in her ears. "Stay here. I'll be right back."

She left her daughters facing the direction they'd been walking so they couldn't see whatever came next. Their cries doubled the instant she stepped out of view, as she knew they would. But she kept going. She pressed the key hard against her palm. Adrenaline surged through her veins.

She stopped a few paces away. The teenage girls must have seen in her eyes that she'd been pushed too far. But they didn't look like they wanted to back down.

Helen squeezed the key in her fist, desperately hoping they wouldn't step any closer. Because if they did, she would fight. And everything she'd ever believed about herself would be gone. She would be the kind of person Tom read about in news stories, shaking his head in shock and confusion.

Her voice was steady and cold.

"This is over," she said. "Do you understand?"

She held her hand tight, even though her fury was making her light-headed. The blond girl locked eyes with her. The sneer on her face said it wasn't over, not for her. She seemed about to respond but was distracted by the sound of a car engine, then of brakes in the street beside them.

It was Nick, Jackie's son. He pulled over and glanced out his open window at the teenage girls. In the stroller, Sophie and Ilona were screaming.

"Hey," he said to Helen. "You all right?"

He got out of the car. His faded jeans hung low on his hips, a chain jangling from his belt loop. The teenagers watched as he went over to Helen in a cloud of patchouli.

"What's going on?"

Helen realized she was still pressing her key into her palm. She shoved it into her pocket. As she returned to her daughters, an icy wave rushed through her. Her legs went instantly cold.

She watched as Nick faced the teenage girls, an eyebrow raised. He was nineteen years old and slight for his age, but seemed not to know it. Jackie was always complaining, and bragging, about the fights he started—bar fights, now that he'd found a place that would serve him. Karl stayed out of it. *Nick's a smart kid,* he'd told Helen. *He can see the right way to go. He just decides not to take it.*

The skinny girl stood with her arms crossed. The blond one planted her hands on her hips. Nick laughed.

"What's the problem?" he said. Not waiting for a response, he spoke to Helen. "Are these skanks giving you a hard time?"

Helen couldn't bring herself to answer him. The two girls watched him with scorn.

"What's your fucking problem?" Nick said to them. He raised his shoulders in an exaggerated shrug. "You deaf? Stupid? Okay, I know you're stupid, so let me spell this out for you. *Fuck off.* Go back to where you came from."

Helen turned to him.

"It's *enough,*" she said under her breath. "We're done here."

The skinny girl's face came to life. Splotches of red blazed on her damaged skin.

"Fuck *you*, asshole," the girl yelled at Nick. "*You're* the fucking skank, the fucking loser who graduated last year but still hangs around at school."

She spat on the ground in front of her. The blond girl waited a few seconds, then gave Helen the finger.

"Later, bitch," she said.

Helen didn't respond. The teenagers turned to go. They moved slowly, making a show of it as they drifted away. Farther down the street, they stopped. The blond girl looked back at them, as if memorizing their features. Then she laughed, that hard laugh, and headed with her friend toward the playground.

As soon as they disappeared, Helen felt a fist unclench inside of her.

"You didn't have to say that," she told Nick. "You didn't have to say *any* of that. You just made things worse." She stopped herself, pressed a hand to her forehead. "Sorry," she said. "I know you were trying to help."

Nick let out a huff but held back whatever he might have wanted to say. He gave a quick, incredulous shake of his head.

Helen breathed in the cool air. She searched in her bag for tissues, found none, and lifted up the bottom of her shirt to dry her face. She turned again to her daughters and held them as they reached for her, straining in their seats.

"Everything's fine," she told them. "We're fine."

Her hands were trembling. Her entire body seemed to shudder with anger and a slowly building sense of shame, each fueling the other in a way that she didn't want to think about.

"Hey," Nick said. "Don't let those idiots get to you." He let out a bitter laugh. "I went to high school with their brothers. None of them are ever going to make it out of this shithole." With a glance at the stroller, he added, "Sorry about the language. I can drive you home."

She pushed damp strands of hair out of her eyes.

"Thanks for your help, Nick," she said. "Really. But we'll walk."

"Then I'll walk with you. Karl would kill me if I didn't. Just give me a sec to park."

She hoped he wouldn't mention this to Karl. Before she could say anything, he was back in his car. He did a U-turn and parked in front of a house with a plastic slide on its lawn.

"It's all right," Helen told her daughters. "Everything's okay."

She held them and kept talking, trying to comfort them. But they weren't crying anymore. They were stunned into silence, their eyes unreadable. She needed to hold them, to feel them close to her, and hoped that this would stop her shaking, end the waves of shock and fear. Because that energy hadn't left her; she felt the pounding in her heart, in her lungs. Finally she released her daughters. She turned to watch Nick fling his army bag over his shoulder and lock up his car. She could smell her own sweat. And she was biting the inside of her cheek, an old habit she thought she'd kicked years ago. As she waited, her jaw tense and working, she tasted blood.

CHAPTER FIVE

Tom would have sprung for a cab to get to Donna's apartment, but there were no cabs, so he'd walked crosstown from the office, taking the long blocks as fast as he could, wondering what was going on with her, what was so important that she had to see him in the middle of the day. At Sixth Avenue, he had a stroke of luck, catching the M5 bus just before it pulled away. As he swung into his seat and the bus weaved through the traffic around Columbus Circle, he couldn't help a smile. *You're making good time,* he told himself. *You're in the clear.*

Smiling and talking to himself. He fit right in with the midday bus crowd.

Broadway to Seventy-Second Street and then north on Riverside Drive. The bus curved down the wide, shaded avenue: graceful buildings to the east, tall trees to the west. Like a boulevard in Paris. Beyond the trees was the terraced park that sloped down to the Hudson. The same river that flowed past Devon, seventy miles away.

He'd always liked the promise the start of fall seemed to offer and had even said something about it to Helen last night, after they'd finally gotten Sophie and Ilona to sleep. But Helen was looking at a bill that had arrived that day, and she had hours of work ahead of her, and all she would give him was a wry smile and a line tossed over her shoulder: *Beginning of shorter days.* And there was that look in her eyes—a mix of resentment and resignation, maybe even a little anger. She went to her office before he could ask her about it, which didn't surprise him.

He would think of something special for them to do this weekend, he decided. Maybe they could somehow carve out some time for themselves. He could surprise Helen tonight, even: bring home some beers that they could drink on their little front porch, under the new fall sky, after the girls were in bed. It amazed him, sometimes, what they had together. Despite all of his mistakes, his accumulated failures.

Tom sometimes thought back on his reluctance to have even one child and wished he could laugh. Within a span of weeks, he'd had to grasp that he would soon be the father of not one, not two, but three daughters. One day at work, when he was still trying to wrap his mind around the results of Helen's sonogram, he learned, thanks to an overheard conversation between Donna and a copy editor, that Donna was expecting a girl.

The copy editor was sorting stacks of papers on a table near his desk. For a few moments—even after Donna breezed away to her office, her eyes on her phone—it seemed all he could hear was that shuffling sound. Finally Tom realized that the copy editor was looking at him. She put down her papers and smiled.

"I know just how you feel," she said. "That sound makes me sleepy."

Tom straightened in his seat, giving her an embarrassed smile as he glanced away.

From that day forward, he resolved himself to focus. Concentrate on whatever task was at hand. Do things *right*. This thing was bigger than he was, and he could not screw up. When Helen was told she could sleep only on her left side, he bought her a pregnancy pillow and relocated to the couch. He wasn't sleeping much anyway. His mind raced with questions. How could he manage to tell Helen? Should he even try? Especially now, when she was feeling her absolute worst? He sat on the couch, sweating, his feet propped on the coffee table while Pussyface paced beneath him, her tail sweeping the undersides of his knees until he was ready to scream.

Bleary-eyed and rubber-limbed, he sleepwalked through his days at work. Donna was round-bellied and glowing. Her hips stayed trim, her arms firm and muscled. She glided between the cubicles, her shoulders thrown back to support the weight of her chest. Sometimes, at the end of the day, he would stop by her office and ask how she was feeling. *Everything's great,* she'd say.

He heard all about her preparations from the conversations around him. Her support network was in place, and ironclad. She had her parents in Westchester; both were successful and prominent lawyers, he would soon learn. She had her younger half sister, Candace, who'd been trying to make it as an actress in L.A. but was now moving to New York. Donna had already interviewed a dozen candidates and secured a nanny. She'd also sold her condo at a profit and put the proceeds toward a prewar apartment on Riverside Drive. Her new home had a room for her sister, a room for the baby nurse, and a room for the baby, which her tight circle of sophisticated, accomplished friends had already furnished with organic linens and educational toys.

No one, to Tom's knowledge, ever speculated about "the donor." Donna was a single mother by choice, the copy editor informed him. She didn't have to add that Donna was a hero to the late-thirties and early-forties single women on the magazine's staff.

One day in her third trimester, Donna called him into her office.

"So," she said. "How is Helen?"

"She's fine."

Tom waited. Donna hadn't called him in here to ask about Helen. She gazed down at her belly.

"Just think," she said. "Two months from now, you'll have twins! We're talking instant family." She grinned as if she were proud of him. "Helen must be so happy."

He'd seen it many times—Donna was a master at gently persuading others to come around to her way of thinking. With the lightest possible pressure, she was touching on his vulnerabilities.

"I'd like to make this official," she said, waving a hand at the distance between them. "You're free and clear, as I've said before. We can sign an agreement that leaves you with no responsibilities, no obligations. No child support, either. Which I imagine is a relief."

She'd always understood him so well. He looked at her for a long time.

"No responsibilities," he said. "I would be out of the picture."

"Yes. It's called a termination of parental rights. There would be no relationship between you and this child."

She was cool and confident. A winner. It was why everyone wanted to be close to her, why they jockeyed for a position at her side. Donna was a winner.

"We've been good friends for years now," she said. "I wouldn't suggest this if I didn't think it was the best solution for everyone. Do you have a lawyer? We can keep this very simple. Just a meeting in an office."

She rested her hands on her desk; she'd done her research, of course. She opened her calendar to schedule that meeting. She was looking at the weeks right after her due date.

Which was just a few weeks after Helen's. By then, he would be a father.

One of Donna's hands had drifted back to her stomach. Tom couldn't help looking there—at what had seemed, from the very start, to belong only to *her*.

She looked up at him. Her eyes softened.

"You can feel good about this," she said. "I've told you: I *want* to do this on my own."

As he faced the enormity of regret, he felt a moment of panic; his doubts gripped him, tugged him by the ankles. But she would be a great mother; he was sure of that. The child would never need to know about him, would never feel a lack of care or love.

"Send me the date," he said. "I'll be there."

Helen beat Donna to the delivery room by three and a half weeks. His first children were hers. He watched as the babies came out: one with eyes open, wide and staring, the other in a gentle snooze. They were held out to Helen and then to him.

Hello, Sophie. Hello, Ilona.

They were beautiful. They were hideous. Staring down at them, he realized he was laughing and crying. He knew his tears were about more than becoming a father or seeing his children for the first time. But the nurses were impressed. One squeezed his shoulder. He squeezed her back.

Don't go, he wanted to say. *I've fucked up everything.*

In those early days, he didn't have much time to think about Donna or the pending meeting. The chaos and constant work at home consumed him completely. Sometimes, though, his mind played tricks on him. When he managed to sleep, he had vivid dreams that corrected his recent history. He had ended the affair after two weeks, amicably and with Donna very much not pregnant. She would come to Helen's baby shower and hand over a check for a double stroller. He would wake in a happy confusion, his affair scrubbed from the record. He tried to stay in those dreams as long as he could.

But one evening, while Helen was using the hospital-grade breast pump that resembled agricultural machinery, he checked his email.

There was the birth announcement: Elana, five pounds, fourteen ounces, born six days ago.

Hello, Elana.

Elana. Just a name she'd always liked, Donna would tell him later. No, she hadn't realized that one of his daughters was named Ilona (named after the girl who'd lived next door in

Philly and had helped out his mom after his father died). Not that it would have changed Donna's decision.

Tom called her.

"Can I come over?" he asked. "Just for a few minutes."

Donna was silent for so long he thought she'd hung up.

"What for?" she said, her voice flat.

He wanted to see her, this newborn Elana. Even if it was just this once, he had to see her. He was sleep-deprived, conflicted, not thinking clearly. This would be all he ever had before he walked away: a glimpse of these early moments, the very beginning.

"I have something for you," he said.

Later, Donna would cite her answer as the first of her own bad decisions. The one she regretted the most. He'd caught her at a rare weak moment, when she was elated and proud but too exhausted to argue.

"Five minutes," she told him. "We need to sleep."

Late that night, while Helen and the girls were in their longest stretch of sleep, Tom took from the closet one of the many duplicate blankets, still in its gift bag, that some relative had sent. He drove from Long Island City to the Upper West Side.

Going out for wipes! his note said. *Back in a few.*

He walked through the dark rooms of Donna's apartment, his heart thundering. He met the night nurse, the half sister, and Donna's mother, who seemed even more formidable than Donna herself. She waved him on and went back to her magazine.

Donna was in the nursery, a cool, moonlit oasis of calm. He placed the blanket on a table, then went over to her and gazed down at the baby in her arms. She looked so much like Donna, down to the wisps of wild hair.

"I told everyone to give me some time alone with her," Donna said. "And now my fucking arm's locked in place."

"Do you want me to hold her?" Tom said.

Donna sighed. Even in the dim light, he could see the weariness on her face.

"Fine," she said. "Every time I think she's sleeping, she starts fussing."

With evident caution, she handed her to him. Elana stirred and grasped his finger.

He knew it was just a reflex. But a connection had been made. A tiny, momentary bond. It was real.

He saw something in Donna's eyes, too, as she looked from Elana to him. Surprise at his confidence, maybe, and also an unexpected warmth. Though that might have been a trick of the shadows.

On his way out, he took a pack of organic wipes from Donna's supply closet.

"I had to go to three stores," he told Helen when he got home.

Helen was on the couch, flat on her back, an uneaten bowl of pasta between her feet. She opened her eyes and gave him a drowsy look.

"That's great," she said.

Every few days, he would call Donna. He usually got her voice mail. Several hours later, he would get a voice mail back.

"Thanks for checking in, bud," Donna would say, with just a hint of forced energy. "We're all set."

But a day before the meeting to sign the papers, Donna canceled because Elana had just come down with a fever. Then Donna got sick. Early one morning, he called from work to see how they were both doing.

"My parents are gone, my nanny is sick, and Candace flew out to L.A. for an audition," Donna said. "I haven't been out of the house for three days and I can no longer even remember what it feels like to wear a clean shirt."

"You need a break," he said. "I'll be right there."

He made up an excuse for the deputy editor and left work to spend the day with Elana: taking her to the little garden behind the building, fixing the mobile and hanging it over her crib. Later, when Elana was napping, Donna came home and they sat together in the living room.

"We need to reschedule that meeting," she said. "But I can't do next week. Too many appointments."

He was secretly relieved. He was even more relieved when she called two weeks later and once again put off the meeting. Elana was going through a colicky phase, keeping everyone up all night, and now Donna's entire household was sick. He pitched in again. He was amazed Donna let him, that she was allowing herself to rely on him, even a little, as a last resort. He was relieved even though he knew that every moment he spent with Elana would make it harder to let go. On the days when he could stop by, stealing thirty minutes or even an hour after work, the idea of signing the papers began to fill him with dread.

Before long, Donna was back in the office. But her schedule wasn't easy. She had the magazine to run and often traveled, and though she managed her time down to the minute, there were entire months when she didn't have a moment to spare. For the first time, she had circles under her eyes. Even with all her resources, the pressures sometimes exhausted her.

Helen, usually a rebounder, was also struggling. After her boss saved her job by moving her off-site and on contract, she often worked at night, after Tom came home. Late one night, when her computer crashed and wouldn't restart, she borrowed Tom's laptop to finish an email to her office.

"I'll just be a second," she told him.

She opened Gmail and, not realizing it wasn't her own account, clicked on the Drafts folder. The only email in there was a note that Tom had never sent but had forgotten to delete.

This is a mistake—we should talk.

It was from one of the times he'd come close to ending the affair with Donna. The address line was blank.

"What is this?" Helen asked.

But she knew what it was. He could see it on her face. He spoke before he lost his nerve.

"It only went on for a few weeks," he said. "And it ended a long time ago."

Helen got up from his desk and went to the kitchen. He followed her. After a few minutes, she spoke without looking at him.

"How long ago?"

"Before you got pregnant."

That was true. He hadn't told her everything, but he hadn't lied. Not exactly, not yet. He felt a speck of relief at coming partially clean and had a sudden desire to tell her everything—to tell her about Elana. But he stopped himself. As he looked at her face, he was sure he would lose her forever.

So he remained quiet while she took it in. He watched her confusion turn to anger and hurt.

"I don't want to see you tonight," she said.

He spent that night in their car. He left with only his wallet and keys, not even a coat. He probably could have gone back and collected a few things. But despite his guilt at hurting Helen—and he would repair that damage, he told himself; he would *not* make it worse—being out of the house brought an irresistible sense of release. His head was throbbing and his muscles ached but the thought was still there: *I can go anywhere I want right now.*

The following night, he crashed at an old college friend's apartment, sleeping on an air mattress that slowly deflated. He woke up on a crumpled pile of plastic. That evening, as he was about to leave work, Helen called.

"Come home," she said. "There's no way I'm doing this on my own."

About a month later, after an afternoon spent carrying the girls up and down the flights of their walk-up and trekking them to the Queens playground, Helen handed him a folder filled with house listings in Devon.

"We could find a place here," she said. "A home we can afford. Like this one." Looking at a photo, she smiled. "We'll be happy there. I'm sure of it."

She must have seen some hint of resistance—she knew he didn't want to leave the city—because he saw her stop, wait. Consider her options. And if she was willing to use them.

A chill ran through him. It had never been this way between

them. They'd never resorted to tactical moves. He could see the resentment and hurt pride on her face.

"Is there a reason why you want to stay?" she said. "Is something keeping you here?" She pressed on. "Or someone?"

Tom knew what it had cost her to ask that question. He conceded immediately.

"No," he told her. "Of course not."

After the move, Donna called him in for another talk in her office.

"We can't leave this hanging forever," she said. "It's as much my fault as yours for letting this go on for so long. Let's set that appointment."

Tom waited. In different ways, he was failing everyone. And he regretted that more than anything. But he had to tell her.

"I've been thinking about that," he said. "Because things have changed."

Donna gave him a steady look. He could tell that she understood and that she wasn't really surprised. And yet he felt the weight of her stare.

"Look, I'm not going to *force* you out," she said finally. "I think it could be good for Elana, having you in her life. And the truth is I like knowing you're around. I didn't expect that, but I do." She waited. "But if that's the way we choose to go, we need to come to an understanding. I want clear boundaries and expectations. That's in your interest, too, if you want to be a part of her life."

He'd considered that: securing his claim. Making weekly,

legally protected visits to his daughter. He also pictured Elana, years from now, looking back and thinking that was all he'd wanted: one hour a week, at her mother's apartment. Would she compare what he'd given to her to the time he'd spent with Sophie and Ilona? (Just the idea of her as an adult tripped him up completely. Would these three daughters meet one day, come to know one another?)

"That doesn't mean I think that's the right decision," Donna said. "I still think the best solution is the one that's simplest for everyone." Her phone hummed, and when she tapped it, a photo of Elana lit up the screen. "You can choose to give Elana a simple, happy life. Or you can give her, and all of us, very complicated lives."

Tom wanted to say that everyone wound up with complicated lives, sooner or later, no matter how much they tried to avoid it. He also knew he was being selfish.

"One more thing," Donna said. "You can be in or out. Not both. If you're in, that means no secrets. I won't be a part of that. It hasn't been a problem for me yet, but it will be." She looked at him. "This is taking a toll on you, Tom. Believe me, I'm telling you that as a friend."

She touched his hand. Hers was dry and cool. He realized they hadn't had any physical contact since the night she'd put the newborn Elana in his arms. Donna left her hand in his.

"We have loose ends," she said. "I don't like it."

Before he knew it, Sophie and Ilona were toddling around the new living room, sporting inch-long crops of hair that made them look like tiny marines. Elana had Donna's wild curls, bright blue eyes, and a mischievous smile. He tried not to look for similarities among them, though they were there, in sudden looks and gestures. He could see the hunger for adventure in their eyes as they stumbled forward, reaching for whatever was new. *What now? What next?*

He was learning too. How to live in a heightened state. How to be careful. He paused before speaking. He checked himself. But the effort exhausted him, and he sometimes found himself forgetting things or gazing around him, unaware of what, exactly, he'd done or said just moments before. Though in some ways, life got easier, or at least the mechanics did. He and Helen had their new house in Devon, and she was hard at work, the way she liked it.

Never mind that he was coming apart at the seams. That was what he told Elana during his visits. He whispered in her warm little ear. While she was small, and the words held no meaning for her, he could unburden himself of his secrets, confide in her as if she were the only one he could trust.

"I'm behind the eight ball," he'd say, lulling her to sleep. "But I can't let you go."

In the moment, the pressures sometimes seemed excruciating, almost unbearable, but those moments became weeks and then months. Donna wanted a resolution, but time was working against her: She was busy with the ever-increasing demands of her job and life as a single mother and was often tired. As the months wore on, he and Donna seemed to settle into a fragile equilibrium. He could sometimes convince himself that his worst mistakes were in the past. The hard part was keeping everything straight, all the tiny details. That was what gave him the slow-burning terrors that kept him awake at night.

One Sunday morning, while he was working on a spreadsheet of their household expenses, Helen gave him a concerned smile.

"You called Ilona 'Elana' while you were getting her dressed," she said. "Did you see the way she looked at you? You said it three times."

He looked at her, his heart thumping with shame.

That talk with Donna was the last they had in her office. The economy stalled and the magazine folded. Tom and Donna were the last two out the door.

"Don't worry," she told him. "No one is going down on my watch."

There followed dark months when he couldn't find a job. Before long, he and Helen were charging everything: groceries, copayments, electric bills. On a night when they were trying to figure out which of their credit cards to use for the family's next health insurance payment, Donna called.

"You've got an interview at seven-thirty tomorrow morning," she said. "These guys start their day early. Science desk, newswire."

That was the first of what would be four interviews. Tom was walking to the train when someone from HR called with an offer. With a dizzying sense of relief, he told Helen the news.

"We're lucky," he said.

"*You're* lucky," Helen said with a laugh. "It's strange. You've always been lucky."

His life was coming together again, but he wore it awkwardly, like a shirt that didn't quite fit. It would take them years to catch up, Helen said, and she was right.

He thanked Donna at his next visit. Together they watched Elana rampage around the living room, toppling towers of blocks and dismantling the toy kitchen. He could have spent hours watching her carry out her destructive little missions.

Donna told him she was dating again. Venture capitalists, social entrepreneurs. There was also a British neuroscientist who was fifty-five and "still fit," Donna said.

"Alan's not exactly my type," she said. "But he's growing on me."

Tom could see she was eyeing this guy for a larger role and was surprised to feel a hint of jealousy.

"What about you?" he asked. "Are you looking for work?"

She was working all the time, she said. Consulting for a content marketer, managing special projects for one of their former competitors. She'd always had various side ventures, but now she was looking at bigger, bolder opportunities. Some of these opportunities might involve travel, she added. "Or relocation."

Tom felt something go slack inside him. Donna gave him a level stare and her warmest smile.

"Send my love to Helen," she said. "Let's talk next week. I'll shoot you an email."

Sometimes he forgot that Helen and Donna knew each other. They'd met at office parties and drinks nights, and all three of them were Facebook friends. One morning, he saw Helen looking at photos of Elana on her computer. He froze behind her, tilted forward on the pads of his feet. He didn't dare to breathe.

"Look at her," Helen said, clicking through the images that Donna had posted. "She's adorable."

The words almost fell out of his mouth: *Thank you.* He coughed, covering his face while he landed on his heels. He felt like someone whose instinct is to dart into traffic in response to a cry of *Watch out!*

Helen gave him a strange look, then turned back to her computer. There was a photo of Elana on a trampoline. An action shot: As Elana bounced, two other kids were getting catapulted onto the gymnasium floor.

"Have you seen these?" Helen asked. She scrolled down. "I didn't know they even made skiing outfits for kids that age."

Other photos showed Elana riding a balance bike and swimming in a pool. Traveling to Paris and Barcelona. Napping at Davos, crawling at Comic-Con.

"Donna's doing this all on her own," Helen said. She glanced at Sophie and Ilona, who were building a tower out of Duplo blocks next to the coffee table. "Are we supposed to be taking them skiing?"

"Of course not," Tom said. "Nobody did that sort of thing when we were growing up. Look at us. We didn't go to Barcelona."

Look at us. That was what she was doing.

"Maybe I'll check out some swimming lessons," she said.

And Helen wanted the girls to go to the more expensive preschool, the one they probably couldn't afford. It was easy for him to forget these stresses. There were always others. He sometimes felt like he hadn't had a clear thought or an unscheduled minute since all of these little girls were born.

He began to look forward to those long train rides between Devon and the city. He would ease back onto the vinyl seat, stare out the window, give himself over to the train's rhythmic sway. He never slept: It was his one chance to lose himself without consequences, to let his mind empty and wander. *Ninety-five minutes each way, that's gotta suck,* Mark said. Tom smiled and shrugged. *You get used to it.*

He was about to embark on the trip home after a late night in the office when he got a call from Donna.

"She's crying and she won't stop." Donna seemed to be holding back tears herself. Her voice quavered, which shocked him. "She's got a fever. She's *honking*!"

The pediatrician hadn't called back. Her sister was out and she couldn't reach her mother or any of her friends. She was thinking of going to the hospital.

"Wait ten minutes," Tom said. He could text Helen, tell her he had to stay another hour and would call from the train. "I'll be there."

Donna's eyes were red when she came to the door. Tom could hear Elana coughing in her bedroom. He knew that cough; both Sophie and Ilona had already had episodes of croup. He opened a window and sat with Elana on the bench beneath it, letting her rest against his shoulder as the cold air hit her face.

"What are you doing?" Donna said. "She'll freeze."

"Trust me."

Within minutes, the coughing stopped. Elana was drowsy but still awake, her eyes on him.

Donna gathered blankets and sat down on the bench beside them. Though she was shivering, her face was flushed with relief.

"Look at that," she said, smiling at both of them. "Daddy helped."

Tom looked at her. For almost two years, he'd managed to remain a pleasantly vague presence, not unlike the woman who came once a week to clean the apartment and also doted on Elana. Donna flinched as she realized her mistake.

That caught Elana's attention.

"Daddy," she said. Seeing her mother's reaction, she repeated it. "Daddy, daddy, daddy."

They put her to bed, leaving the window cracked open, the humidifier sending up puffs of cool mist. After she fell asleep, Tom sat with Donna in the kitchen. Donna poured them each a whiskey and pushed a glass toward him.

"I don't know what came over me," Donna said. "I must be delirious from lack of sleep."

"She won't remember. By next week it'll be forgotten."

"I saw that look. She'll remember. What am I supposed to tell her?"

Donna finished her drink. He poured her another.

"I should have forced us to settle this long ago," she said. "Even if that meant dragging you to court. But I always thought we'd be able to work it out on our own. What the hell was I thinking?" She picked up her glass, then put it down again. "What the hell are *you* thinking, Tom? Do you really believe this can go on much longer?"

She got up and emptied her glass in the sink.

"You're running out of time," she said. "We're going to reach a point where I'll have to make this decision for you. And it might not be the one you want."

Helen had forgiven him a short affair with a nameless woman who was never coming back. Sometimes he wished he'd told her everything. She knew him better than anyone. How many times, desperate for advice, had he wished, perversely, that he could turn to her? Helen was practical, resourceful. She was good at solving problems; she would know what to do. He could almost imagine what she would tell him: *You should have come to me right away. Or not at all.* But now, at this stage, the whole truth was so much harder to forgive. She would make a decision, and Helen's decisions were final.

"Stop worrying," she said once, after they'd bickered their way through the morning routine. "We can't *afford* to get divorced."

When she saw his face, she told him she was kidding. But as he left for work, he felt that some part of him had finally broken.

There wasn't a day when he didn't think about what Donna had proposed from the very start. He could walk away. Wash the slate clean while Elana was still young enough to forget him. It was the difference between one lie and years of lies.

He wasn't a liar, he told himself. He was as loyal as a dog.

And Donna was right. Elana's life was full—of activities, family, love. But the time was coming when she would ask questions. Was he really her daddy? Why didn't he live at home with her like the daddies in her books?

"You want to tell her it's because you already have a family?" Donna said.

That was at his visit two weeks ago. Tom sat stiff-backed in her home office. She knew she had him.

"She's three now," Donna said. "But there's still time for us to do the right thing. She will forget. I know it hurts to hear that. But she will forget, and she will be fine."

"How can you say that?" Tom was so angry he almost couldn't get the words out. He sprang up from the couch. "I've been part of her life for three years. She wouldn't just forget me overnight."

Donna pressed her palms on her desk.

"My sister moved back to L.A. six months ago," she said. "The first week she was gone, Elana asked about her all the time. Then she stopped. She still calls the guest room *Aunt Cammy's room*, but if I ask her who Aunt Cammy is, she gives me a blank look."

Donna leaned back and pushed her hair over her shoulders.

"I'm not telling you this to hurt you," she said. "I'm actually trying to make you feel better."

Tom couldn't listen anymore. He left Donna's office and went to Elana's room. He stood at the door and watched her wave a hand through the particles of dust that swirled through the air. She saw him and tackled him around the knees and pulled him inside.

He let her play one of her favorite games: knocking him over. He sat down on the floor with his legs crossed and let her push him again and again. She squealed with delight, never tiring.

Her eyes twinkled and gleamed. With her, he never screwed up. He could do no wrong.

Daddy's little bruiser.

Tom rooted her on until, exhausted, he collapsed on the corduroy cushion. He curled on his side and pretended to sleep.

Elana plopped on the floor beside him and studied him for a moment. She patted his hair, touched his face. Then she placed her small hands square on his back and pushed with all her might.

"Daddy," she said. "I pick you up."

CHAPTER SIX

HELEN, 12:50 P.M.

Inside, door shut. For a few minutes, Helen forced herself not to think about the teenage girls. She lost herself in the usual tasks: removing backpacks, untying laces, fielding demands for something to eat. The only thing she wanted was to peel off her stinking, sweaty clothes and escape to the shower, where she would turn the water as hot as it would go. She didn't care if it hurt.

Then she would get back to Mega Crux. She still had time if she moved fast.

Her cell phone rang. Ryan was already talking when she picked up.

"So how's it going?" he said. "You wouldn't believe how many times I've had to stop the sales manager from calling you."

"I have to call you back," she said, and hung up.

She settled the girls on the couch. Gave them PB&Js and cookies and glasses of milk. Pulled the curtains and put on Sesame Street's *Peter and the Wolf*. The living room was cool and dark, in shifting shadows.

She had to talk to Ryan, but first she had to clear her head. She went to the basement, stripped off her clothes, and tossed them in the machine. The shower helped, but not as much as she'd hoped. By the time she came back downstairs, the cookies and milk were gone, the sandwiches pushed aside. The girls had claimed their usual spots: Sophie on the giant pillow that Helen had owned since college, Ilona curled up with her elephant and sucking her thumb. They were already drifting off. Helen sank down onto the bottom of the stairwell and watched them breathe.

She was at her desk, trying to make some progress that she could report to Ryan. But her thoughts kept returning to the playground. She could see it all so clearly.

The blond girl's fury as she spat out each word: *Fuck you, bitch.* The skinny girl grinning down at Sophie, like they were two of a kind. The sound of the rock hitting the ground behind her. The rock that—*what was she thinking?*—she'd put into the stroller and brought into her home.

She pressed her hands to her forehead. *It's over now,* she told herself. Though even as she thought the words, she sensed this wasn't true. She could still feel the heat rising up her spine, the electricity racing beneath her skin, the key between her fingers. She would have used it, too, though her hand had been shaking, her arm trembling with adrenaline; she had been that angry, that frightened. It terrified her even now, thinking of how close she'd come to making a terrible mistake. She could *see* herself, returning their stares, checking over her shoulder as they followed her down the street. She had been inside and outside, tasting acid, breathing in the metallic smell of her own sweat.

It's over. Done. She hadn't made that mistake. They were out of her life. She had to move on.

She stood up from her desk. Checked her phone: no messages. Downstairs, she saw that Ilona had dropped her elephant and was sleeping with her back to the TV. Sophie was on her stomach, the way she'd slept when she was a baby, making fussing sounds. Bad dreams.

Helen kneeled beside her and traced circles on her back until Sophie settled deeper into sleep.

Last week, she'd passed by the girls' room during naptime and saw that Sophie had left her bed. At first, she hadn't been worried. She thought she heard noises down the hall, in the spare room that had become a playroom. Sophie liked to be alone; Helen had gotten used to finding her in a bedroom or hallway, surrounded by her books and animals, pretending to read to her dolls.

So she'd gone back to her office and gotten to work, trying to finish up some project. A few minutes later, she stopped. The house was too quiet. She listened for sounds of Duplos or crayons spilling onto the floor. Nothing.

She looked in the spare room. It was empty. She checked the girls' room, her bedroom, and the bathroom. There were no signs of Sophie.

"Sophie," she called out, keeping her voice soft. She didn't want to wake Ilona. "Sophie."

She still wasn't worried, not really, not yet. But she moved faster, her pulse accelerating as she looked in the bedroom closets and under the beds. She was checking the hallway closet, looking behind dusty luggage and stacks of unpacked boxes, when the doorbell rang.

She ran down the stairs and opened the door. On the front step, a young man held Sophie by the hand. Sophie was staring straight ahead, wide-eyed, torn between squirming away and wanting to see what would happen next.

Helen rushed forward and took her. The sudden move made Sophie burst into tears.

"It's okay," the man said. He looked from Helen to Sophie and back again. "Everything's okay! Didn't mean to scare you." He backed away, hands raised, and gave Helen a nervous smile. "I found this little lady on your lawn. Picking dandelions."

Sophie looked down at the flowers in her hand. She squeezed them into a pulp and threw them to the floor.

When had Sophie gotten big enough to open the door? Helen held her a foot away and looked her over. As soon as she released her, Sophie darted past her and fled to the couch. Ilona came downstairs, joining her sister in tears, deafening shrieks that reverberated through the rooms.

Helen looked at the man on the porch. Clean-cut, mid-twenties, brown uniform. The UPS guy. He was getting redder by the second, seemingly embarrassed for both of them. Helen pressed a hand above her eyes. She thought of strangers. Cars. Strange men *with* cars. She stopped there.

The girls' cries echoed in her ears. She couldn't think straight.

"Give me one second," she told the guy. He gave her an awkward half-smile.

Leaving the door open behind her, Helen darted into the kitchen, poured some watered-down juice, filled bowls with goldfish crackers. Sophie and Ilona took the cups and bowls and carried them into the living room, knowing they could get away with anything now.

She went back to the UPS guy, who was still waiting on the porch.

"Thanks for bringing her in," she said. "She's never done that before."

He seemed relieved.

"Don't worry about it," he said. "The same thing happened to some friends of mine. Except they found their kid on the roof of their apartment building."

Helen didn't want to hear that story. In the living room, the girls overturned a mesh basket of toys, sending them clattering to the floor. They were spilling half of every handful of crackers, crunching them under their feet.

"Are you okay?" the guy said. "You kinda look like you're having a heart attack."

"I'm not." She took a breath. "Having a heart attack, I mean."

"Okay." He looked like he didn't believe her. He picked up a package from the porch. "Helen Nichols?"

"Yes. Thanks." Her heart was still racing, but she was glad to see that her hands were steady as she signed the electronic clipboard. She put the Zappos box on the table. As if she owed him an explanation, she added, "They're just moccasins."

As soon as he left, she called a locksmith and had a dead bolt installed. It was high enough that Sophie and Ilona wouldn't be able to reach it for years. That evening, when Tom came home, he looked at it, puzzled.

"It seemed like a good idea," Helen told him. "That's all."

She wanted to tell him what had happened, but she couldn't.

"Great," Tom said with an affable shrug. "Glad one of us is on top of things."

Helen went to the kitchen and heated up the last of the coffee. There was a tension in her neck, a soreness in her limbs. Lingering effects from the playground.

But she had to admit it was more than that. Her body seemed to ache in recognition of what was becoming impossible to ignore. She was losing control. Making bad decisions. All that slow-burning anger she'd felt these last few years was finally coming to a boil.

Even small things were slipping out of her grasp. Like their backyard. From the window over the sink, she could see the uneven slope of their lawn. The grass was a little high, the flowering shrubs a little wild. At the edge of the property stood an old doghouse that had been left by the previous owners. It was in bad shape and getting worse, with gaps in the roof that allowed water to collect inside. They'd decided to tear it down when they moved in, but somehow still hadn't gotten around to it. On those rare weekends when they had a spare block of time, they always thought of a reason to do something else.

"If we tear it down, where will I sleep when I'm in trouble?" Tom once said. He never made that joke again.

Two years later, it was still there. Early that summer, Butch had stopped by the house while Tom was at work and offered to help them get rid of it.

"You don't want to wind up with animals in there," Butch

said. "Or termites." He scratched his shoulder, reaching under his muscle-T. "Besides. It don't look good."

"Thanks," Helen said. "We'll take care of it. Really." He was giving her his typical look, hostile and suspicious. "It's on the list."

She and Tom would tear it down tonight, she told herself. They would tear it down, then drink beers on the porch under the dark sky, the only sound the faint notes drifting from Glenn's wind chimes across the street.

She wouldn't tell Tom about the girls from the playground. Just like she hadn't told him about Sophie's escape. She was sure he would try to make her feel better, tell her it wasn't her fault, that these things happened, that no one got hurt. But maybe he'd ask himself the same questions that kept coming to her. What if Sophie had wandered off their front lawn? What if the teenagers had had more nerve, or better aim with the rock? What if she'd hurt somebody with that vodka bottle or used the key?

———

Helen took her coffee to her office and turned on some music to try to keep any thoughts and images of the playground at bay. She willed herself to focus, and to her surprise, it worked. Finally she was beginning to make progress, and though she wasn't close to where she should have been, she thought she could make her deadline.

She dialed Ryan's number.

"Sorry about earlier," she said. "It was a bad time."

"Don't worry about it! We all have those days." Ryan lowered his voice, the way he did when he had bad news. "Speaking of...how far have you gotten on Mega Crux?"

"About halfway there."

"That's a relief. Sort of! Because they're changing it again. And here's the thing." Ryan paused, as if bracing himself. "It'll be an hour before I can get you the changes. At least. They haven't even started the conference call. And Lou still wants to circle back with you before he leaves." He groaned. "In case he wants to change it again, I suppose."

Helen closed her eyes. Not only had she wasted time, but she could already feel the pressure she would be under to complete the edits once she received them.

"I'm really sorry," Ryan said. "But you'll like this. I'm pulling together an ad for the next issue. There's a new line of protein products."

Despite herself, she smiled. It was how they'd always cheered each other up during crazy days in the office.

"Go on," she said.

"Man Patties! Protein patties for mass-building muscle heads." Ryan was twirling in his chair; she could hear it squeaking. "You know, you could use some mass, Helen. Maybe you should fry one up and sprinkle it over one of your watercress-and-almond salads."

"Thanks," Helen said. "But about the Mega Crux deadline—there's no way."

"Of course there is." Ryan's voice was bright. "You'll be fine. You always are."

She *used* to be fine. She paced around her office, her frustration building with every step. She knew she should use this unexpected delay for other, less pressing projects. But her concentration had been rattled, and she could feel her anger, undirected, just below the surface. She kept seeing the blond girl's cold, hard smile. *Like I give a fuck.*

She needed a break, she decided. From everything. Then she would come back and do her work in half the time, and with better results. She'd go for a run, free herself from this downward spiral.

She checked to see if Monica's car was in Karl's driveway and made another call.

"Any chance you could babysit for a little while? I'm on deadline."

"Sure," Monica said. "Right now?"

"That would be great."

A cap clicked on a pen.

"I'll come around back."

Helen went down to the living room, where Sophie and Ilona were stirring. They followed her to the basement, dragging their dolls behind them. The girls loved Monica. They liked to play with her hair and go through her bag, looking at her books and highlighters and makeup. Monica didn't mind. She was the oldest of four sisters and was, it seemed, unflappable. Her occasional babysitting was one of the many jobs she squeezed in between her classes at the local college and shifts at her dad's pizza parlor. She'd turned down an offer from a better school after one of her sisters—one of the middle ones, Crystal—got pregnant. Their mother had left years ago, so Monica took her sister to appointments and helped keep the household running.

She was a straight-A student with choppy hair that she cut herself, most recently bleached a white blond.

Helen waited on the back porch. Over at Karl and Jackie's, the side door opened. Monica came across the lawn in cutoffs and a tank top, an old backpack hanging from her shoulder. She wasn't wearing any makeup or the silver and leather bracelets that were usually stacked on her wrists. If it weren't for her hair, she would look fourteen years old.

The door behind Helen was open. Inside, Sophie and Ilona were playing with their toy kitchen, the tiny plastic plates and fake pizza slices clattering onto the floor.

"Thanks," Helen told Monica. "Everything's piling up today."

"No problem. So you'll be in your office?"

"First I need to get out of the house for a while. Then I'll get to work."

Monica nodded. Helen glanced behind her, though she knew the girls weren't listening. Even if they could hear her, they wouldn't understand what she was talking about.

"I finally finished off that bag you sold me," she said.

Monica laughed. "The one from last winter?"

"That's the one," Helen said. "I don't have cash on me right now for another. But how about next week?"

Helen remembered sitting on this porch one night a year or so ago, after a long day working on some forgotten project. Monica had come out from Nick's and was standing in the backyard, smoking a bowl. When she saw Helen, she smiled and strolled over. They sat for a while and Monica passed her the pipe. She didn't seem surprised at all when Helen took her up on her offer.

"Next week's fine," Monica said. "But hey, if you want to chill out now, I've got a joint back at the house."

Helen sat on the porch swing while Monica went back to Karl and Jackie's. She returned with the joint and a lighter. Helen walked to the edge of her yard, out by the doghouse. A few puffs, that was all it took, and a soft weight fell upon her. The world went quiet and distant and still.

She came slowly back across the lawn.

"Thanks," she said. "That helped."

Monica put the lighter and the rest of the joint in a tin box. She slipped that into her bag.

Helen gazed at the shimmering expanse of her neighbors' yards. Over at Butch's, the chemically treated grass seemed to glow with an almost neon intensity. For the first time, she found herself paying attention to how nice his yard was, how much work he must put into it. There was a certain precision to the paving stones, in the unvarying pink of the petunias, even in the way the red maple was reflected in the birdbath. Something about that made her feel bad about herself, though she wasn't sure why.

"I'll be back soon," she said. "I'm going for a run."

"Okay. Give me a minute to take this back to the house. I'll meet you inside."

"Sure. And, Monica? Thanks for everything."

She pushed herself. Ran at a fast pace, as if she didn't know or care where she was going, as long as she got away.

But she knew where she was going.

At first, she'd told herself she was going back to a lane of warehouses she'd explored a few months ago. She liked the light there, the way the abandoned buildings curved into the distance, the muted red of the brick against the blue sky and so many shades of green. She could take photos with her phone—she had it with her, in case Monica needed to reach her—and work on a painting later, maybe even this weekend, if she finished her assignments. She'd wanted to go back for weeks now, and this was the perfect chance, the perfect way to turn this terrible day around.

But while she was changing her clothes and tying her running shoes, a different idea had come to her. She'd tried to push it away, told herself it was another risk she shouldn't take. And yet she couldn't let it go.

She headed south, then east. Soon the streets of vinyl-sided colonials and split-levels gave way to an undeveloped stretch of land near the river. Farther south was what remained of the town's industry: the recycling center, the auto salvage yard, the wastewater treatment plant. She'd walked down there once, kicking up dust on the shoulders of desolate avenues, stopping to look at the blistered paint and cracked surfaces.

But today she followed the road along the residential edge of town, diverging from all of her familiar routes. She slowed down, eased into the road's steep decline, until it flattened out near a short bridge.

It was the last of the many bridges that crossed the creek, the unofficial cutoff between the nice and not-so-nice parts of town. This was where she should turn north, continuing her run on a wide loop that took her home.

But she kept going. As she crossed the bridge, her sneakers

landing hard on the concrete, she looked down at the water shining in the narrow channel. The banks of the creek were thick with willows and tangled vines, the textures softened yet overly bright. Around her, the light was hazy, the air hot and dense. She could feel her energy sapping as moisture left her skin. She knew she should stop, turn back. But she kept running.

She had to see where they lived.

Hollyanne and Tiffany: the girls from the playground. Nick had told her about them as he'd walked her home. Hollyanne was the skinny one with the bad teeth and bitten nails. Her older brother, who was Nick's age, had gotten kicked out of school for pushing a teacher down a stairwell. Tiffany, the blonde, was the only girl in a house full of stepbrothers; one had just spent a month in Rikers for punching an off-duty cop in the city. Their families lived next door to each other on a street that ended at a former coal silo.

"They're nothing," Nick said. "Forget about them."

Just a few nights ago, he'd gotten into a fight with one of Tiffany's stepbrothers—"a total fucking idiot," he told Helen, "but not the one who just got outta jail"—at Morey's, a bar on East Street where a lot of nineteen- and twenty-year-olds managed to get served. It started with an argument inside the bar. "About *politics*." Nick laughed. "I just couldn't stop myself— he's so fucking stupid." After trading insults through last call, everyone stumbled out to the parking lot. "There was all this pushing and jostling around, and he says I shoved him," Nick said. "The guy's got fifty pounds on me—I didn't shove him. But someone pushed *me*, and I guess I fell into him a little." As the guy was winding up, ready to throw a huge drunken punch in Nick's face, Nick darted away, moving as fast as he could. The guy fell forward, and Nick ran for his car, managing to escape only because the guy's friends, who were wasted, were already beating up someone else.

"Anyway," Nick told Helen. "Total idiots, all those guys." He shrugged. "Like their skanky sisters. Not worth thinking about."

On the other side of the bridge, the road rose up again, curving around a stand of trees. Helen ran along the road's gravel edge. Small frame houses sat close together on irregular lots, separated by strips of grass or concrete. At the top of a hill was an apartment house with a porch divided by orange construction netting. Two men sat on either side, drinking on their lawn chairs. Their eyes followed her as she swerved onto the sidewalk. It was threaded with weeds and ended in the middle of the next block.

She ran past cottages divided into rentals, homes with planks over their windows. Streets ended in empty lots or in half-finished construction sites with corrugated trailers. When she saw the silo, she turned and slowed to a walk.

A few houses away, an old man came out of a basement apartment. He was thin, his face ashen. A middle-aged woman with a gray ponytail stepped out to see him off. She gave Helen a long stare. Helen stopped, stared back, unblinking and stoned.

The woman went back inside, letting the door slam on her tinderbox of a house. This was their street—Hollyanne and Tiffany's. And maybe it was the sun and the heat, but for an instant, Helen saw it: the street swept by fire, the flames leaping from house to house, porch to porch. It was late at night and everyone was sleeping. Soon men and women were running out to the street in their T-shirts and underwear, holding children, clutching phones. Lights from the fire trucks swept over the houses; sirens and alarms filled ears. Babies cried while their parents shifted their feet in the gravel, littered with splinters of glass from their own broken bottles.

It was just a fleeting vision, burning away as fast as it had come.

Helen stood at the edge of someone's lawn and looked all around her. She saw what Hollyanne and Tiffany saw when they came home, when they looked out their bedroom windows, when they ran outside and let the screen doors slam. Duct-taped gutters, missing shingles. Crooked blinds and torn screens. Rusty cars in the driveways.

She didn't want to understand them. She didn't want to know about their violent fathers and brothers or their neglectful mothers. She wasn't sure exactly why she'd wanted to see where they came from, where they lived, though she'd hoped that it would somehow stop the relentless replaying of the scene in her head. They'd intruded into her life, and she would trespass in theirs. Maybe she'd thought that would give her some control of the moment. Give her the perspective she needed to file it away and put it to rest.

But she had been wrong about all of that. Now that she was here, she was sorry. Sorry to see how bad it was.

She remembered how she'd stared at those girls, what she saw in them. The blond girl—Tiffany—had let out that cloud of smoke and stared back. Helen now thought she understood the message behind the girl's scorn. *Tell me something I don't know.*

She felt a sudden dizziness. She was sorry and angry, transfixed and repelled. As she looked down the street—at their block, their homes—only one thing seemed clear: She had to get out of this place. She didn't want to be here any longer.

She pivoted quickly and was about to break into a run, but the edges of her vision were refracting into rainbows. She took a few steps and leaned against a telephone pole. Shapes shifted when she looked at them directly, dissolving into zigzags and herringbones.

She'd had migraines before and knew the warning signs. She would be fine. But she needed to go home, get out of the sun. Drink some coffee; that usually worked. And then take it easy.

A smell drifted from one of the nearby houses. Fabric softener, lavender scented. She wanted to sit, close her eyes, wait for the dizziness to pass. She squinted at the house where the smell was coming from. It stood out on the street, very small but well kept, with a swept porch and potted flowers. Behind a low fence was a tiny but elaborate garden with a miniature trellis, a wagon wheel, and a mechanical waterfall that sent a trickle of water over colored stones.

She held on to the fence. As she tried to steady herself, an older woman came out of the house.

"You all right, miss?"

Taking careful steps, the woman came up the slope of her driveway. She was wearing a man's shirt and sweatpants. The lavender scent wafted off of her. Helen tried to answer, but for a moment couldn't speak.

"You stay right here," the woman said. "I'll get you some water."

She turned, about to head down to her house again. Helen rushed to stop her.

"No, thank you. You don't have to do that. I'm fine, really."

"Are you sure?" the woman said. "You don't look fine to me. Is there someone I can call for you?"

From a few houses away came the sound of footsteps on gravel. Helen turned to look, but she was too late. Whoever had been there was already gone. She reached for the fence again, gripped it tightly.

"You really ought to sit down," the woman said.

"I'm fine," Helen said. "I'm very sorry. I should go."

Without another look, she turned and walked away, feeling steadier with each step that took her away from here. She could feel the woman watching her until she rounded the corner and disappeared.

CHAPTER SEVEN

Tom got off the bus at Ninety-First Street. He paused for a moment, taking it in. Twelve stories of pale brick, arched windows, wrought-iron doors. It was like someone's dream of New York, not a real place where a daughter of his was growing up. He couldn't have given Elana any of this. Not the landscaped park, or this avenue of grand buildings, or the effortless affluence that seemed to emanate from every dappled leaf and muffled footstep. She was on a different path, with a different trajectory, than any he'd ever known.

A different path than Sophie and Ilona, maybe. Or at least a different starting place. That was what Helen would say.

He was like any other parent. He wanted the world for his daughters. All of them.

There was a jangling sound. A guy was coming up the street, walking a beagle.

"Tom?" the guy said. "Tom Foster?"

It took Tom a moment to place the guy, in his off-hours Adidas T-shirt and baggy jeans. His heart accelerated until he came up with a name.

"Oh, hey there, Dan." The weekend editor at the newswire, who worked Saturdays through Tuesdays. A decent enough guy but very plugged into the office gossip, and also a source of it. "Sorry, didn't recognize you at first."

"You off today?" Dan grinned, one hand shielding his eyes against the sun. "What're you doing up here?"

Tom thought fast. "Doctor's appointment."

Dan started to look a little uncomfortable. Plenty of doctors, many of them shrinks, kept offices on the ground floors of the nearby apartment buildings. But Tom wouldn't mind Dan thinking he was off to a much-needed therapy session. That was not something he was likely to repeat.

"Ah!" Dan said. "Well, I won't keep you. See you Monday."

Dan raised a hand and tugged at his dog's leash. The dog wouldn't budge. He planted himself on the sidewalk and gave Tom a doleful stare.

"Come on, buddy. Time to go."

Dan pulled the dog's leash, managing to drag him a few steps before the dog flopped down again and stared at Tom.

Dan shook his head. "I don't know what's wrong with this guy."

Tom gave the dog a quick pat and headed to Donna's building. It could have been worse. He could have bumped into someone who knew Helen. But even though he thought he'd handled it well, he still felt like he'd been caught. He could feel Dan watching him—Dan and his sad-eyed beagle—as he went to the door.

———

Candace, Donna's half sister, was waiting in the doorway of Donna's apartment. He and Candace had always gotten along in their limited encounters, but today she was giving him an odd little smile that he didn't understand.

"Candace," he said. "I didn't know you were back in New York."

"Oh, I'm just visiting." She glanced away, as if embarrassed, and waved him in. "I'm going home on Monday."

Tom followed her to the living room, an open space with high ceilings, gleaming floors, and tall windows with views of the park and river. Above the fireplace, a series of black-and-white portraits showed Donna holding Elana when she was just a few weeks old. A low bookcase against an exposed-brick wall displayed Elana's collection of Japanese vinyl figures. (*Who bought them for her?* Tom always wondered.) There wasn't a sound from the street below or from the rooms within.

Candace sat on the sleek modern couch, her back straight against the shallow cushions. Tom waited near the coffee table, refusing her invitation to join her. But something about the way she was looking at him—that strange, coaxing smile—kept him from heading down the hall to Donna's office.

"So," Tom said. "Where is everybody?"

Candace answered with an apologetic shake of her head. As she rearranged her hair over her shoulders, she looked like a smaller, and softer, version of her sister. Though she was very close to Donna—she'd wound up staying for two and a half years to help with Elana—she'd never seemed to judge him for his amorphous role in her niece's life.

"Donna's on a call," Candace said. "She should be off in a few minutes. And Elana's in her room. Naomi's trying to settle her down for her nap."

"I'd better see her now, then. If she falls asleep, I won't get a chance before I go."

Tom started to turn, but Candace reached out a hand to stop him.

"Donna asked if you could wait," she said. "I know she needs to talk to you."

"And she knows I need to get back to the office."

"Her phone's always ringing," Candace said. "You know how it is." She wouldn't meet his eyes. "Can I get you something to drink? Iced tea, maybe?"

"I'm fine, thanks."

She seemed on edge for some reason. Tom tried to put her at ease.

"So how's L.A.?"

"Well, I'm not acting anymore," Candace said. "I decided to go back to school and get my teaching degree." She let out a self-conscious laugh. "Do you think it's a bad idea? Me, as a teacher?"

There was something practiced about her lines, as if she'd anticipated things they might talk about, while the real action went on behind closed doors. Tom played along and listened for any sounds escaping from down the hall.

"Not at all," he said. "Come on, you're a natural. You've always been good with Elana."

"Well, thanks—but you're *great* with her. When I've seen you with her, I can tell you're a great dad." She glanced down at her hands, acknowledging that she was treading on difficult territory. "With your other daughters, I mean. With your family."

His other daughters. He'd never known how much Donna had told her, though he wasn't surprised. She was Donna's sister and, like the babysitter, probably knew more than he realized. He had been very lucky that—out of respect for Donna or concern for Elana—no one had decided to use whatever they knew against him.

"Hey, Candace?" Tom said. "Let me ask you a question. What's going on?" He'd never spoken an unkind word to her, and from the expression on her face, he wondered if anyone ever had. "Why are you keeping me out here?"

Her face flushed. Before she could respond, a door opened, and Donna came down the hall, her bare feet slapping on the hardwood floor.

"You guys all caught up?" Donna glanced at her sister, then turned her attention to Tom. "All right," she said. "Let's do this."

Donna's office was in the sunroom, a small, light-filled box that looked out on the avenue. Hazy streaks of sun fell across the glass expanse of her desk and the awards she'd won at the magazine.

Instead of taking her usual spot behind her laptop, Donna sat with him on the couch, a narrower and harder version of the one in the living room. She stretched out her legs in front of her. Her toenails were painted a bright orange. She was wearing a silky top and slim jeans that skimmed her thighs and calf muscles and a heavy gold bangle around her wrist. She shoved it high on her arm, where it would not move.

"Thanks for taking the time for this," Donna said. "I know it isn't easy to break out of there."

"Why was Candace stalling me? And why did you schedule this during Elana's nap?"

"I need to talk to you. Without Elana running around."

"Well, here I am." Tom tried to ignore the tension that was building in his neck and shoulders. "Though if I don't get back soon, I'll be out of a job."

"I'll get you a car. My guy's a maniac. He'll have you there in ten minutes." Donna rested an arm along the back of the couch. Her hand almost reached him. "I have an offer in London," she said. "A good one."

Tom went cold. He returned her neutral stare.

"Congratulations," he said.

"I'd have to leave in a month."

"Leave?" he said. "For how long?"

Donna kept her eyes on him, her face free of emotion.

"This is a job, not a project," she said. "I'm talking about relocating. Moving to a new home. Enrolling Elana in a new preschool and hiring a new nanny. Though Naomi has already agreed to stay with us for the first month, to help with the transition. Which is a huge relief."

A dull pain throbbed in Tom's chest. She'd had many offers over the years, going back to her earliest days at the magazine, but she'd always refused to leave the city.

"Why would you do this?" he said. "Why now?"

Donna gave him a look that was sympathetic but didn't hide her frustration.

"Because I found a *job*, Tom. More than a job. This is a new opportunity for me. A new platform." She stopped herself. "Because it's a new beginning. An *ending* and a new beginning."

She was watching him closely, making sure he was taking in every word.

"I have a call with the principals on Monday," she said. "As long as they're willing to make a few changes, and I'm guessing they are, I plan to sign the contract. And unless I get a call from your lawyer by next Friday, I'm going to have my attorneys start a family court proceeding. Because I don't want this issue hanging over me when I'm gone."

Her words squeezed the air out of his lungs.

"You're *suing* me?"

"I'm seeking sole custody of Elana. It's effectively what I have already. But this will make it official, without any questions left unanswered." She paused. "I've told you before: You can be a part of Elana's life, and we can still come to an agreement that will work for me. Or you can step aside. This day has been coming for a long time, Tom. Get yourself a lawyer. We'll set a date for next week, and we'll settle this, one way or the other. Privately. That will save us both a lot of trouble."

For a moment he had an urge to run to Elana, to see her now, to make sure she was really there. That she hadn't already been spirited away, out of reach.

"So I have a week," he said. "A week to figure out if I want to fight."

"To fight? What's there to fight about?" Her voice was light, but he heard the steel behind it. "Let me give you some advice. I'm being more than generous." She stopped and stared past him. Tom couldn't remember a previous time when she wouldn't look him in the eye. "I want to be clear. It's not that I want to take her away from you. I think it could be *good* for her to have a relationship with you. But I'm not going to let her grow up feeling like a secret, thinking she's a mistake you're trying to hide. If you want to be in her life, there has to be a commitment. Out in the open. It has to be real." She looked at him. "And even though that could be good for her, it doesn't mean that's what's *best* for her. Or best for you." With a wry smile, she added, "Somebody ought to look out for that. Clearly, you're not."

Donna didn't take cheap shots; he knew that. But his muscles were tense with panic. Once she left, she wouldn't look back.

"There are laws about this," he said. "You can't just take a child out of the country."

She let out an angry laugh.

"Of course I can take her out of the country. I've done it many times before. She has a passport. Your name isn't on the birth certificate." She gave him a long, hard stare. "Get yourself a lawyer, Tom. I don't know what you're thinking of *fighting* for, but you can't afford a fight, and you wouldn't win. In fact, you have a lot to lose. Think about that. I'm not even talking about the money."

Those were the last words he was willing to hear. He got up and walked out of the room. He rested his forehead against the wall in the cool, dark hallway.

A wild cry from Elana broke the silence.

The door was open. Elana was spinning around her bedroom, her shirt stuck over her head, both arms trapped. She lurched from side to side, crab walking, as she tried to wrestle her way out. Her exposed stomach looked taut and wiry.

Naomi, the sitter, let Elana spiral around her, glancing off her bed and desk and wardrobe, until she tripped over her Magna-Tiles and landed on the giant corduroy cushion.

"Okay, Elana. Can I help you? Just a little bit?"

"*No* help! I can do it *myself*!"

Naomi kept out of the way. She was petite, with strawberry-blond hair that she kept in a frizzy halo, and was wearing a threadbare T-shirt, shredded jeans, and sandals that looked like they were made of seashells. She was the cool babysitter with the work ethic of a junior partner. Donna wouldn't let any other parents near her.

As Elana scrambled to her feet, Naomi reached out and gave the girl's shirt a quick, imperceptible tug that made it fall into place.

Elana, suddenly free, whirled around and gave Naomi a stern look, suspicious that help had been given. Tom couldn't stop himself from laughing.

Naomi turned toward the doorway. Elana dashed forward and flung herself into him.

"Come here!" Elana took his hand, throwing her weight into it. Her wild hair swayed in a disheveled ponytail between her shoulder blades. "I want to show you!"

He let her pull him into the room. It was almost the size of the studio apartment he'd lived in during his first years in the city. Pale walls, sheer curtains, cotton rug that was just beginning to fray at the edges. Her bed was heaped with stuffed animals; wooden racks held her books. In one corner of the room sat a small circular table, two matching chairs, and a plush miniature armchair monogrammed with her initials. Almost everything in the room looked simple, even plain, but this was misleading. Tom knew that each item cost far more than it might seem, and he wondered how much Donna's lawyer parents had helped with the expenses.

Elana was digging around in her school bag—not a ladybug or a froggie, like the backpacks worn by the kids at Sophie and Ilona's preschool, but a canvas satchel that could accommodate a college textbook. Naomi stood beside her.

"Nice move," he told Naomi. "I was sure that was heading toward a total meltdown."

Naomi acknowledged the compliment with a silent nod. She stayed in position next to her charge, instead of slipping away as she usually did when he appeared.

"I'm heading back to my office soon," Tom said. "So I'd like to visit with Elana for a few minutes."

"Is Donna in her office?"

She had been told to stay; he could tell. That was why she was here, hovering like a chaperone—along with Candace, who was still guarding the living room. He could hear her padding around, making her presence known. In case he tried to do something crazy, maybe? Like take Elana and run? Or was it just a show of resources, of everything that Donna could provide, of the family and network that stood behind her?

"She's in there," he told Naomi. "Go ahead and check if you want."

She swept past him. He heard her knock on Donna's door.

Elana found what she was looking for in her bag. She whipped out a piece of construction paper.

"I made you a picture!"

She rushed over to him. The paper had been dated by one of the teachers at her preschool.

"It's me! And you!"

Tom studied the two figures. He was the tall one whose head was cut off by the top of the page. She'd drawn herself as a multicolored scribble.

"Can I keep it?" he asked, though he already knew the answer.

"No! I made it. It's mine."

He nodded. "Could you keep it for me?"

She took the drawing and went over to the flat files that stood beside her desk. She stuck the picture in the bottom drawer. That was where she kept all of her drawings, right down to the earliest attempts with just a wobbly line or two.

The apartment had gone silent around them. He wondered what Donna was telling Naomi in her office.

Elana picked a book from the rack. And another. And another.

"Do you want me to read to you?" he asked.

She gave him the books and climbed into her armchair. Tom eased himself onto the beanbag next to her. His back pinged, reminding him that he'd slept on the couch the night before.

"How about we start with Pooh?"

He'd given her the book and could read it in his sleep. As he turned the pages, he thought about Donna. If he tried to get a lawyer to challenge her in any way, she would fight back. They would hurt each other and everyone around them.

He remembered what had happened to Suzanne, an old work friend. A photo editor at the magazine. She was divorced and lived with her teenage daughter in a tiny apartment on First Avenue. She told him once about how much she wanted to move to Seattle, where most of her family lived. But her ex-husband had sued to stop her, and won.

"Nothing I can do about it," she told Tom. "He's a selfish prick. But he's still her father."

At the time, he'd felt horrible for her. Now all he could think was, *The guy had won.* That selfish prick had sued, and he'd *won*.

He might win too. There was a chance. A small one, but still—a chance.

Though that was probably wishful thinking. The truth was, he didn't know what his rights were. Or if he had any rights at all. He'd never asserted any legal claim. If he fought Donna's move—however hopeless that seemed—then all his secrets would be revealed. To Helen, the person who would be hurt the most. He would have to tell her.

But if he really could win, *did* he want to fight?

He thought of what Donna had suggested, the option he'd rarely allowed himself to consider: that he could be a part of Elana's life, without any secrets or deception. He could be there for her, through all of the years to come.

But that meant talking to Helen. Telling her everything he'd failed to tell her years ago, when he'd learned Donna was pregnant, and later, when she'd discovered that email.

He hadn't been willing to take that gamble then and felt even less capable of taking it now. The stakes were too high. He thought of everyone and everything he could lose. Helen. Sophie and Ilona. His home, his friends, his reputation. His pride, what was left of it.

Donna wanted him to do what was simplest and easiest for everyone: walk away. *Free and clear. No obligations.*

Though he would never be free and clear. After three years, he couldn't just walk away. Even if he did, how could Donna imagine him simply disappearing forever from Elana's life when it was so easy to find someone, for lives to intersect? Even if Elana moved away, that didn't mean their paths would never cross. What if they passed each other on the street? He would know her; he was sure of that. Would she recognize him? He would be so easy to find, if she ever came looking. *Would* she look for him?

He didn't know the answers to any of these questions. There was only one thing he understood with any certainty: *This* life, as he knew it, was coming to an end. These stolen hours that he'd spent checked out from the never-ending pressures of his all-too-real life. Time that had meant so much to him that he'd risked losing everyone he loved and everything he'd ever thought to be true about himself.

Coming to an end. Maybe that would be a relief.

He pushed the thought away as soon as it surfaced. Elana moved closer and rested her head against him, then bounced up and propped her elbow on his shoulder, hitting a tendon or nerve that might never function properly again. He shifted in the beanbag; she settled.

She'll be fine, Donna would say. *More than fine.*

Tom turned the page and finished the chapter.

"Read it again," Elana said. "Again."

He thought of the messages piling up at the office, the stories waiting in the queue. Elana squirmed around to look up at him, her eyes dark and huge.

"Okay," he said.

He started from the beginning. The words were putting him into a trance. Elana was holding her stuffed pig, her fingers playing with its chewed tail. Just like Ilona played with the frayed ear of her elephant.

As he looked at that ragged toy, his regrets came rushing over him. Three years of regrets. If he wasn't careful, he would sink under that weight.

The book slipped from his fingers. Elana poked him in the shoulder.

"Wake up!" she said.

But instead of trying to make him read, she rolled from her chair onto his beanbag, landing in his lap. She stretched out across his chest.

"Just what I needed," Tom said, and smiled. "A blanket."

He held her until she fell asleep, and then carried her to her bed.

"Close the door," Donna said when she saw him in the doorway. "Unless you want Candace and Naomi to hear what you have to say."

She was at her desk. Tom sat across from her and waited until she finished whatever she was working on. It was just like one of their meetings at the magazine.

"I have to get back," he said. "But we need to talk."

"We can talk now."

He'd been away from the office for too long. He could feel the seconds ticking. But there were things he had to know.

"How long has this been in the works?" he said. "This job of-fer. This move."

Donna shut her laptop.

"If you really want to know, this wasn't my first choice. Moving to London. I've lived *here*, on my own, since I was nineteen. I don't want to leave. But forty-seven-year-old women don't always get their pick of amazing offers. I might not get another chance like this."

It was something he hadn't seen before: Donna taking herself down a notch. Fearless, unconquerable Donna was making compromises.

"The timing is good, though," she continued. "Elana hasn't started real school yet, and we have a place to stay."

"And where's that?" Tom asked, though he'd already guessed the answer.

"Alan has a town house. Or a terraced house, whatever they call them. He's been trying to get me to move there for months now."

Alan, the still-fit neuroscientist. Of course he owned a town house.

"We visited a few weeks ago," she said. "Elana loved it. It's a charming house on a quiet street that's a few blocks from a park. And he's agreed to make the place more kid-friendly. She'll have her own bedroom and a playroom and the run of the garden."

Donna was scrolling through photos on her phone, as though showing him photos of Alan's charming town house would convince him to sign away any claims on his daughter. Tom didn't bother to look.

"Anyway." She put the phone down. "It's a very nice place for a child. Kind of Old World, not my style, but it'll work. At least for now."

"For now?"

"It's a two-year contract, with an option to renew. But the

company is thinking of this as a long-term commitment. And I know Alan is hoping for a permanent move." She paused. "Look. I'm not talking about forever. But I can't give you a deadline. I can't promise that we'll be back in two or three or even five years."

Tom was watching her closely. She would play her cards. With regret, but that wouldn't stop her from winning the game.

"One of the good things about us—maybe the *only* good thing about how we've handled these last few years—is that we've always been respectful of each other," Donna said. "For the most part, we've both at least tried to do what we thought was best for Elana."

"Of course we have. That isn't going to change. That's why I don't want you to take her away."

He was expecting a flare of anger, but her eyes were cool and clear.

"What we've been doing these last few years—that *isn't* what's best for Elana," Donna said. "Or for me. And that's a factor now."

Tom felt another wave of regret, but he wouldn't retreat.

"I don't want her to go," he said. "You're not going to change my mind."

Donna rested her palms on her desk.

"There's not a lot you can do about that," she said. "I don't want to ruin your life, Tom. But I have my own life to consider. Mine and Elana's."

As they stared at each other across the glass slab of desk, neither of them willing to make the next move, they heard feet scampering down the hall—first Elana's, followed by Naomi's.

There was a cry of joy, then a crash, then tears. Elana's howls echoed through the rooms. Naomi murmured to her, soft little words that they couldn't understand.

He and Donna shared a glance, even a hint of a smile.

The moment passed. Donna reached for her phone.

"You must be late," she said. "I'll get you that car."

———

Outside, Tom stood in the shade of the building. He was sweating. Not a healthy sweat, but a clammy, nervous sweat that made him cringe within his clothes, shrink away from himself.

He leaned against the bricks and tried to ignore the hollowness in his stomach. Across the street, a man was watching him. Middle-aged, square-jawed, hair that was still thick and still blond. Wearing expensive but tasteful athletic gear, one broad hand resting on a bright new basketball. He was sitting on a bench, pretending to talk on his cell phone.

So this was Alan, Tom realized. Where had Donna found a British guy who looked like that? One who exuded health and happiness and success, who looked like he skied and sailed boats and climbed mountains. And played *basketball*.

Was he posted there on Donna's orders, as a last defense against some crazy move?

Fuck him.

But it was worse. This guy wanted to have a conversation. Alan was putting his phone away and offering an affable smile. It was meant to show his good-natured acceptance of their difficult situation and his confidence that they would rise above it. Like men.

He was coming over.

"Hey there." A soft accent, not too posh. "Got a minute?"

Tom didn't want to talk. Not now, not ever. Without looking, he crossed the side street and came within an inch of getting plowed down by the livery car that Donna had summoned for him. Alan was watching him, one hand still beckoning, a puzzled look clouding his craggy features. The livery driver was watching him too; he shouted behind his closed window. But Tom kept walking, aware only of the sounds of his shoes on the pavement. With every step, the sidewalk seemed to slip farther away. And that was fine with him, because he was out of there. He was gone.

CHAPTER EIGHT

HELEN, 2:30 P.M.

She'd caught him at a bad time.

"Hold on." Tom, on his cell, sounded out of breath and distracted. "Why are you bringing this up? Why *now?*"

"We can talk later if you're busy."

"I don't get it," he said. "You know we can't afford to move."

Helen was in the bedroom. She'd called him as soon as she got home, not stopping to shower or change her clothes. The girls were downstairs, on the couch with Monica, working their way through a stack of books. Monica's voice drifted up the stairwell: *"'And for all I know he is sitting there still...'"*

"We could cut our losses," Helen said. "We can accept the fact that we made a mistake and move on."

She hadn't told him about the teenage girls in the playground. How could she tell him about what she'd seen in those girls and what she'd seen in herself? But the answer to her problems had come to her, with a sudden clarity and certainty, as she'd run home: They could leave. They could leave their problems behind and start over somewhere new. And she could return to a time when she knew herself. When she trusted herself.

"This is a terrible time to sell," Tom said. "You know that. Our house isn't even worth what we paid for it. Not even close." Traffic blared in the background. "And where are you thinking of moving *to*? Back to the city? Or to some other town or suburb that we barely know?"

She felt a flash of annoyance at him, and then at herself, because they could have discussed this when he came home, after she'd had a chance to organize her thoughts. But she hadn't been able to make herself wait.

"I don't have the answer to that right now," she said. "Let's talk later. I have to get back to work."

Sirens echoed in her ear, then faded away. Tom let out a breath.

"You know, we're still settling in," he said. His voice was softer now; it seemed like he'd slowed down to talk to her. "Do you remember how excited you were to move to Devon? You were so happy when we got the house. Don't forget that." He paused. "Did something happen?"

For a moment she considered telling him. Not all of it, maybe, but enough to make him understand what she'd experienced that day. But at what point should she draw the line?

She could hear the sounds of city streets: the wheeze of a bus, car horns, blasts of music. Floating above these sounds, filling the gaps and silences, was the unmistakable jingle of an ice-cream truck.

"Where are you?" she asked.

"Right outside the office." The background noise grew muffled, as though Tom had cupped a hand around his phone. "I just stepped out to get some air. But I've got to get back to my desk. I don't want them to start looking for me."

Before he hung up, Helen heard a few last notes of that jingle. She tried to picture an ice-cream truck on Park Avenue, idling in front of his Midtown office tower.

———

She was still standing at the bedroom window when a battered old car came down Crescent and stopped just past her house.

It was a gray Buick that looked like it had survived both fires and floods. One of its doors was charcoal black; the others were streaked with rust. She couldn't see the driver, only the guy in the passenger seat and the one in the back. They were both young, early twenties at most; their wiry arms hung out the windows. The guy in the passenger seat was eating something out of a small bag. He poured the last of it into his mouth, then tossed it onto the street.

He was looking at Karl and Jackie's house. Or maybe at her house.

Helen moved to the side of her window, where she couldn't be seen. As the driver gunned the engine, her heart raced. There was screeching of brakes as the car turned off Crescent.

She'd seen that car before. The unpainted door, the veins of rust. Had she caught a glimpse of it on her run?

Had someone seen *her* and followed her home? She was trying to remember, call up the visual details she normally wouldn't forget, when there was a knock behind her. Monica was at the bedroom door.

"Hey. Just wanted to let you know. I can only stick around for another hour or so."

Helen glanced at her phone.

"Sorry. I lost track of the time."

"Normally it wouldn't be a problem," Monica said. "But I just started a new job, and they were nice enough to swing me a Friday shift." She shrugged, then ran a hand through the feathery tufts of her hair. "Fat Pete's. I'm waiting tables. Buckets of Miller Lite and fiesta fries. But the tips aren't bad."

Helen laughed. "How many jobs do you have these days?"

"Besides working for my dad? I guess two. Officially." Monica glanced behind her. "I'm saving up as much as I can for next year. I'm transferring schools. Starting over, really, because I can't use my credits."

Helen tried to hide her disappointment. She was losing her babysitter. (*And her pot dealer,* she noted.) Though Monica was half her age, Helen considered her a friend, or almost a friend, and almost-friends had come to mean a lot to her these past two years.

"Where are you going?" Helen asked.

"Rhode Island School of Design. I could have started this year, but I put it off because of my family."

RISD. At Monica's age, Helen had wanted so badly to go there but hadn't even let herself apply, because she didn't think she would get in. It took her a moment to respond.

"That's great. I didn't know you were into graphic design."

"Well, I started taking Photoshop classes back in high school. I had some great teachers there."

Helen smiled. She stepped back and looked at Monica, with her home-bleached hair and chipped nails. And the clothes she bought off the junior racks. She pictured her at RISD. They would love her there. She wouldn't have to change a thing.

She reached out and gave Monica a hug.

"Congratulations!" she said. "Your dad must be so proud of you."

"Thanks. He is. My mom will be proud, too, once the news gets out to her."

Monica had never spoken about her mother before. Helen thought of the photo by the register at her father's pizza parlor: a plain woman surrounded by her four beautiful daughters. There was something painful about the look on the mother's face, her distant eyes aimed straight at the camera.

Helen wasn't sure what to say.

"So you're in touch with your mom?"

"Not really," Monica said. "But I talk to my aunt, and I guess she gives her a call every once in a while." Her face revealed nothing. "She lives in Denver I think."

Monica spoke the last words all at once, in a way that left no room for follow-up questions. Nineteen years old, and she'd already mastered the art of giving away just enough information to hide herself completely.

"You'll do so well there," Helen said. "Though I'm glad you'll be here for one last year. The girls will miss you."

She thought of Monica's sisters, three coppery blondes with themelike names: Amber, Crystal, and Jade. She often saw Crystal driving around town, so clear-eyed and young she didn't look old enough to be at the wheel. And then you saw the baby seat in the back.

Monica's dad would take it hard, Helen guessed. He seemed to live behind the counter in his pizza shop, in his white shirt and pressed jeans and with a small silver cross around his neck. And what about Nick? She could guess the answer to that. *Tough break, Nick.*

"Will it be hard for you to leave?" she asked.

She expected the answer she would have given herself: *It will be fine.*

Monica grinned with disbelief. "Are you kidding? I can't wait."

As she took that in, Helen felt a shift.

Monica was moving up.

And she was going down.

Somehow, Helen managed a laugh.

"I'll have to take you out to celebrate! Once I find a new sitter."

"Don't worry," Monica said. "There's time for that." There was a soft thump downstairs, then a cry from Sophie. "I better get down there."

"Okay. I'll take over soon. Just give me a few minutes to get organized."

Monica left and closed the door behind her. Alone again, Helen sat on the bed and rested her face in her hands.

She was stuck. Ryan had finally sent the changes for Mega Crux, and for thirty minutes she had been working on one slide, trying to animate three lines of text along with a bar chart and a spinning globe. A painstaking task. But it didn't stop her mind from wandering.

That rusty Buick. Where exactly had she seen it?

The only sounds coming from downstairs were the wordless babbles and squeaks of *Pingu*. When Monica left, Sophie and Ilona had turned to Helen with disappointed looks, knowing she would be unable to sustain the level of entertainment that Monica had provided. With a too-familiar pang of guilt, Helen took her daughters by their hands and asked their favorite question: "Who wants to watch a cartoon?"

It had bought her some time, but she hadn't used it well. She left her office and meandered through the rooms, going from the girls' bedroom to her own. She looked at their bed, remembered that Tom had fallen asleep on the couch yet again last night, and thought of how he'd sounded on the phone: *I've got to get back to my desk.* Something about that—his frustration, the urgency—made her think this wasn't a question of stepping through the door. He wasn't right outside of his office.

She knew him: He wasn't a liar. But he was hiding something. Which, itself, was strange. He wasn't like her, who had always kept so much hidden away. He'd never liked secrets.

Years ago, not long after they'd met, Tom took her to see his childhood home in Philadelphia, the tiny apartment he and his schoolteacher mother had moved to after his father died. He used to joke that you could sit in the center of any room and touch all four walls. (Their house in Devon was, by far, the largest space he'd ever lived in.) There had been no room for secrets in that apartment.

Afterward, on their drive back to the city, they'd stopped at the Street Road Inn—day rate: $19. They drank in the bar until it closed, then walked down the highway until they came to a convenience store. Its blinking sign advertised half-pound cheesecakes, cigarettes, soda, lottery tickets, ice. "We could live here," Tom said as they loaded up on supplies to carry back to the motel. They stayed up all night and woke up late the next day with crushing hangovers.

And she was happier than she'd ever thought was possible.

For most of her life, she'd kept herself at a distance from everyone around her. She couldn't say why, except that guarding her words and her space felt natural and necessary. Both her mother and father believed in maintaining well-defined boundaries—buffer zones, really—between themselves and others, and she had followed their example.

It was only later, through friends and boyfriends and during those early years on her own in the city, that she began to bridge that distance. And then she met Tom, who had no need for barriers, whose first instinct wasn't self-preservation. She trusted him and let herself feel closer to him than she'd ever felt to anyone.

In recent years, though, she'd retreated again. She'd buried her doubts, regrets, and fears and told herself it was easier that way. She'd wanted to protect herself.

She looked at Tom's untouched pillow. Something was wrong.

He wasn't a liar. And he wasn't a cheater, though she knew he'd cheated once. He'd made a mistake and they'd moved on. She'd known cheaters, and Tom wasn't like them. He didn't live his life beneath the surface: His honesty and openness were still there, all these years later.

She thought of the day she saw that email. How she'd flinched away, not wanting to let it touch her. Wishing she could forget the words as soon as she read them and knowing it was too late.

This is a mistake—we should talk.

The address line was blank.

Even that day, when she confronted him, she wasn't curious

about the details. It was over and that was all she needed to know. The less she knew, the less significant it would be. Her refusal to hear anything about it, her lack of interest, kept it small.

At the time, she wondered if this refusal to hear him out was her way of hurting him back. She could tell he wanted to tell her more. When he realized he was caught, he'd seemed almost relieved.

But she didn't want to hear it. After two days, she took him back. She didn't want to break up her marriage or family over a mistake, and that was what his little affair felt like: a mistake.

Besides, there were times when she believed that she owed him one. She thought back to that long-ago conversation in their Queens apartment, when he told her, or almost told her, that he didn't want children. As if she hadn't caught the hints he'd dropped for years. Even in that moment, when she'd thought they'd come to a new place in their marriage, that they were ready to start a family, she could see it still on his face: He would be happier without them. And she pretended not to see.

Later, after those months of trying, she showed him the tests.

His voice caught. "Are you sure?"

"I took three of them."

Helen let him look for himself. For just an instant, she saw the mix of emotions on his face. Pride and excitement, but also disappointment. And fear.

That was almost four years ago. He was now the great father she always knew he would be. But she could see that his own life had contracted, almost to the point of disappearing.

He loved their daughters as much as she did, perhaps, some

days, even more; it seemed to come so naturally to him. She was sure he wouldn't change a thing.

Probably.

That was the small voice she could never silence. Despite how much she wanted to believe that he had no regrets, her doubts crept in. *He was always so tired.*

All those nights on the couch. Last week, she'd watched him nod off while rewinding the DVR to see the parts of *The Daily Show* he'd slept through the first time. Once, she'd found him under his desk, where he'd fallen asleep while trying to fix the Internet cables.

She thought of the energy he used to have, how he'd take her all around the city, street after street, pointing out things she'd never seen before. These last few years had exhausted him. She knew that—she couldn't help seeing it—but she didn't understand it. She hadn't felt tired like that since those chaotic early months after the girls were born. She even wondered if he was sick somehow, but his doctor had given him a perfect bill of health just a few months ago. She considered their money problems, his commute, the pressures of the newsroom. But no matter how much she thought about it, she couldn't figure out why he was so tired.

———

Helen checked her email. Kristen, the sales manager, had sent three follow-ups in the last hour: *Just wanted to circle back! ETA? Hope to see the revisions soon—thoughts?* Ryan, who had been cc'd on the emails, had sent one of his own in mock business-speak: *It may be time to do some bar-setting for these people. Forgive me,* he added. *I'm so overcaffeinated I can see the insides of my eyeballs. Which are itching.*

As she studied the latest demands, trying to determine where to start, a loud whirring filled her ears. She went to the window. There was Butch, armed with his leaf blower. He was working his way across his backyard, his T-shirt rippling across his stomach, his shoulders exposed to the sun.

She knew from previous experience that closing the window would do almost nothing to muffle the noise, though it would at least keep tiny particles from migrating across the lawns and into her office. But she stayed by the window. Every few minutes, Butch would stop to examine some imperfection in the azaleas or firethorns. Then, after the silence had settled, he would start up the motor again.

Her cell phone rang. She looked at the number; Lou never bothered with her office line. She took the phone to the bedroom. Even Lou's booming voice couldn't compete with the leaf blower.

"Jesus Christ, these fucking *people*," Lou said. He had her on speakerphone; she could hear him stabbing at his keyboard like it was a manual typewriter. "If they 'ping me' again, I'll shoot them for sport. So! How are we doing on Mega Crux?"

"We're doing great, Lou."

Helen stood at the window. She glanced out at the street, then looked again. The Buick was back, idling in front of Karl and Jackie's driveway. Black plumes rose from its tailpipe.

"I'm serious," Lou said.

Helen stared at the car. She still couldn't make out the driver, just the other two guys. Young, wiry. That was all she could say about them.

"One more hour," she said. "I'm going through the last of the edits right now."

"That's what I like to hear! Look, I got a few more changes I'd like to go over with you. You got a pen?"

Helen pressed a hand to her head. "One sec."

The driver of the car was gunning his engine. Just as he hit the gas, a small white dog began running across Crescent. The car accelerated and swerved. Helen couldn't tell if the driver was aiming for the dog, or even if he saw it. In an instant, the dog collided with the right side of the car's front bumper and flipped backward, moving down the length of the car. It landed on the asphalt and then sprinted out of view.

Helen looked out at the empty street and gasped. With a sickening feeling, she realized that the little dog was the one that had belonged to her former neighbor. Tom still looked for it whenever they passed that house. He'd driven around the neighborhood the day it disappeared, calling its name. Cotton Ball.

"Lou," she said. "Can I call you back? I think a dog just got hit in front of my house."

"Christ. I'll send you an email about the changes. But don't keep me waiting—I just got out of a twenty-minute meeting and I've been instructed to give you a brain dump."

"Great. I'm looking forward to that."

She hung up and went downstairs. On the TV, the animated penguin was squawking at its mother.

"I have to check on something outside," she told Sophie and Ilona. "I'll be on the front lawn. Right outside the door. Okay?"

They nodded, their eyes on the screen. Helen took her keys and closed the screen door behind her. She didn't want them to see this and needed to take care of it before they left the house again. She walked onto her lawn, then stopped. The dog had crept back from where it had run, leaving drops of blood along the way. It was now lying at the edge of the driveway. The smell hit her, a stench of urine that seemed to go right into her lungs.

A door opened at the yellow ranch house across the street. Glenn came down the steps. Helen wondered if he had been keeping an eye on the car, peeking through his venetians.

He walked over, smoothing his fine hair over his forehead. Aside from Karl and Jackie, he was the only neighbor who'd welcomed Helen and her family the day they'd moved in. There had been a boyfriend back then, but he was long gone. *Back to the city,* Glenn said with a sad shrug when Helen asked about him later.

He crouched down beside the dog. He was in his work-at-home accountant's clothes, an Oxford shirt and pleated corduroys.

"I still have Debra's number somewhere," he said. "I'll call her. Poor little Cotton Ball."

"Is she still alive?"

"Just enough to suffer."

Helen looked at the dog. Her fur was filthy and matted, but that was definitely Cotton Ball.

"Should we take her to the vet?" she asked.

Glenn folded up his shirtsleeves. He lightly touched the dog's head.

"She wouldn't survive the trip." Glenn's eyes looked watery behind his glasses. "There we go, there we go," he said, whispering to the dog. "It's almost over. There you go."

Glenn gave the dog a few last pats, then got up and brushed

his hands together. The dog seemed smaller than she had just a few seconds ago, as if she'd shrunk beneath her fur and skin.

"Did you recognize those kids?" he said. "It seemed like they were here for a reason."

Helen glanced away. She felt a surge of guilt, like she'd been caught in a lie. But she *didn't* know them. Or didn't think so, at least.

"They drove by here a while ago," she said. "They were checking out Karl and Jackie's house, I think."

"Why would they check out Karl and Jackie's house?"

Helen glanced at him. "How would I know?"

"Not sure." Glenn shrugged. "I saw them that first time, too, and they were in front of the driveway. They might have been looking at your place."

Helen's face burned. She didn't want to believe he was right. Glenn gave her an apologetic look.

"Sorry," he said. "It's hard to say what they were doing. I'm probably wrong. I'm just upset about the dog. Fucking monsters, those kids."

"Well, I don't think I've seen them before," she said with more certainty than she felt. "I don't know why they were here."

Glenn rocked on his heels. He stuffed his hands in his pockets, blousing out the pleats of his corduroys.

"I'll get an old blanket," he said. "I can take her to the vet. Dispose of her properly."

"Thanks, Glenn. For taking care of this."

He gave her a weak smile, then turned away. As she headed for her door, she saw Ilona there, staring out at the dead dog.

Helen tried again, though she had been trying for five minutes now and had gotten nowhere. Ilona's cries had turned to shrieks, and while Helen wanted to comfort her, she could feel her patience wearing under the waves of tears.

"I want to see the dog!" Ilona cried out.

"It's hurt," Helen said. She couldn't say the dog was dead. "Glenn is taking her to the vet. The dog doctor."

"I want to help!"

"You can't," she said. "I'm sorry."

Her phone rang, but she couldn't answer it while Ilona was bellowing. She wished Tom were here; it was hard not to be envious at times at how children's crises didn't intrude upon his workday. On the couch, Sophie was happily watching cartoons. *Pingu* had rolled into *Caillou*.

Ilona gave her a last furious look.

"You're mean!"

Then she stormed off and settled on the couch beside her sister. And Helen, though she wished she could stay there, try one last time to soothe her daughter, let the TV do that job instead.

She ran up to her office and checked her email. She read the long list of changes that Lou had sent—not just for Mega Crux, but for a new assignment he wanted her to work on, and could we have a first look by Tuesday? Though of course Monday would be better.

Fuck you, Lou.

She stared at the email until the words blurred on the screen. Then she slapped her hand, hard, against the surface of her desk. Her coffee cup fell to the floor and shattered. She sprang up from her chair and stepped onto Pussyface, who hissed, scratched her bare ankle, and went back to sleep.

Fuck!

Butch was still going at it with his leaf blower, making neat little piles and scattering dust at maximum volume. Helen watched him from her open window. He'd finished his own yard and was now starting on Karl's, or at least the part that bordered his own property. He was over near the azaleas, blowing away the remains of last year's leaves that had been left to rot.

She went to the closet and took out the water gun that Karl had given her that morning. Kneeling beside her office window, she narrowed her eyes and fired.

Pow, pow, pow.

It wasn't filled with water, but just pulling the trigger made her feel better. She lifted the screen and leaned out the window, the gun against her shoulder, and tracked Butch as he worked his way across the grass. She aimed at the baseball cap he wore low on his forehead, at the sweat-soaked back of his muscle-T, at his ankles above his soccer slides. She fired away as he poked around the bushes, kicking up clouds of dead leaves.

Her cell phone rang. It was the receptionist from the preschool, wanting to know if she was still planning to come by with a check, or maybe she wanted to try splitting the bill with another card after all? Because if they waited until Monday, there would be a late fee. And she didn't think she could get it credited back a second time.

"Of course," Helen said. "Can you hold on while I get my card?"

She waited a moment, then hung up. An instant later, her office line rang. And her cell rang again. She listened to the dueling ringtones until both calls rolled into voice mail. Then she sank to the floor under the open window and let the sound of the leaf blower fill the room.

CHAPTER NINE

Tom entered the lobby, glancing at the time as he badged in. He didn't know how he would explain himself to Mark, or Rita, or anyone else who'd noticed his absence, which had been so much longer than planned. He'd finally caught a cab, but it had gotten stuck in endless traffic, so he'd run through the park and then walked the last sixteen blocks to his office, his heart racing against the clocks in the newsroom.

Alone in the elevator, he thought of that call from Helen, how frazzled he'd sounded as he marched down Fifth Avenue, maneuvering through the crowds as fast as he could. He was flushed, still sweating. The office AC blasted him, vacuum-sealing his skin.

He had to pass through the kitchen to get to the newsroom. He was starving, but there was no chance of getting lunch, so he scanned the snack bins. On the counter sat the MUST BE 40!!! mug, with the muddy remains of a midday Flavia. He was glad to see it, this small mystery in an office where everything was accounted for, tracked with badges and analyzed on spread-sheets. He was about to stock up on energy bars when one of the general assignment editors, a slope-shouldered guy with braces on both wrists, came up to him.

"You that editor on the science desk? Not Mark, the other guy?"

Tom was already cringing. He took a step in the direction of the newsroom.

"Yes. Tom Foster. Why?"

The GA editor nodded. His eyes flickered, as if a bit of errant data had shifted into place.

"No reason," he said with a tight little smile. "Just wanted to put a face to the name."

───

Mark was at his desk, typing at maximum speed.

"All okay?" Tom said in a low voice.

"Amazingly, yes." Mark squinted at his screen. "You were lucky. Huge screwup on the bond desk. Everyone else is off the radar." He gave his keyboard three sharp taps. "Though if you ever take a break like that again, I hope it's for a job interview."

"No one asked for me?"

"Just Tadpole, once, and I managed to deflect. He's putting out fires. I doubt he even remembers what he wanted."

"Thanks," Tom said. "I owe you one."

"You owe me dozens, and I plan to cash in one of these days. I feel like going on a bender." Mark looked up. The finance team leader was approaching. "Back to work."

Tom scrolled through the queue. He edited a news summary and sent out an update on the superbugs. He worked fast, and well, checking every edit, at times reading the words aloud. Yet despite how hard he tried to concentrate, he couldn't silence Donna's voice in his head.

This day has been coming for a long time.

He'd known that. But every time he saw Elana, and she lifted her arms or climbed into his lap, he'd push his doubts and fears away.

He typed, backspaced. Cut a paragraph, pasted it back in.

What he needed was time. With a few days to himself, he could clear his head; he could find a solution. A way to stay in Elana's life, without sacrificing his family. He could find a lawyer. (*With what money?* Another problem to figure out.) He could talk to Donna.

He again let himself consider talking to Helen. Where would he even begin? He imagined her questions, everything she'd want to know. How the fling with Donna had started, and ended. Why he'd lied. (No, Helen wouldn't ask that. The answer was clear.) Would she ask about the time he'd spent with Elana? Would she want all the details? What he dreaded most was the possibility that she wouldn't ask anything at all. That before he had a chance to explain himself, they would be over. Done.

He needed time. Space to breathe.

"Where's Rita?" he said.

"Who knows?" Mark said. "She keeps disappearing."

As soon as she came back, he would ask her for a few days off. He scrolled through his emails. There was a message from Charlie, the general assignment team leader.

Come see me when you get back. Provided you're not too busy.

Charlie had apparently noticed not only that he'd stepped out, but also for how long. With a jolt, Tom remembered that

Charlie was friends with Dan, the editor he'd seen near Donna's building. They ran the softball team together.

Tom looked over his monitor. Charlie was at his computer, just two rows away from Tadpole's desk. No one liked to go up there, risking Tadpole's attention. But he had to see what Charlie wanted.

"I'll be right back," he told Mark. "Quick talk with GA."

Tom got up from his desk and went down the center aisle. He passed the real estate and pharma teams, then stocks and bonds. As he neared the front of the newsroom, he saw heads lifting, everyone glancing his way to see if he was someone worth watching. Even Charlie turned from his screen. He shot Tom a look, eyebrows raised. *Later.*

Tom stopped. Tadpole was hissing into the mouthpiece of his headset, berating whoever was on the other end of the line. Soon he was yelling; his voice shuddered and broke. He jumped up from his desk, shouting a string of curses.

The newsroom froze. One voice could be heard from the back. A reporter, unaware of the silence around him, was finishing a call: "Have a super weekend, Stan!"

Tadpole circled his desk. His face was bloodless with fury. He tore off his headset and hurled it at the wall behind him. Not satisfied, he swept both arms across his desk, shoveling its contents to the floor.

He stormed off. It was so quiet that everyone could hear the elevator ping. Soon the silence was filled with the usual tapping and patter of voices.

Tom went back to his desk and sank into his seat.

"You had a prime view of that one," Mark said. "Who was the victim?"

"No idea."

Not for the first time that day, Tom missed the science magazine, where no one was crazy and everyone got along. Where the only bad thing that had ever happened was a short-lived affair in which he'd impregnated his boss, who was now preparing to take their child out of the country. And out of his life.

I'm not talking about forever, Donna had said.

Tom knew what she meant. He also knew that if they left, they would be truly gone. In that sense, it was a permanent move.

It was a new beginning, like she'd said. And an ending.

He didn't begrudge Donna a new beginning. Not at all. But he wanted to come up with a different ending. A better, happier ending.

It was the time of day when the mixed fumes of coffee, sweat, and adrenaline hung like a fog over the newsroom. Rita had come back and left again before Tom could speak with her. Mark was checking the headlines, taking advantage of the Friday afternoon lull.

Mark, who had been through two divorces. And could probably recommend a lawyer. Tom tried to picture how that conversation might go. Mark wouldn't ask why he needed a lawyer. At most, he'd say, *Sorry to hear that. Hope it works out.* But something held him back.

He must have been staring at Mark. Because Mark was now staring at him.

"Fall asleep with your eyes open?" Mark said. "If you're looking for something to do, I'd be happy to pass you a story."

Tom turned back to his monitor.

"Sorry," he said. "I was just about to ask you something."

"Go right ahead." Mark folded his hands behind his head and leaned back in his seat. "I'm waiting for an update on the tornado feature. For the next three minutes, I'm all ears."

Tom looked around him, at the rows of reporters and editors hunched at their desks, breathing in the recycled air. He felt like he had more than three years ago, when he sat in Donna's office, agreeing to a meeting that never came to pass. The feeling he'd had again just a short time ago, as he read to Elana, the book slipping from his fingers. He was terrified of making a move he would regret. He could almost see himself, immobilized in his Aeron chair, his heart galloping while he stared ahead, unseeing. He was inside and outside, watching himself sink.

He wouldn't let that happen. He couldn't stay here, at his desk, a moment longer. He printed the story that was on his screen.

"You know? I really should talk to—"

He got up and took the long route, hoping Mark wasn't watching as he passed the printer and left the newsroom. He kept going, through the kitchen and past the elevator bank and down the hall to the stairwell. He opened the door, stepped inside, and went up three flights, as high as he could go.

He emerged in a quiet space of gray-carpeted cubicles. Research, analytics, tech support—they were all up here, each team in its dimly lit domain, separated by fuzzy moveable walls. Tom kept his head down. No one would look at him unless he looked first. He walked on, not caring where he was going, as long as it provided a brief escape. He just needed to be in a place where no one could find him. He turned down a hall lined with storage closets and came to a small alcove. On one wall was an oversized casement window. To his amazement, it was unlatched and slightly open, letting in an inch of air.

It looked wrong, the way a sleeping cat or a child's toy would have looked wrong. Here, on the nineteenth floor of a Midtown office tower, was a window that *opened*.

Outside was a small terrace that held gray-boxed machinery. Tom listened for footsteps, then swung the window open on its side. The space was just large enough for a person to squeeze through. He climbed up, hoisted himself out, and closed it softly behind him.

The afternoon sun hit his face. He stretched and felt the tension ease in his back and shoulders. A gust of air rushed over him. Above him was the cloudless sky.

He moved to the edge of the terrace, on the other side of the wood screens that hid the ventilators. Stretching to the south and east were roof gardens with tables and lounge chairs, leafy plants and potted trees. A few flights below, two women stood at a rooftop's edge. They were smoking cigarettes, sprinkling ash down on the street.

He felt like a kid who'd found the perfect hiding place. The wind swept around him, ruffling his clothes. He watched the women across the street toss their cigarettes, then head inside, their hair and skirts whipping. As he gazed down at the slowly moving traffic, he heard a voice behind him.

"Well, what do you know. Tom Foster."

He seized the low wall in front of him, then spun around, his heart juddering. It took him a moment before he saw her there, sitting on the pebbled ground near the ventilators, her legs stretched out, sunglasses shading her eyes.

"Jesus, Rita."

"Do me a favor," she said. "Step away from the edge. I can't afford to lose half of my team."

She waved a hand, indicating the space beside her. Tom sat on the uneven surface. Rita reached into her jacket and took out a pack of cigarettes.

"You mind?"

"Not at all."

"It's just to settle my stomach," she said. "I did something bonkers today. I went out at lunch and bought a hot dog in Central Park."

"You're kidding." Tom stretched out his legs beside hers. "I didn't think you ever left the building for lunch."

"I know. I've been told I work too hard, even for this place." Rita exhaled a cloud of smoke and slowly fanned it away. "You don't have that problem, do you?"

Tom turned to face her. She was staring up at the sky.

"Is it something you want to talk about?" she said. "Heart-to-hearts aren't really my thing, but it's affecting your work. So I suppose, if it would help, we could give that a try. Or you could just take care of whatever the problem is. And not lose your job."

Tom straightened his back, feeling almost light-headed as he stared into the distance. Far below them, a fire truck was making its way down Park. Sirens echoed in the canyons between the buildings.

"I'll take care of it," he said.

"Good," Rita said. "Well, since you're here, I'll let you in on a little secret. I'm giving notice on Monday. As soon as I walk in the door."

For the first time, she smiled. She pulled up her legs and folded her hands beneath the knees of her black jeans.

"You found a new job?"

"That's right," she said. "At the *Times*. All that hard work is finally getting recognized. Not here, of course."

Tom wished he could see her eyes behind her sunglasses.

"Congratulations, Rita. You deserve it."

"Thank you," she said. "I start next month. You know what happens when you give notice here? Some twenty-three-year-old in HR gets you to sign some papers. Then security escorts you out the door. The whole thing takes about fifteen minutes, if you're lucky."

"Sounds harsh."

"It's great. They pay you for your last two weeks, even though they won't let you work. As soon as I'm out, I'm going shopping. I need a bathing suit. I'm going to spend ten days in Costa Rica."

Tom pictured the plane, the hotel, the beach. It was too tempting to imagine.

"Mark's going to take this hard," he said.

"You'd think he would have noticed me clearing out my stuff this week. When I leave tonight, there will be nothing left but a pencil."

She stubbed out her cigarette and tossed it on a pile a few feet away. He wondered how long she had been coming up here but knew better than to ask.

"This place won't be the same without you," he said.

"That's true. You'll have to do a much better job of watching your back, for one thing." Rita turned to him, pushing her glasses to the top of her head. "You know Charlie? You're on his list."

"He sent me a message asking to see him," Tom said. It was hard to meet her gaze. "But Tadpole was having a meltdown."

"Well, Charlie needed some backup a while ago, and you were out," Rita said. "And I guess this wasn't the first time. He waited for me outside the women's restroom to tell me about it. I'm surprised he didn't barge right in."

The slope-shouldered editor in the kitchen was Charlie's right-hand man. Tom pictured him churning out headlines, his wrist braces propped in front of his ergonomic keyboard.

"I wouldn't let Charlie down again," Rita said.

"I won't," he said. "I realize this is a terrible time to ask for anything, but I was hoping for a few days off next week. To take care of that problem."

Rita studied his face.

"I'll see what I can do."

"Thanks, Rita. I appreciate that."

She got up and brushed the dust off her clothes. At the window, she stopped and looked back at him.

"Anything I should know before I go in there?"

"Screwup on the bond team. And Tadpole probably needs a new headset."

"Thanks. Maybe I'll take the long way back."

She climbed inside, leaving the window open behind her.

He was back at his desk and had the row to himself. Rita had disappeared again, and Mark was filling in for her at a meeting in the conference room.

Tom worked on a story for the pharma team. In a few hours,

he would have some time, at least, to figure out what to do next. He just had to get through this day. But as he tried to focus, a voice kept breaking in. Vanessa, in the row ahead of him, was talking on her cell phone.

"Yeah, well, I might go to that party," she was saying. "I mean, I could, but there's also Brendan's thing. So there's the party, and that opening, and Dominic's band is playing. But that's later." She tilted her head, typing with one hand as she spoke. "Okay, we could do that, or just the opening, and then stop by Jessie's party instead. You know her. So do you want to get dinner first?"

Listening to her, Tom thought he would give anything to have that feeling again, just once—of being off the clock, able to go wherever the night might take you.

"And don't forget tomorrow," Vanessa went on. "There's that show. No, not that one. The one in the park. Well, we could do both. Then we really should meet up with Alison and Steve, because we haven't seen them in forever."

Tom didn't realize he was looking at her until she glanced into the mirror attached to her computer. She flashed him a smile.

He looked away, his face burning, cursing himself for making that mistake again.

Mark came back from the meeting and clapped Tom on the back.

"You might want to try using your keyboard every once in a while," he said.

Tom blinked at the message that appeared on his screen. It was from Jim Blivet, the pharma team leader.

Still waiting on the fever-vax story. What's the holdup?

Tom read the story again from the top. He fixed the headline, edited the lede. Cut one quote, moved another. He checked the codes and tickers and sent it to the wire.

His lack of sleep was catching up with him. He reached for the coffee that had been sitting on his desk all day. It left his mouth feeling like it was coated in wax. When was the last time he'd had anything to eat? He was about to head to the kitchen when he heard a rippling of voices in the middle of the newsroom. Up at the general assignment desk, Charlie rose from his seat.

"Where's Rita?" he said. "We've got a problem."

Mark scrolled through the stories they'd sent to the wire. He opened the one that Tom had just edited.

"Crap."

Mark started typing.

"What is it?" Tom said. His jaw tightened as Charlie approached. "What's wrong?"

"Got it, Charlie," Mark called out. "The correction's on its way." He turned to Tom and said with forced cheer, "Just a coding problem. You put in the wrong ticker. Blivet's gonna want your head on a platter, but no one else will care."

Charlie reached their row. He rested a hand on the back of Rita's chair and gave Tom a grim smile.

"Just the man I wanted to see."

Before Tom could respond, Jim Blivet, a slight man whose round face was currently mottled with rage, came down the aisle. He stood behind them, his hands planted on the hips of his Friday chinos, his lower lip trembling. Later, Tom told himself, he might remember the way Blivet looked right now and laugh. But not while Blivet was glaring at the screen over Mark's shoulder, blinking in disbelief.

"What the fuck, guys?" Blivet said.

"Don't worry, Jim," Mark said. "It's a two-bit biotech in Buffalo. And the correction is already out."

Rita appeared. She stopped at the end of their row. Charlie removed his hand from her chair.

"Is there a problem?" she said.

"Mix-up with a ticker," Charlie said. He gave her a long look. "Mark's taking care of it."

"Good." She looked at Blivet. "Then, if you don't mind, I'd like to get back to work."

Blivet, still hovering behind Mark, huffed out a breath. He turned on his heel and brushed past Rita, speed walking back to his desk.

Charlie looked at Tom.

"You left me in the lurch earlier," he said. "Can't remember the last time I've had to say this to an editor, but maybe you should ask Mark or Rita to look over your stories before you send them to the wire. Sometimes it helps to have a second set of eyes."

Tom didn't respond. After Charlie left, Rita straightened her folders.

"I'll send you the correction," Mark told her.

"That's all right." Rita sat at her desk and took a travel magazine from a drawer. "I trust you."

She placed the magazine in her lap and slowly turned the pages. Mark stared at her, openmouthed.

Rita paid no attention. After a few moments, Mark turned his stare to Tom.

"Look, I'll be more careful with the tickers," Tom told him. "Sorry you had to deal with that."

Mark gave him a weary smile.

"How about I take our stories for the rest of the day?"

"You don't have to do that."

"Or I could check over your stories for you. Like Charlie said."

"Thanks," Tom said. "But I'm fine."

He glanced at Rita. She'd put on her headphones, but that didn't mean she wasn't listening. She placed her magazine face-down on her desk and started looking through her filing cabinet.

"I'd just like to keep both of us out of trouble," Mark said. "You could work on advance obits. Tadpole was hounding us about them this morning. Pick one, give it a read, and add this code." He shot him a message. "Then the editors will know it's ready when we need it."

Tom ran a hand over his eyes. Editing advance obits was dreary work. They were often written by the newest reporters, who got roped into making uncomfortable calls to the colleagues of aging public figures. There was a different folder for the very old and very sick—the ones "circling the drain."

"I can handle our stories," Tom said. "And whatever Jim or Charlie sends to us. You don't have to pull my weight."

Mark lowered his voice. "I don't mean to pry," he said. "But you seem to have a lot on your mind." He leaned closer, his voice almost a whisper. "Let's not rattle any cages."

Mark was right. Charlie was gunning for him, and now so

was Blivet. Not to mention the Hong Kong bureau chief. Any of them might raise their concerns to Tadpole, if they hadn't already.

He just had to get through this day. And he could *not* lose this job.

"Fine," he said. "Obits. I'll work on obits."

Tom opened the folder and picked a file from the middle of the list. A three-term senator, late sixties. His obit—six blunt, dry paragraphs—had been submitted by a reporter in the D.C. bureau. Cranked out to meet the quota. Tom checked the names and dates, read the quotes and anecdotes. It had all of the pertinent details, except, of course, the senator's age. *DEAD AT TK.* Tom added his initials to the end of the file.

He went back to the folder and searched for another obit to edit. At the bottom were government officials who were in little danger of dying soon but who'd made the cut because of their prominence. With any luck for everyone involved, none of these files would be revisited until years from now, when, Tom hoped, he would be long gone from this place. The last on the list was the Fed chairman. Not yet sixty, no health problems. A safe bet.

Tom got to work, though the words were swimming. He had to clear his head before he faced Helen. What would she *want* him to tell her? He needed to steal an hour, get some food, and come up with the beginnings of a plan—before he rushed to the train and returned home. He had to figure out something by Monday or Donna would move forward.

He sent Helen a text.

Crazy day here. Might be a little late.

A text from her came at almost the same time, as if she'd not only sensed him thinking about her, but had also picked up on signals, from seventy miles away, that he wanted to come home late.

I'm on deadline for Lou, her message said. *You'll do bath & bed, right?*

Tom stared at his phone. Even on his most exhausting days, he always rallied for the end-of-day routine with Sophie and Ilona, as long as he got home on time: giving the girls their bath, then reading their bedtime stories and making up a story of his own to tell them as they fell asleep. Yet the thought of performing those activities tonight, while his mind raced frantically elsewhere, seemed to instantly drain the last of his reserves. But he couldn't let Helen down.

He would make it up to her. Somehow, he was going to make up for everything.

OK. Be there as soon as I can.

And again he had the ridiculous desire to ask Helen for advice. He was so used to talking to her.

He was turning back to his computer when a reporter breezed down the aisle. A young woman, just out of college, with wild, dark hair held back in a ponytail. The images came to him despite his resistance. Elana, starting kindergarten. In middle school. As a teenager. As a young woman, fully grown. She would be tall and strong, like her mother. Confident. Well adjusted.

Elana would become a whole, complete *person*, and if Donna took her away, she wouldn't know who he was. She wouldn't remember that he'd ever had a part in her life. That her father had been more than just an anonymous donor.

Tom's eyes stung as he gave the Fed chairman's obit a last read. For the third time, he checked the codes. Then he hit the string of function keys and pressed Send.

This time, he knew he'd made a mistake. He knew it instantly, in his guts. The room seemed to pitch, and he felt himself float a little, as if the severity of his mistake had rendered him weightless.

The headline scrolled at the bottom of his screen.

"Rita." Tom kicked his chair back and spoke to her behind Mark. "We've got to pull something from the wire."

He clicked on the obit, unable to believe it was really there. It was a detailed and nuanced piece, written by the top reporter on the economics team. There were sections on the chairman's childhood in South Carolina, on his years in academia, on the doctrine that bore his name. He was married to a schoolteacher and loved baseball. He liked to bike to work from his home in the suburbs, even in winter, which drove his wife crazy. Tom opened the photo attached to the file. It showed a vigorous man with salt-and-pepper hair and warm, intelligent eyes, crinkled at the corners. He was laughing—the reporter had described his deep, booming laugh—though considering the state of the economy, it was hard to imagine what was so funny.

Rita was fast. The first retraction, highlighted in red, appeared on his news feed. It remained for a full five seconds, a measure of time that seemed to last an eternity. Rita sent a second red headline as she replaced the story with a one-paragraph correction.

Waves of gasps and murmurs spread through the newsroom. One reporter let out a hoot that ended when a fist hit a desk.

Mark whirled toward him.

"Are you fucking kidding me?" he said. "You sent the Fed chair's obit to the wire?"

Tom gripped the arms of his chair, as though he were in a car that was about to crash. He could hear them coming before he could see them—the top editors and their deputies. Others who Tom didn't even recognize, their faces livid, eyes sparkling.

Tadpole was the first to arrive. His voice thundered in the silence of the newsroom.

"What the fuck's going on here, Rita?"

Tadpole swept through the row ahead of them, his hands clenched into fists. He stopped in front of Tom's desk, glaring down as if he planned to send him out on a stretcher. Tom cleared his throat, about to speak, though he had no idea what he would say. His head was throbbing and blank.

Rita waved a hand to get Tadpole's attention.

"My mistake," she said. "I was working on the obit with Tom and sent it to the wire while I was showing him how to code it."

Mark gave her another openmouthed stare. Tom swallowed hard but kept his eyes straight ahead, gazing through the men who were filling the space around him, walling him in. The finance team leader, a former Wall Street analyst, was sweating through his bespoke suit. Dick Maddox, top of the top editors, had appeared, his face blazing from his hairline to the seam between his shoulders and head.

Tom watched the headlines roll, his muscles coiled. If he could have pushed back his chair without toppling the editors behind him, he would have walked out, leaving his badge at the door. Because that was where this was heading. There was no question about that, only about how much humiliation he would have to endure before they swung the ax.

As if reading his mind, Dick Maddox moved behind him.

"C'est la vie," Maddox said, speaking over Tom's head to Tadpole. "C'est la fucking vie. You'll have to ream this guy out later. We've got to hit the phones. Who wants to call the dead chairman?"

"He's in Bridgehampton for a wedding," the finance team leader said, whipping out his cell phone. He turned to Rita. "I'll apologize on your behalf."

"That's so generous of you," Rita said.

Tadpole stepped over to her desk. "If it were anyone else—"

"You'd say you understood," she said. "Because mistakes happen."

Tadpole coughed out a laugh.

"Not to you, they don't. You kill me, Rita." He gave Tom a last withering stare. "We're not done. We're not even close."

Tadpole sprinted down the aisle. The rest of the editors followed. Half of the newsroom was already on the phone, trading gossip. Reporters snuck glances in Tom's direction and looked quickly away. Tom's phone number was at the end of the published obit; all three of his lines were blinking.

"Don't answer," Rita told him. "Maddox will send out a statement. No one else talks."

Mark spun his chair toward her.

"Talk about taking one for the team."

Rita narrowed her eyes at her screen, refusing to look at him. Mark turned to Tom.

"You are the luckiest bastard I've ever met."

Mark shot up from his chair and stormed off.

It took Tom a few minutes before he could face Rita. When he tried to speak, she gave a very slight shake of her head.

"Don't thank me," she said. "Don't apologize. Don't say anything."

Tom studied her profile as she fired replies to the messages popping up on her screen. Each arrived with an insistent ding.

"Rita," he said. "You didn't have to do that."

"No, I didn't. But I didn't want to send you off to the firing squad on my last day."

"Thank you." Tom managed to get the words out before she could stop him. "I know you paid a price for that."

He thought of her previously unblemished record. Though Rita kept her face turned, Tom could see that her eyes were red. He looked down at his desk.

"I'm sorry," he told her. "I'm so—"

Rita cut him off with a wave of her hand.

———

The newsroom was shutting down around him.

Tom took the last of the science team's stories, finishing the ones that Mark had left open on his screen as, row by row, the desks emptied. The stocks and bonds teams were the first to go, signing off an hour after the markets closed. Soon the other teams started to peel away. As stories came out from competitors, each having a good laugh at their expense, Tom expected Tadpole to come back and escort him to the fishbowl for a public firing. But all he got was a single message:

My desk Monday morning. Don't be late.

On Monday, Tom realized, he might be getting a lot more time off than he'd hoped for. But even his fear and shame couldn't compete with the guilt he felt about Rita. She hadn't said another word to him, never moved her eyes from her screen. Mark came back to claim his messenger bag and shut down his computer.

"Hey," he said. "Whatever this is, take care of it, okay? For your sake, and ours."

Tom nodded at his screen.

After Mark left, Rita took a few papers from her filing cabinet. Tom gathered the rest for her and dumped them in the recycling bin. When he got back to his chair, he saw that she'd placed a single pencil in the center of her desk.

She came over to him. Tom pretended to read a news summary as she lined up the folders beside his phone. He wished again that he could tell her how sorry he was, but he knew that she wouldn't want to hear it.

She was looking at him. "Well."

"I hope you have an amazing trip, Rita."

"Oh, I will." She reached for his phone cord but released it in its usual tangle. "Look, I'm not going to say goodbye, but I want you to know that I wish you the best of luck." She made a failed attempt at a smile. "However that luck might manifest itself."

He thought about it.

"Thanks, Rita."

She gazed at the rows of empty desks.

"Please tell me you're not planning on spending the night here," she said.

"No," he said. "I'll head out in a few minutes."

"Good."

And without another word, she walked off, motorcycle helmet in hand, backpack over her shoulder.

Tom listened to the fading sounds of the newsroom. The machinery around him was switching into lower gear. Computers buzzed and went dark. Soon all he could hear was the whirring of the ventilation system. It was hard to believe it had been there all along, hidden in the background, beneath all those other sounds.

The quiet was broken by a rhythm of heels.

He looked up to see Vanessa striding down the length of the newsroom. Coming back from the bathroom, carrying her purse. She'd fanned her hair over her shoulders and fixed her makeup. Her lips were a bright red.

Friday night, out on the town.

She was coming toward him. How many times had she caught him looking at her that day? Never intentionally, but she wouldn't know that.

She stopped at the end of his row. She gave her blouse a self-conscious tug and crossed her arms over her chest.

"Sorry to bother you," she said. "But I'm supposed to stay until the last editor leaves." She waited. "So do you think you'll be leaving soon? You don't look... busy."

"Sure," Tom said. "Sorry. I didn't mean to hold you up."

She moved a step closer and glanced at him, as if daring herself. Her face took on a confident look; her hands moved to her hips. She gave him that same smile he'd seen before, when she caught him looking at her in the mirror.

"Maybe I'm wrong," she said. "But I bet you could use a drink."

CHAPTER TEN

O h, I'm not busy," Karl said. "Just sitting in traffic, waiting for this guy who's trying to cut a U-ey to get out of everybody's way." He added, his voice cheerful, "Yeah, fuck you, too, buddy. Not you, Helen. This guy."

Helen could hear the Allman Brothers playing on Karl's car radio in the background. She was in her living room, watching Sophie and Ilona take apart their dollhouse.

"I need to tell you something," she said.

She moved closer to the window, away from her daughters. Then she told him about the car that had stopped across from their houses, and the guys who were in it, and how they'd killed the dog.

Karl was quiet for a few moments. Horns blasted over the line.

"Well, that's horrible about Cotton Ball," he said. "I'm very sorry to hear that. But I don't think there's anything to worry about. A bunch of freaky-looking dudes in some junker car? We have no idea what they were thinking."

"I thought they were looking at your house," Helen said.

"Though Glenn thinks they might have been checking out mine."

"Glenn? You guys have some kind of neighborhood watch meeting about this?" Karl laughed. "And what's he mean by checking it out? Like, *casing* it? I don't think so."

Helen covered her free ear. Sophie and Ilona had littered the floor with tiny chairs, a bedroom set, and the compartments of a four-inch-high entertainment center. Now they were fighting over one of the dolls, a spindly figure with a few strands of yarn sewn into a ponytail. As they twisted her, trying to make her stand up without falling over, one of her legs popped out of its socket. Immediately both girls started to cry.

"*Stop,*" Helen said. "I told you not to do that." She picked up the doll and stepped away, landing on a miniature toilet. She barely managed to keep her curse under her breath. *"Fuck."*

"Hey," Karl said. "You all right?" He waited. "Is it the dog?"

If Karl were there, she might have told him everything. Because she didn't think she could keep it inside any longer. She would have told him about the playground, and her run, and how she was willing to bet that the guys in the rusty Buick were the brothers of the teenage girls, and that the only thing she didn't know was whether they were looking for her or for Nick. But her daughters were crying, and her emails were piling up, and if she didn't get back to work *right now* she would have no hope of meeting her deadline. She would have no hope at all.

"I'm fine," she told Karl. "I just thought I should let you know about that car."

"Well, like I said. It's probably nothing. Let's face it—you, me, and Glenn? We probably all spend too much time looking out our windows. Give us a few years, and we'll turn into Butch. Measuring the height of the grass in our neighbors' lawns."

Helen was looking out her window right now. Karl and Jackie's front lawn was freshly mowed and watered, an even two inches high. If Butch was keeping an eye on anyone's lawn, it was hers and Tom's. *This weekend,* she told herself. They would mow the damn lawn.

"I better get off the phone," Karl said. "You know that young cop, the one that sometimes directs traffic in front of the high school?"

Helen did. He was blue-eyed and apple-cheeked, like the police officer in her daughters' Playmobil set.

"He's looking like he wants to give me a ticket," Karl said. "I'll be home in a couple of hours. If you see these guys again, give me a call."

"Okay. I will."

He hung up, leaving Helen watching her daughters, who were happily tearing off the limbs of their remaining dolls, tossing the pieces to the floor with the ravaged furniture.

Her phone rang. Helen wished she'd had a chance to finish one more Mega Crux slide before facing another call from work. But when she checked the screen, she saw that it was Tom.

"Hey there," she said with a surge of relief. "Please tell me you made the train."

He didn't respond. There was a crackling sound, followed by a burst of music. Then a man's voice, muffled, coming from a distance.

"Tom?" Helen said. "Are you there?"

A siren, a truck backing up, that crackling again. Then she heard the voice again. Was that Tom? It was hard to tell.

"Hello?" she said.

The man stopped talking. Helen heard a young woman's voice, girlish and high, the words running off into a flirty laugh. Then the connection went dead.

Helen tried calling him back. She got his voice mail.

It was a pocket call, nothing more. But she could still hear that girlish laugh, its high pitch echoing in her ears. Still, she didn't allow herself to be suspicious. It was a matter of principle, like her parents' insistence that everything would be fine.

Or was it just pride?

She stopped herself. That was not a path she wanted to follow. It was just a pocket call. Maybe he was waiting in line somewhere, making small talk with another commuter on his way home. Or maybe it wasn't even Tom, and he'd lost his phone again. A year or so ago, after a late night at work, he'd drifted off on the train, slept right through to the end of the line. And, he'd explained, it was only later that he realized that everything had fallen out of his pockets—not just his phone, but his wallet and keys and even the pink bracelet that Sophie had asked him to carry around all day.

Sometime that year, he'd even lost his wedding ring. She'd discovered it was missing one day when Tom was heading out the door, already late, cursing because he'd forgotten his watch. She went upstairs to get the watch from the wooden box on his night table and noticed that the ring wasn't in its usual place. And he wasn't wearing it. Neither of them wore their rings very often, but they usually brought them out for special occasions.

His hadn't made an appearance in months. Not even on their anniversary.

The loss was probably harder on him than it was on her. He was the one who was sentimental, who couldn't bear to throw anything away. (He saved every toy, every book that belonged to the girls. Every photo he'd ever taken of them, no matter how blurry, was on his computer.) She wanted to tell him she knew about the ring and that it was okay. *They could have a replacement made!*

She would let him know tonight. When they had those beers on the porch. She could try to explain how she felt about moving, see if she could make him understand. And they could talk about whatever was bothering him, why he always seemed to have too much on his mind.

She'd been wondering about that for hours now, turning the problem around in her head even as she looked after the girls and worried about her work. But she was no closer to an answer. She tried to imagine what would make him stare out the kitchen window, the way he had last night, lost in thought while setting up the coffee. Not even realizing she was still there, watching, as he stacked the dirty dishes in the drying rack and let the faucet run.

She tried calling Tom once more, still hoping that he'd made the next train. Again she got his voice mail. In three years of long days and late nights, she had never felt this thoroughly depleted. Somehow she made it through dinner, checking her email as she served up the pasta and broccoli, but she hadn't been able to come up with a response to Ryan's last urgent message: *If you're alive, I suggest you reply to your emails from the Mega Crux team, b/c they are apoplectic.*

As she hurried the girls into the tub, she tried not to let herself wonder too much about where Tom was, what had happened. On a day this stressful, she could already guess when he'd turn up: the moment after the girls fell asleep, right when she had to get back to work.

She must have been more distracted than she realized, because it took her a few minutes to understand the game her daughters were playing. Sophie would reach for the shampoo bottle, and Ilona would then knock it out of her hand, sending it splashing into the water. Each time, with increasing aggression and enthusiasm, Ilona would cry out, *Bam!* Then they would do it again, reenacting the scene they'd witnessed in the playground.

Helen grabbed the bottle from Sophie so quickly that her daughter recoiled, bumping her head lightly against the soap dish. Ilona's mouth trembled.

"Don't do that," Helen said, her voice an icy hiss. "I *never* want to see that again."

Her daughters, crying, slid their eyes away, too frightened to meet her stare. She watched them, scared and shivering in the cooling water, and felt her heart break.

"Mommy's sorry," she said. "I'm sorry, sorry, sorry."

A washcloth floated in the water. Helen pressed it to her face, though it was too late. They had seen her cry. She pulled the stopper and let the water go down the drain.

She made it up to her daughters with books. The same three books, their favorites, read in her best, most soothing voice, over and over. She wedged herself between them on the floor, Sophie on her left, Ilona on her right, and let their elbows press into her as she turned the pages. Tomorrow she would have little bruises below her ribs. *Good,* she thought. At last they climbed into their beds, and she turned off the light and turned on the stuffed turtle. The ceiling glowed with purple stars. They were asleep before she left the room.

Though of course making it up to them came at a cost: There was no longer any chance she would make her deadline. If she didn't send the file to the printer before nine, Lou would land in Pittsburgh and learn that the spiral-bound copies wouldn't be ready for his morning meeting.

She could offer no excuses. She couldn't explain her failure.

She sat at her computer, typing and deleting notes of apology that would only seal her fate. Possibly, she could risk a call, but Lou was famous for his temper, and her years of work would mean nothing if she cost the company a chance to get more business from a major client. He would fire her. And without her job, her family's shaky finances would collapse.

She searched through her emails for the version of the wrap deck she'd completed earlier in the week, the one the sales manager had rejected outright. She slapped on the first slide, changed the headers, and threw in the video without testing it, hoping for the best. She sent one file to the printer in Pittsburgh and another with the video to Lou, then sent Lou a second email about the hardcopies.

They'll be ready at 7 a.m.

She didn't know if the sales manager had ever shown the earlier, rejected version to Lou. But it was too late to worry about that now.

Lightly Chilled. That was the title of Karl's album. She closed her email, put on the music, and lay down on the floor of her office. As the downtempo beats lulled her into a trance, she let it all fall away. The teenage girls in the playground. Their brothers in the rusty car. The enormous error she'd just made at work. The many times she'd yelled at her daughters or hadn't been there for them.

She got up and stopped the music. She played the last track again. Karl hadn't titled any of the songs, but she was sure she'd heard this one before. Hadn't he mentioned something about the fifth track that morning, when she stopped by to pick up the CD?

Finally it came to her: It was a cover of "Endless City Streets," a sentimental rock ballad from the late '70s, and almost unrecognizable until the very end, when a few notes hinted at the guitar solo. The song had come on the radio one afternoon when she and Tom and the girls were at Karl and Jackie's. Karl, who was working the grill, had caught her singing along. *Don't stop on my account,* he said with a smile, meeting her eyes as he added, *I didn't know you could sing.*

And something about the way the words came out made Helen glad that Tom was already drifting off in his lawn chair. And that Jackie was inside, refilling the pitcher.

Karl could sing. She and Tom had gone out a few times to see his band play at Trax. She thought of the photo in Karl's studio of him as a teenager: feathered hair, Led Zeppelin T-shirt, faded jeans. There was also that photo of his sons, who lived out of state and had children of their own. He didn't talk much about his life before Jackie, but he'd let a few details slip. There was a time when he'd lived in a cabin upstate. Years had gone by when he didn't speak to either of his sons. His ex-wife was somewhere else now, out of the picture. Off the grid, from the way Karl described it.

He had a past in a way that she did not. Her days had followed, in a more or less uninterrupted line, from where she'd started. But she hadn't wound up where she'd expected. Looking back, she was amazed at how naïve her expectations had been. That hard work would be rewarded. That those who followed the rules wouldn't slip behind. That there was some value—a trade-off, even—in focusing on goals, not dreams.

What were her dreams, before she came to believe that the best goals were within reach? She didn't know; she couldn't remember.

The doorbell rang. The sound floated through the rooms.

Helen wasn't sure how long she'd been lying there, listening to Karl's music on endless repeat, wondering about the song he'd recorded for her. Where was Tom?

She checked her phone: no missed calls. She went to their bedroom window, afraid she would see a police cruiser and an officer waiting on her doorstep. Or that car again. But the street was quiet, with no signs of anything unfamiliar. It had to be

Tom. He must have walked home from the train station, having lost not just his phone but also his keys.

Downstairs, in the dark of the living room, she glanced out the window at the porch, then let the curtain fall. It was too late to pretend she hadn't heard the bell. She took a deep breath. Composed her face. And then she opened the door.

He stared at her from under the porch light, his broad arms crossed over his chest. In one glance she took him in, from his muscle-T to his soccer slides. His basketball shorts were cinched below his thick waist; his shoulders were sunburned and peeling. For the first time she noticed that she was at least half a foot taller than him. Even if she weren't standing above him, at the edge of the short step that led into the house, the top of his head would barely clear her chin.

"Evening, P.J.," she said. That was his real name, or at least the initials that were on his mailbox. There was no way she was calling him Butch. "Everything all right?"

He stood there, his mouth in a tight line. Helen steeled herself for another lecture. About their lawn, probably. Or their rotting doghouse, which he blamed for every mosquito in the neighborhood, or maybe that strange wild plant at the back of their yard whose shoots were drooping under their own weight. He had registered so many complaints in the past two years that it was hard for her to pretend they were still on civil terms, let alone friendly ones.

Whatever his problem was, she would handle it quickly and get him off her porch.

"It's late," she said when he still didn't speak. She kept one hand on the door. "Is this something that can wait until the morning?"

Butch stared at a point over her shoulder, as if he resented having to look up at her. Or maybe he was seeing if anyone else was home.

"Pat saw you aiming some kind of weapon at me today," he said. "From a window."

At first, Helen could almost believe he was kidding. Pat, his wife, was a sturdy woman with an ash-blond bob who always stared right through Helen when she said hello. They'd had only one conversation, about a year ago, when Pat went door to door down Crescent, asking if anyone else was bothered by an unfamiliar bird that had nested in one of the sidewalk trees. "It's a very *loud* bird," she told Helen. "And it sounds like it brought friends."

Helen had never heard a thing. But she smiled.

"Well," she joked. "There goes the neighborhood!"

Pat had left without another word. "Don't worry about it," Jackie told Helen later. "That bird probably lives in her head." But that was all she would say. Jackie never really made fun of Pat, wouldn't even speculate about what Butch did in his garage all day. They were Pat and Butch, married right out of high school; their fathers and uncles had worked together at the mills until the day they closed. "Those two, they're *from* here," Jackie said, and Helen left it at that.

But now Butch was on her porch, staring at her, challenging her to explain herself. She couldn't figure it out. How had Pat even seen her? Did the woman spend her afternoons hiding in the bushes, spying behind the cover of the azaleas? Helen felt the entire weight of her day pressing on her shoulders. She reminded herself: *Handle it quickly.*

"It was a water gun," she said. "For the squirrels. Maybe it was hard to see that from wherever Pat was standing. But really, it was just a toy." She tried a smile. "It wasn't even loaded."

Butch kept staring, his eyes hard and dark, his stubbly chin jutted out.

"That don't explain why you were aiming it at me."

His lips were white. All at once, Helen saw herself, and her family, through his eyes. With their less-than-perfect yard, their dilapidated doghouse and its buggy little puddle. All the little repairs they didn't have money for or even time to think about. They were the bad neighbors, the ones bringing down Crescent Street. *(There goes the neighborhood!)*

Her heart was racing. The way he was staring at her—his bald desire to intimidate her, *shame* her—seemed intended to ignite her own anger. He might as well have tossed a lit match. But she swallowed that back, reined herself in.

"You're right," she said. "Please accept my apology. To you and to Pat. I was fooling around with a kid's toy, and I had no intention of upsetting either one of you. It was a mistake. I've had a long day, and that's no excuse, but that's all it was. A mistake."

He didn't blink. He kept giving her his outraged stare, as if her apology had only stoked his fury. His feet were planted just below the step to the door. His hand moved to the doorjamb. He spread his fingers, leaned into his palm. Helen saw this without looking and pretended not to notice. For the first time she felt how alone she was, standing at the threshold of her house, the rooms dark and empty behind her, while upstairs, her daughters were sleeping.

She thought fast. She could slam the door, though if she tried, he might block her. And if he didn't, the door might break his fingers. How would she explain that to his wife or the cops or Tom? *He came to the house and seemed like he was about to force his way in.* She didn't want to have that conversation with anyone. What if Pat talked to the police and brought up the water gun? Even though it was a toy, she was sure it looked bad. She would be the one who'd menaced a neighbor.

Butch was studying her, as if considering whether to accept her apology.

"I hope you don't think it's a joke," he said. "Playing with guns. Because there's nothing funny about it. Sometimes you can't tell the difference between a toy gun and a real gun. Aiming one at somebody is a good way to get yourself killed."

Butch took his hand away, but he wasn't done. He folded his arms and stayed just outside the door. He was so close he had to tilt his head to glare up at her.

He could stand out there shivering in his muscle-T all night if he wanted. She wasn't going to take it anymore.

"I agree with you," she said. "There's nothing funny about guns. And I see how you could have mistaken it for the real thing. But I wouldn't have expected that anyone was watching my window so closely." She locked eyes with him, trying to show he didn't scare her, even if he did. "Again, I'm sorry, and please let Pat know I'm sorry too. Now, like I said, I've had a long day. Good night."

Helen waited. She couldn't understand what was keeping him there. The look on his face said he wanted to air some additional grievance, pursue some new line of interrogation. Her anger flared, and she thought of the many questions she could ask him, if she felt like it. What did he do in his garage all day? Why had he retired at the age of fifty, and why didn't anybody talk about it? Why the hell was Pat staring up at her window?

Butch's face seemed to harden. Something was still bothering him. But whatever it was, she didn't want to hear it. Not now. Not today.

She was about to close the door—in his face, since he'd left her no other choice—when he unfolded his arms and moved his hand back to the doorjamb. She saw his fingers curl in, gaining purchase, and she tried to think of the moves Joe had taught her. But it was like her memory had been wiped clean. Butch probably outweighed her by sixty pounds. She thought of telling him, *You don't know how loud I can scream.* She hoped Karl was home. Or Glenn. Her heart pounded, fast punching in her chest.

She could do it. Slam the door. Crush his fingers.

But instead of retreating, she opened the door wide and moved toward him, stepping down. Heading right for him.

Butch stepped back instinctively, his feet shuffling in his soccer slides. His fingers left the door. As he stumbled backward, losing his balance, he reached for her. His hand landed on her arm with a soft slap as he tried to stop himself from falling. The touch seared her skin, drawing all her rage to that point of contact. In an instant, she swung her arm, a violent shake that dislodged his hot, damp hand, forcing him away as she freed herself. And then it was too late. His foot missed the first of the four low steps that led down to the grass. His arms spiraled as he fell to the ground.

He landed on his back with a soft thud. Helen gasped. Her heart was beating even faster now; there was a pulsing in her head and limbs. An energy coursed through her that she hadn't felt in years, not even when she was boxing at Joe's or when she ran so hard and for so long that her muscles burned.

For a few moments Butch blinked up at the sky, furious and amazed, catching his breath. Then he scooted away on the grass, causing his shorts to slip down. He grabbed the waistband, tugged them up, and propped himself up on his elbows.

She came down the stairs and stared at him. She held out a hand.

"Here," she said. "Let me help you."

A screen door creaked on its hinges. Pat had come out of her house in a bathrobe. She seemed on the verge of running toward them. Even two houses away, Helen could see the fear and accusation on her neighbor's face.

"He's fine," Helen called out to her. She hoped it was true. "He fell, but he's fine. It was an accident."

Butch was still on his elbows. Again she offered a hand, but he ignored her. He hoisted himself up, yanked his clothes into place, and searched the grass for the soccer slide that had come off in his fall. He shoved his foot back in.

He walked to the edge of her lawn, breathing hard, glancing over his shoulder. When he reached the sidewalk, he stopped.

"Crazy fucking bitch."

He turned away and went down the sidewalk. He gave her a last look when he reached his own front lawn. Then he marched down the flagstone path that curved in a tight *S* shape from the sidewalk to his porch, not once straying onto the grass.

Helen sat on her porch and stared out at the dark sky.

She'd gone into the house and taken the rock from the stroller. She held it now, turning it over in her hands. Across the street, the wind chimes at Glenn's house were playing a tuneless series of notes. She remembered Jackie saying once, after a third drink, *One of these nights, I'm gonna cut down those chimes. So help me God, he's gonna make me do it.*

Though she was cold to the bone, she wasn't ready to go inside. Toxic waves were washing over her. She was thinking about Butch. She was lucky that he hadn't hurt himself badly. That he hadn't jumped up and done anything to hurt her.

She'd flung him away, knowing that he would fall. And she'd felt an unexpected thrill—the thrill of losing control, the impulse she'd been fighting for so long.

She held the rock, ran her fingers over its surface. She got up and threw it as hard as she could, sending it into the shadows of the street. She shivered, a full-body tremor as the adrenaline left her limbs.

As if in response, a car came down Crescent. Headlights swept across the trees. But it wasn't Tom's car. It was the rusty Buick, slowing down as it approached Karl and Jackie's house. Helen went to the side of her porch to get a better look. But they drove off, gunning the engine as they headed for Elm. Maybe they'd seen her.

She tried to catch the plates, but it was too late. They were gone.

The street went quiet again. The wind chimes stirred in the breeze.

CHAPTER ELEVEN

"Can you hold this?" Vanessa asked. "I'll be back in a sec."
They'd stopped in front of a bodega on a block of pizza parlors, nail salons, and cell phone stores. Before Tom could answer, she passed him her cigarette and dashed inside.

Tom looked down the street and wondered, not for the first time, what he was doing here. When they left the office, there was still light in the sky. Now there was only a faint trace of orange between the buildings to the west. They'd strolled down Park Avenue, taking it slow—her shoes were *killing* her, she told him—and turned onto Fifty-Ninth, passing the subway entrance at Lex. That was where he should have made his excuses, offered his apologies as he broke away. He could have run down those stairs and caught the express to Grand Central and the next train home. Though he'd already missed his chance to see Sophie and Ilona before they went to bed; his last hope of getting home at a decent hour had departed with the six o'clock train.

He hadn't even checked his phone, sent a text to let Helen

know he would be later than expected. How could he type another apology, another excuse, about the office? He might not have a job next week. That realization brought a flood of shame that drowned out all other feeling.

And so he'd walked on, Vanessa's words washing over him as she told him how happy she was that he'd accepted her invitation for a drink: "No one in the newsroom ever goes out!" Talking fast, she described how hard she found it, even after three years there, to really *connect* with people, to meet the editors, to get any sense of where she was going or of what options were open to her. She had a bright, beaming smile that tended to disappear completely when she thought he wasn't looking and that she could turn back on in an instant, though it was always a beat too late. Glancing at the shop windows and at the shop girls taking smoking breaks, she told him that she often felt stuck and sometimes even hopeless. Then she laughed at herself, saying she didn't want to dwell on any of that. "It's just so nice to escape from the office!"

Wasn't that what he'd wanted? To escape his real life for a while? Back at work, when Vanessa asked if he wanted a drink, she'd caught him at the exact right moment—when he was exhausted and overwhelmed, consumed by thoughts of Donna, Elana, his own mistakes. He was ready, for a moment at least, to bask in freedom.

They'd zigzagged down the streets and avenues until they wound up here, east of Third. Vanessa came out of the bodega. She bent down to adjust her shoe, and her skirt went tight from her hips to her knees. Then she reclaimed her cigarette.

"Thanks so much for waiting," she said, and flashed him that smile. "This bar is great. You'll love it." She looked him over, and he could see the insecurity in her face, that hesitation in her eyes. "It's relaxed, almost a dive, but not too divey." She paused, studying his reaction to see how this description was going over, then added, "Good beers on draft. Nothing fancy or pretentious. And not too expensive!"

A teenage girl walked past, tall and slim in her new fall clothes, a private school girl with flowing hair that fell almost to her waist. Down the block, a thirtyish businessman in an expensive suit sat on the steps of a cream-colored town house, a glass of wine in his hand. Even now, after so many years in the city, Tom felt distinctly out of place when faced with extraordinary wealth. Only models in catalogs looked like that private school girl; only in magazines did a man drink a glass of wine on the steps of his cream-colored town house.

Vanessa crushed her cigarette and looked around for a trashcan. Seeing none, she put the butt in her purse.

"So the bar's around the corner," she said. "But would you mind if I stopped by my apartment first? It's right down this block. I've got to get out of these heels."

She rocked from one foot to the other, illustrating her pain as she studied her ankle. It was another opportunity to refuse, to say he was tired, busy, running late. *Let's do this some other time— soon!* But he saw her face, how nervous she was, second-guessing herself for giving him an out.

"Sure," he said. Relenting, as he knew he would. "Of course."

They walked down the tree-lined street, past brownstones with wrought-iron stairwells, balconies overflowing with vines. As they got closer to Second Avenue, the block changed, the museum-like homes giving way to apartment buildings. Vanessa stopped in front of a gray brick tenement, six stories high, with a double set of fire escapes facing the street. On one side was a grassy lot, surrounded by construction fencing. At the corner was an Irish pub.

"We could go there," Tom said. He calculated how long it would take him to get to Grand Central. "That looks fine to me."

"Oh. No. Sorry, I can't." Vanessa placed her hand on his arm and just as quickly took it away. "I sort of have a history with the bartender." She smiled, then shrugged. "Besides, we're here." She glanced at the gray building, then added, "I love this block. Though I'm thinking of moving over there. A super told me about a place in one of those buildings."

She pointed across Second Avenue to the next block, which was divided by the off-ramp of the Queensboro Bridge. Passing trucks blasted their horns.

"Wouldn't it be loud?" Tom said. "With all that traffic?"

"Well, the apartment's in the back, so it wouldn't be too bad, I hope. Though I guess that means there'd be a lot less light." Vanessa reached into her bag. "Anyway. I was flattered to get the tip. Grateful, really. I think it could be a really good move!"

Tom guessed that it wouldn't be a good move and wanted to tell her that. But what did he know? He hadn't made the right decision about anything in years.

Vanessa was watching him. Tom shifted his messenger bag, filled with a day's worth of newspapers he would never read, on his shoulder. The strap kept unbuttoning the second button of his shirt. He had a sudden urge to crawl out of his clothes, out of his skin.

"Okay," he said. "Well, I'll just wait for you here, then. While you change your shoes."

"Come on up. It's only the second floor."

She went up the stairs and unlocked the door, not turning to see if he would follow. Tom hesitated. Did he want to stand there, waiting, while the conversation with Donna played in his head? He caught the door behind Vanessa and followed her inside.

They entered a hallway tiled in various shades of brown, the tans and beiges echoing the thick paint on the walls. Vanessa scooped up her mail and newspapers—she had them all, the *Times* and *Journal* and *FT*—telling him, "I'm at the office before these even get here." She climbed up a steep stairwell, one hand on the railing, the other holding her newspapers to her chest. When she reached the landing, she adjusted her skirt and straightened her blouse, checking to make sure that everything was in place.

"I'm warning you." She fumbled with her key. "It's small. But I'm just so glad to have a place of my own."

She opened the door and turned on the lights. It was a tiny studio, almost as high as it was wide, with a Pullman kitchen, an alcove for a bedroom, and two tall windows that looked out to the street. Despite its size, it was open and bright, the overhead fan turning a light cool breeze. Against one wall sat a velvet couch with gold feet and a curved wooden frame. There was a coffee table, a small desk between the windows, and several side tables that held potted plants and dozens of framed photographs.

"Nice place," Tom said.

"Thanks. It's my first real apartment in the city. The first without any roommates, I mean." She waved at the couch. "Go ahead, have a seat. It's the only place to sit, besides the bed."

Before he could stop himself, he glanced at her bed, visible in its alcove behind a sheer hanging Indian print. Vanessa kicked off her heels. Tom didn't want to sit—and give the impression that he would be staying—but he also didn't want to hover in the small room. He perched on the edge of the couch and tried not to watch as Vanessa crossed the apartment in her bare feet, putting her bag on the desk, her keys in a bowl. She had a good walk, he noted, in the micro-instant he allowed himself to look. Loose-limbed and fluid. She went to the fridge and took out a bottle of beer that she opened and set in front of him in one seamless motion.

"My last roommate?" she said. "She lived on the couch. Ate there, slept there. Kept her clothes there. I used to find her underwear stashed between the cushions."

Tom couldn't help a quick glance on either side of him.

"Don't worry," she said. "It's new. I didn't take much with me. I didn't want any drama. You know? I'm too old for all that."

He didn't know how old she was and would have guessed she was in her late twenties to early thirties, like so many people in the newsroom. With the way she dressed, her red lipstick and vaguely retro clothes, it was hard to tell. But now, watching her flip through her mail, frown at a bill, he wondered if she was older than he'd thought. Maybe thirty-five, thirty-six. Not much younger than him, really. But she had so much freedom, she might as well have been from another generation. All those phone calls at the office. Didn't she have plans? He was about to ask when she checked her phone.

"Great," she said. "It's still early. There's more beer in the fridge, if you want another. Be right back. Now that I'm here, I might as well change."

And she was off to the alcove, shifting the Indian print into place. It did almost nothing to hide her.

What the hell was he doing here? Though he wished he could flop down on the couch and descend into a dreamless sleep, he sat with his heels digging into the floor, as if that would somehow stop him from plummeting. He turned so he faced the kitchen, preventing himself from catching even an accidental glimpse of her, and studied the shelves above the sink as though nothing were of greater interest to him than kitchen cabinetry. Vanessa was moving around in her little alcove, rattling hangers, pushing them aside, and he wondered how she could possibly fit a closet back there. He took a long drink of his beer, then checked the label. It was a high-end microbrew, with more than double the alcohol of the Beck's he bought in discount four-packs at his local Key Food. The beer hit his empty stomach and went straight to his head. He felt light-headed and drowsy and dazed.

Vanessa talked to him from behind the Indian print.

"I've had so many bad roommate situations. The last girl was always throwing herself at my boyfriend and bad-mouthing me behind my back. So I left. I wound up living with my stuff in a rental van for almost two weeks before I could move into this place."

Tom pictured her driving around the city, cruising the dark avenues in a van stuffed with aloe plants and beaded pillows.

"Where did you park?"

"On the Upper East Side. I figured it was the only chance I'd get to live on Park Avenue."

She was slipping her legs into jeans. It was an intimate sound to be heard from such a short distance. Tom stared down at his shoes. His bottle of beer was still half full. Was it the lack of food, lack of sleep? Somehow it was already working on him.

"You couldn't find anyone to stay with for a few days?" he said. "What about the boyfriend?"

He regretted the question as soon as he spoke the words. He thought of what Mark would say, the warnings he'd fired at him just that morning. *Watch out,* he'd said. *Volatile.*

"Oh, that was over," Vanessa said. "We'd been together for two years, and here he was, flirting with this roommate that I hated. I thought it was the real thing—that we'd get married, not right away, but that was where we were heading. But I could never manage to talk to him about it. So one night I had a ton of drinks and called him up at two in the morning and just sort of yelled at him, 'Where is this relationship going?' That did the trick. I had my answer."

She laughed, a deep, genuine laugh, and Tom was relieved to hear it. He made the mistake of looking in her direction. There was a gap between the edge of the print and the wall, and he caught a glimpse of her in profile—from her bare waist to the cup of her bra—as she pulled on a shirt.

Jesus.

"You always think you have friends who will help," she said. "I have good friends—really *great* friends, girls who are like sisters. Not that I have sisters, but you know what I mean. But sometimes no one can help. Or they can but they won't. Which is something I should have learned a long time ago."

She pulled up a zipper. Tom studied his hands.

"Anyway, that's all in the past!" she said. "Sorry about all the low vibes. Give me one minute. I'm almost done here."

Tom turned to the photos on the table beside him. Travel

shots, mostly: Amsterdam, Paris, San Francisco. In one, a close-up from what looked like a wedding, Vanessa was laughing as she hiked up a strapless dress. Her hair was falling from its complicated arrangement on her head. Her mouth was open, her eyes squeezed closed in happy abandon.

She came into the room in torn jeans and a T-shirt, artfully distressed, from a band he'd never heard of. Somehow he had the impression that she looked more like herself, though he'd never seen her look like that before.

"Isn't that a great shot?" she said. "An old friend took it."

He hadn't realized that he'd picked up the frame. He put it down, his face hot, knocking over two other photos as he tried to set it in the right place.

"Sorry," he said. "I'll fix that."

"That's okay. Let me do it."

She put the photos back in order, picked up his empty bottle, and got another from the fridge. He couldn't remember finishing the first one. Was he actually getting a little buzzed? Vanessa went back to the kitchen and fixed a drink for herself.

"That picture was taken ten years ago," she said. "Right after I moved here. I was going to journalism school, part-time. I'm still taking classes, just to defer my debt."

"You can do that?" Tom thought of all the debts he'd like to defer.

She came back with her drink, what looked like vodka or gin and tonic, and sat on the edge of the coffee table, facing him.

"Sure," she said. "Of course, the total debt keeps getting bigger. But I'm hoping to keep rolling it over until I die." She lifted her glass. "Cheers to that!"

She clinked her glass against his bottle. Her hair was gathered over one shoulder. She'd changed her makeup somehow, added glitter around her eyes. She seemed so comfortable, so relaxed, that he wondered if she'd already snuck in a drink. At work, she was always radiating nervous energy: observing herself, trying to read others' observations of her. Maybe it was just being in her apartment that put her at ease. She was talking to him as if they were the kind of old friends who spent all night on endless phone calls, hashing out their futures over drinks. He was on her couch and she was on the coffee table. Eye to eye, knee to knee.

Bad move. A bad decision, agreeing to that drink and, worse, coming up to her apartment. It was as if things had gotten so bad, the pressures so overwhelming, that he'd cast aside even the possibility of repairing the damage. Told himself he had nothing else to lose.

When that wasn't true at all. He had plenty to lose. There was always more he could lose, farther he could plunge.

Vanessa laughed, and an embarrassed look came over her face.

"You know what I'd like to do?" she said. "If things don't work out for me in the newsroom?"

She crossed her legs and rested her hands on one knee.

"Okay," he said. "What do you want to do?"

"I'd like to move down to the Jersey Shore and spend the rest of my life making macramé lampshades and collecting seashells."

"Now that doesn't sound too bad."

She laughed. He drank his beer. He hadn't come here just to escape his problems, he realized. He'd wanted to pretend that every moment of his life wasn't already accounted for and claimed.

Vanessa leaned forward. She had an earnest look in her eyes. "Can I ask you something?"

Here it was: the cost of his rebellion. In his experience, nothing good ever followed that question. Tom smiled, trying to keep it light, his brain fizzing under the influence of double-digit-proof microbrews.

"What's that?" he said.

"How'd you end up at the wire?"

He let out his breath.

"Just luck, I guess. Though I think I might have run out of that."

Vanessa nodded, her face serious again.

"I used to believe in the whole make-your-own-luck idea," she said. "Send positive energy out into the universe, and it will come back to you. When really that's just exploiting the sad dreams of all the sad people who are trying so hard. I've felt a lot better since I realized that."

Tom had no idea what she was talking about, but now that they were back on even ground, he didn't mind keeping up the illusion that he was following along. He saw the clock blinking over the stove; he felt the minutes ticking and the loss of each departing train. *He had to get out of here.* There was still a chance to leave before this took a turn for the worse. The first step was putting down that beer. Every sip sank him deeper into the sofa cushions.

"There's something else I wanted to ask you," she said. "I mean, I know this maybe isn't the best day for you. But I've wanted to talk about it for a while now. If that's okay."

Tom didn't even try to hide his look of alarm. He leaned back, attempting to increase the distance between them. She spoke before he could stop her.

"What do you think my chances are for moving up in the newsroom?" she said. There was a spark in her voice. She looked game, ready for anything. "Getting a reporter's job. Any beat, any team. At this point, I'd take whatever they'd give me."

At first, he felt a surge of relief. That didn't last, because Vanessa was now staring down at her drink, and he had a sense that tears were coming. But he didn't dare reach out to her. He could not touch an arm, a knee.

"Or should I just give up?" she went on. "I don't want to wake up three years from now as a forty-year-old newsroom clerk."

She waited, her leg kicking a slow beat, her ankle bare above her tennis shoe.

"I'm just looking for an opinion," she said. "An objective reading of where I'm going. I feel like I can't really *see* myself anymore. Do you know what I mean?"

He sure did. But he didn't know what to say. Because he feared that if they offered her anything—if Tadpole ever stopped to consider her fate—it would be something she didn't want. It would be the overnight shift, or covering palladium on the commodities team, or tracking the movements of the Canadian dollar. At first she'd be excited—*flattered*, she might say— thinking it was a rung on the ladder. But there wasn't a ladder, not in that place, not for her. He'd seen it happen so many times. There were plenty of crappy jobs in the newsroom, and if she pushed hard enough she might get one. And before she knew it, she'd wish she'd packed her bags for the Shore.

Or maybe he was wrong. Maybe he would pick up the *Times* a year from now and see her byline on the front page.

He saw the look on her face. She was hoping he wouldn't let

her down. He sensed that there was a right answer, and only one. He couldn't get this wrong.

"Well, after what happened today, I think I'm the last person anyone should ask for advice about working their way up in the newsroom," he told her. "I'm sorry to say that. But it's true."

He raised his bottle. There was maybe an inch left in it. He tried to think of something else to say—he had to offer her something better, or *more*—but he was on the verge of the spins, a sensation he hadn't experienced in years. The velvety textures of the room were beginning to streak and blur. He was missing another train. He had to get out of here, and he had to call Helen.

Vanessa smiled a little sadly.

"I hear you," she said, taking his bottle. "You want another? Or are you ready to go out?"

Tom felt his brain shutting down of its own accord. Exhaustion had taken him to a place beyond embarrassment.

"This is going to sound strange," he said. "But I think I need to lie down."

Vanessa played with a rip in the knee of her jeans, running her fingers under the threads.

"Do you mean in my bed?"

Tom couldn't retreat fast enough.

"No!" he said. "No. I meant here, on the couch. Just shut my eyes for a few minutes."

She saved them with a laugh.

"That's fine. No problem. Take a little nap."

At that moment, she looked so easygoing, so receptive, that he had an urge to tell her everything. All the secrets of his last three years. But that would take more than a few beers.

"I'm sorry," he said. "I've just had a really hard day."

"Don't worry about it. Take as much time as you need."

She got up and headed to the kitchen, taking the bottle and her glass.

"Go ahead," she told him. "I'm serious. Make yourself comfortable."

It was all he needed to hear. He took off his shoes and emptied his pockets and stretched out as best he could on the too-small couch. The pillows beneath his head were studded with tiny mirrors and beads. He could hardly feel them.

Vanessa opened the fridge. Maybe she was fixing herself another drink. Tom heard clinking ice cubes, running water. Though that changed, and the ice cubes sounded like broken glass, and the water was rushing, crashing in a waterfall. He was going down. It was a relief somehow. At last, he was going under.

CHAPTER TWELVE

HELEN, 10:00 P.M.

A cross the shadows of the driveway, a screen door rattled shut. Helen watched from her porch as Karl came down his front steps. He glanced over his shoulder, as if out of habit, in the direction of her house. Seeing her there, he gave a second look.

"Helen?" he called. "You all right?"

He came across his lawn and over to her, stopping right where Butch had hit the ground. Karl was in a button-down shirt, which he rarely wore, and was holding himself in an odd, stiff way. But he gazed up at her with his usual easy smile. She moved down the steps, closer to him.

"Are you waiting for someone?" he asked. "Please tell me you're not on the lookout for suspicious cars."

She decided not to answer that question.

"Tom hasn't come home," she said. "And I can't reach him."

He should have been home two hours ago. Just after eight, if he'd caught the six-thirty. She'd tried his cell again and his work line; both went straight to voice mail. She told Karl about the pocket call, leaving out the part about the woman's laugh. He listened, nodded, looked down the street.

"I'm sure he's fine," Karl said. "He's probably still in the city, having a few drinks with people from work. Or by himself. I mean, it's Friday."

"He would have called. And he would have answered his phone when I called."

"So he forgot. And it's too loud in the bar. You know, it wasn't so long ago that I was staying out late and not hearing my phone on a regular basis. Then one night I came home care of an old cop friend, and Jackie said that was it for me. Only drinking I do now is at the house." Karl smiled again. "Don't let it get to you. I'm sure he's fine."

He studied her face in the dim light.

"That all that's bothering you?"

Helen glanced at Butch's house and shivered in the cool breeze. Standing on her porch this last hour, hoping to see Tom and hoping that she wouldn't see that car, she'd wondered, with increasing dread, if others would pay the price for her mistakes. What if the brothers of the teenage girls had learned a little about her life, as she'd learned about theirs? What if they'd come across Tom in the train station parking lot or on his way home?

She was tempted to tell Karl everything that had happened. She'd thought of him as someone who understood her and wouldn't judge her. But she didn't want to risk finding out she was wrong.

"I fucked up today," she said.

He let out a soft laugh.

"Yeah," he said. "Well. I know what that's like."

"It's true. I really fucked up. And I don't think I can fix it. Any of it."

Karl nodded.

"Okay," he said. "You fucked up. I believe you. But don't beat yourself up about it. It's never as bad as you think." He grinned. "Except when it's worse."

Helen looked past him, at his house. All of the windows were dark. None of the usual cars were in the driveway, only Karl's old Honda out front.

"You want to talk about it?" he said.

If only she knew where to start.

"Not now," she said. "But maybe sometime I will."

"Well," Karl said. "When you're ready, you know where to find me."

She could feel the warmth between them. For a moment she thought he was about to reach toward her, touch her arm or shoulder.

"I'd like to drive to the station," she said. "See if Tom's car is there."

Karl was looking back at her like she was a little crazy.

"You want to see if his car's there," he repeated.

"That's right," she said. "I want to see if anything's happened."

Not just in the parking lot, she meant. On his walk along the dark and empty streets, if he'd lost his keys. (Where there *had* been a mugging once, a commuter struck in the head and left unconscious at the side of the road near the station. Neither she nor Tom had been able to forget about that one.) But she couldn't explain that to Karl. At this time of night, she knew the route to the station would be almost deserted, as would the lot itself. Every hour would bring home a few last stragglers, fewer getting off each train until sometime after three, when the last train came in from the city.

Karl massaged his shoulder. For the first time she noticed how pale his face looked.

"Are you all right?" she asked.

"Oh, I'm fine, probably. Just cooped up inside for too long, sitting at my desk till the blood don't flow." He rocked on his heels. "I was going to take a walk, maybe give a quick call to that clinic on Emerson. But look, you want me to stay with the girls for a few minutes? You can drive down to the station, see what the story is. Though I don't know if that'll make you feel any better." He checked his watch. "Tell you what. Do me a favor and stop at Wiley's on the way back, pick up some Tums at the counter?"

She couldn't tell how bad he felt. But Karl wouldn't tell her to go if he didn't mean it. He wasn't someone who told people what they wanted to hear; he wouldn't try to hide the truth. It reminded her of what had drawn her to Tom so long ago.

"Are you sure?" she said. "You'll be all right?"

"Yeah. Why not."

"Thanks," she said. "Thanks for this. Can I get you anything else from Wiley's? Six-pack of Smithwick's?"

"No need for that. Just the Tums."

She ran into the house to get her wallet and keys and came back down the steps.

"I'll be back before you know it," she said. "Promise."

She reached out to him, just a light touch on the arm, and then backed away. He seemed to flinch a little, almost as if she'd hurt him. But he was probably just surprised. In all the time they'd spent in the tight space of his studio, they'd never so much as brushed against each other.

"The girls are sleeping," she said. "Call if there's any trouble."

She could feel him watching her as she walked to her car.

———

She took the Elm Avenue route to the train station, the one Tom would have taken that morning. She scanned the sides of the road, slowing as she passed the streets of newer, low-slung apartment buildings. The complexes ended at a strip mall—liquor store, dollar store, Laundromat—and that was where she turned, taking Lenox up the hill past a stretch of modest houses, doubles and singles with small lawns enclosed by fences. Soon the road narrowed and the river came into view. Driving slowly, she followed the winding road to the station. There was nothing, no one.

She turned into the lot. Tom had parked in a permit spot at the end of a now-empty row. She drove in a wide arc, passing the five or six other cars still in the lot, and parked near Tom's car, leaving a space between them. At first she was relieved to see it there. But as she opened her door, she looked around her, not entirely convinced that she was alone. She circled his car, an ancient wagon they'd bought after the move, taking in the details she rarely noticed anymore—the dents in the fender, the scratches on the front passenger door—then moved back a few steps before bending down to check under it. Out of nowhere, she remembered those stories she'd heard as a kid: urban legends about men with razor blades who hid under cars, slashing ankles in parking lots. She listened for footsteps, on alert for the faintest sound.

It was so quiet that she could hear the low hum of the security lights. She walked to the front of the lot, where a dank-smelling pedestrian tunnel led to the platform. Even twenty feet away, a tension in the air kept her back. She thought of Tom, who wouldn't want her to be here, in this empty parking lot, at this hour.

Why hadn't he called her? Why hadn't he come home?

There was a blast of horns, then clanging bells. She moved to the center of the lot, where she had a view of the platform. The train from the north roared past, heading to the city. A few minutes later, the Poughkeepsie-bound train rumbled in and came to a stop. The doors opened and four people stepped out: a woman from one car, three high school boys from another. The doors clanked shut and the bells rang as the train departed.

Helen waited for the passengers to emerge from the tunnel. First came the woman: tall, early thirties, dyed-blue hair, platform boots. The woman kept moving, crossing the lot toward her car.

A few moments later, the boys came out. They were in school uniforms, white shirts billowing over thin arms and concave chests. They looked drunk, about to get sick, if they hadn't already. They staggered forward.

One of them, the smallest, slapped his hand in his palm and nodded in the direction of the blue-haired woman.

"I'd tap that," he said.

The others laughed.

"Don't make me puke," another said.

One of the boys spotted Helen. He jabbed an elbow at the kid next to him.

"Hey, Owen, is that your mom?"

"You fucking wish!"

"Hi, Mom!"

Helen ignored them. The small one shrugged.

"Come on, let's go to Jerry's," he said. "I haven't eaten shit all day."

They slumped up the hill and out of the lot, heading for Main.

She listened to their fading footsteps, then went back to Tom's car. She looked through the driver's side window. There was the thermos in the cup holder, the crushed remains of Cheerios and animal crackers in the car seats. The doors were locked, the windows up. Had something happened to him in the city? Seeing the car confirmed only what she already knew: He'd left and hadn't come back.

She drove down Main. She passed the police station, the municipal building, the little strip of park where the three high school boys had stopped. They were on a bench, one of them puking, the others laughing.

On the next block was Wiley's, the convenience store. Helen pulled into the lot but didn't get out of her car. She was pushing away a hundred questions that she wasn't ready to ask herself, and instead was focusing on one small thing she didn't want to forget: She had to tell Karl how much she liked his music. That had been the best part of her day—lying on the floor, her eyes closed, listening to the songs play over and over.

She leaned back in her seat, the yellow light of the lot washing over her face, and let herself imagine a different life. One in which she'd somehow wound up with Karl. A man twelve years older, who wore his hair pulled back into a short ponytail. Who sang in a classic rock cover band.

She pressed her hands to her eyes and waited for the tears to dry and the redness to fade. And then she got out of her car.

Over on the side street, some kids were hanging out beside a parked car. Two young guys and a girl. Before Helen had even locked the door, one of the guys was peeling away, telling his friends, "Hold on. I *know* her. She lives next door."

Helen recognized the voice and the stoner's gait. Nick came into the lot, grinning at her.

"Hey there," he said. "We keep running into each other."

He was baked. She could have smelled it a block away. He gazed at the store. On the other side of the plate-glass walls, a woman with short gray hair sat behind the counter, reading a newspaper propped against the cash register. She didn't look up, though it was clear from her posture, the stubborn set of her broad shoulders, that she knew they were looking at her.

"I'm picking up something for Karl," Helen told Nick. "He's with the girls."

"Oh yeah? That's cool."

"But I'm glad I saw you." She waited, giving him a chance to focus. "A car drove by your place three times today. Or my place. I told Karl, but he wasn't worried about it." Now that she was able to talk about it, she felt the full extent of her fear. "It was an old gray Buick with three guys in it. They were looking for us. One of us, at least."

Nick nodded, a series of movements that seemed to require deep concentration.

"Let me guess," he said. "This car was a total piece of shit and had a junkyard door on the front passenger side."

"So you know them." And then she asked, though she'd guessed the answer hours ago: "Who are they?"

Nick brushed his hair out of his eyes. A strand slid back over his eyebrow.

"The idiot brothers of the skanks." He shrugged. "They were looking for me, not you. They drove by my place a couple of nights ago too. The day after that fight. Nothing happened." He let out an awkward laugh, glanced at his friends, then turned back to her. "They're waiting for me to show my face at Morey's again. But what are they going to do, get themselves thrown out of the only bar that'll serve them? It's all head games, stupid macho shit."

Helen could feel his friends watching her, though both were pretending to look somewhere else.

"What makes you so sure of that?"

"They haven't done anything so far," he said. "They really wanted to, they could find me. I mean, look, I'm *around*. Where do I ever go?"

Nick's eyes were dark, his pupils huge. Helen was getting a little buzzed just being near him.

"I feel like I've gotten you in a lot of trouble," she said.

Nick laughed.

"Nah, I'll be fine. I can take care of myself." He was calculating now, but with such effort that Helen could almost see the gears shifting. "You *could* do me a favor. Help keep me out of more trouble."

He cast a conspicuous look over his shoulder at the store.

"Really," Helen said. "What did you have in mind?"

Nick hooked his thumbs in the pockets of his jeans. He was posing a little.

"I was hoping you could buy us some beer. The lady in there already turned us down. I guess everybody picked today to be a total hard-ass."

Helen heard a creaking of wheels behind her. An aging hippie in a tie-dyed shirt and pajama pants was riding his bicycle down Main. She watched the way the light fell on his flowing hair as he weaved across the lanes.

"I don't want to drive," Nick said. "And I should probably wait a few more days before I go back to Morey's. Look, if you get us a case, we'll spend the rest of the night hanging in Rob's basement. Listening to some music. You know."

He reminded her so much of those stoners from high school. The ones who said, *You want to hang out?* And she'd gone with them. Not every time, but just enough that it was still where she returned when she wanted to sit and stare at the world around her. To escape without leaving.

Nick gave her a crooked smile. She remembered how young he was, just nineteen years old. But she could see the circles under his eyes, the hollows in his cheeks. Already the boyishness was beginning to leave his face. She felt a little sorry for him, though she knew she had no right to feel that way. She didn't know what the years might bring—for all she knew, he might wind up far away from this place, thriving, pursuing his dreams. As he should. A decade from now, she didn't want to find herself here, in this convenience store parking lot, wondering if the *Times* had come in.

She glanced at the store. The woman behind the counter had pulled a cardigan around her shoulders and put on her reading glasses.

"You know I'd rather have you drinking in your friend's basement than in a bar," Helen said. "But there's no way I can walk in there and buy a case for you. She's seen me talking to you."

"So? Nothing she can do about that. You buy a case and load it in the trunk of your car. We'll meet you around the corner. It's none of her business what you do once you're out of her store."

"Look—"

A car pulled into the lot. It was Ms. Penny, from the preschool. The teacher kept her eyes straight ahead, pretending not to see Helen as she hurried into the store.

"Just wait till it's clear," Nick said. "You've got nothing to worry about."

She owed it to him. That was what he was thinking. And maybe, in a way, he was right. She'd made so many mistakes, let so many people down, that it would be nice to make one person happy.

Inside the store, Ms. Penny was putting her items on the counter. A single grapefruit and a container of cottage cheese. She placed her purchases in a woven bag and left the store, staring down at her phone as she returned to her car.

"Coast is clear," Nick said.

Helen checked her watch. She had to get back to Karl.

"All right," she said. "But I don't want to hear that you got in your car after drinking beer that I bought for you. You better walk home at the end of the night or crash in your friend's basement. And watch out for those guys."

Nick couldn't hide a look of triumph.

"I'll crash," he said. "That's the plan." His face relaxed, his eyes beamed. "Thanks, Helen."

He gave his buddies a thumbs-up as he swaggered back to

the car but quickly dropped his hand, glancing at the store to see if the woman behind the counter had seen him. The woman gave no indication. She turned the pages of her newspaper.

Helen crossed the lot and entered the store. The sudden brightness made her eyes sting. She turned down the store's single aisle, feeling a curdling in her stomach, as if she were about to shoplift a bag of Corn Nuts. At the self-serve coffee stand, she hovered for a moment, reading the little signs above each thermos. She turned the corner and surveyed the refrigerators. There were six-packs in there, but she'd agreed to a case. Feeling the woman's eyes on her, she moved on, drifting over to the rack of newspapers near the door. She stared at the headlines without reading a word.

The woman behind the counter cleared her throat.

"Help you find something?"

Helen stuffed her hands into her pockets. She felt as awkward as a teenager.

"Have the weekend sections of the *Times* come in yet?"

"You're standing in front of them."

"Oh. Right. Now I see them."

The woman watched her over her reading glasses. Helen picked up a newspaper. Her face was flushed, her ears burning. As she tucked her paper under her arm, she saw the cases—they were stacked beside the counter, near the ice cream freezer and the fruit stand. She made her way over, wondering if she, like Ms. Penny, should buy a grapefruit.

The back of her neck was tingling. She turned and saw that the woman behind the counter had taken off her glasses and was staring at her. Her eyes were a startling shade of blue, hard and bright.

"You thinking of buying a case?" the woman asked. "You probably want one that's refrigerated."

Helen cringed, silently cursing herself.

"Yes. Refrigerated. That would be great."

The woman crossed her arms over her chest.

"You've been coming in here for two years now to buy your paper, but I don't believe we've spoken before," she said. "So maybe you think I don't know who you are. You live on Crescent Street, in the Gordons' old house. You sure did make the Gordons happy. I don't think in a million years they ever expected to get that kind of money." The woman tapped her fingertips on the counter. "At least you got yourself a good house. Plenty of space for you and your husband and your little girls."

Helen stared at her. This was her chance to get out of here. She could put down her newspaper and walk out the door. But she couldn't make herself move. She seemed to have been neutralized by the woman's stare.

"Now, you might not know that my husband's a retired state trooper or that my son is a police officer," the woman said, "but I'll do you the favor of telling you. Those kids out there sure know it, which is why they don't dare come back in here."

The woman shifted in her straight-backed chair. Helen thought she'd never seen a face so plain. It was like a drawing of a face, round and symmetrical, the eyebrows tilted into a sharp brown V of disapproval.

"You *do* know it's a crime to buy alcohol for a minor," the woman said. "Surely I don't have to tell you that."

Helen was tempted to bolt out of there. Nothing was keeping her in this place, listening to this lecture. She'd had enough. More than enough. As the woman droned on, Helen felt her muscles tensing. She wanted to slap down her newspaper and leave.

But she didn't. As she scanned the shelves, she saw the rolls of Tums stacked below the counter. No. Just once today, she would make a good decision. And she would not get angry. She approached the counter. She was determined to try, at least, to get this right. Even if the gesture seemed so small. She wouldn't keep making the same mistakes.

"You're right," she said. "We haven't spoken before. My name is Helen Nichols."

She held out her hand. Kept it steady. The woman made her wait a few seconds, but she took it.

"I'm Mary Cullens." She pursed her lips in what appeared to be an attempt at a smile. "So. Just the paper, then?"

Helen returned the smile, then reached below the counter.

"And this," she said, holding up the Tums. "Thanks, I don't need a bag."

She paid and went out the door, feeling a slight burst of elation at her private victory. She took out her keys as she headed to her car. Nick ran over to her. This time he stayed on the sidewalk, staying clear of the store's property line.

"Hey...wait," he said. "What happened?"

"It didn't work out." Helen opened the door and got behind the wheel. "I've got to go. Karl's waiting for me."

"But what *happened*?" Nick said. "Did she refuse to sell to you? Because she really can't do that."

Helen could hear the outrage beneath his confusion, and she remembered the way he'd spoken to those girls from the playground. How once he started, he didn't know when to stop. Unless she was wrong, things were only going to get harder for him.

"You want my advice?" she said. "Take off before she calls the cops on you."

"For what? We're on the street. We're not bothering her."

Helen was sure the woman in the store was watching them. At home, Karl was probably counting the minutes, wondering what was taking her so long. Why she'd broken her promise.

"I'm sorry, but there's nothing I can do," she said. "I really think you should go."

She closed the door and pulled away, leaving him standing under the lights. She turned quickly onto Main, then braked hard. She had come within inches of hitting the hippie on the bike.

The hippie did a U-turn and came back toward her, steering with two fingers. He rolled to a stop beside her car.

"Hey, sister," he said. "No harm, no foul."

She'd driven only a few blocks when she heard the sirens. A fire truck was approaching. There were no other cars on Main, no signs of anyone on the nearest side streets. Still, she waited at the intersection, not wanting to block the engine's path if it came this way.

Where was Tom? It hit her again, hard. *Where was Tom?* She checked her phone, knowing there wasn't a message, that she hadn't missed any calls. Except for the time he'd fallen asleep on the train, he'd never come home this late. And he always called.

The fire truck wasn't far away but now seemed to be heading west. She listened to the sirens, heard the pitch and fall. With a quickening in her pulse, she wondered if it was near Crescent

Street, where she lived. But it could just as easily be going to the station.

She drove through the light and made a sharp left at Elm. As she curved down her own street and saw the police cruiser parked in front of her house, she felt herself turn cold. Soon she couldn't feel anything at all. She was hovering above, where nothing could touch her, watching herself as she pulled over, her eyes focused, her hands gripping the wheel.

Lights from the police car whirled around her. Streaks of red fell upon the trees.

She got out of her car and moved forward, trying to summon a reasonable answer for what she saw. The vibrations from the fire truck had set off car alarms down the street. Butch's SUV competed with the sirens. Thoughts flashed through her head, sudden and wild. *Was it Butch? Had he come back to her house? Or was it the brothers?* She looked around frantically for the car. But Karl was there. He wouldn't have let anything happen to her daughters.

The door to her house was open. EMTs rushed around a stretcher. A tall guy with a shaved head saw Helen. In an instant his face became blank and efficient.

"Are you Mrs....?" He checked the driver's license in his hand. "Walker?"

She didn't answer, barely registered the question. She could see the stretcher, and that was enough. The body was far too big to belong to a child.

It's Tom, she told herself, and the thought brought a measure of relief, small and hard and infinitely dense. *Not Sophie or Ilona.* Not one of her daughters.

A short woman with spiky brown hair came down the stairwell.

"I was going to stay here until we reached you," she told Helen. "The children are upstairs. They're fine, sleeping." She moved closer, put a hand on Helen's shoulder to steer her out of the way. "Guess they can sleep through anything."

There was a commotion around the stretcher. Helen stepped back as the EMTs wheeled it out the door.

"Move, move!" one of them yelled.

"Wait," Helen said. "Stop."

No one stopped. But as the EMTs passed, she saw that it wasn't Tom on the stretcher. It was Karl. His face was slack and his skin was the color of clay. And though she felt she was far away, something dark and terrible reached her: *You'll be all right? Call if there's any trouble.*

"We're taking him to Lambert," the tall guy shouted over his shoulder. "You can follow us there."

Helen reached out to the spiky-haired woman, seizing her arm to stop her from leaving.

"Is he going to make it?" she cried out. "I need to call his family. I need to let them know." She had to make this woman understand. "Please tell me he's going to be okay."

"He's in good hands. I've seen a lot worse. Look, I think he called just in time, is what I'm saying. You're not his family? Tell them to go to Lambert."

The woman seemed far too calm. Helen let her go and ran up to her daughters' room and opened the door. It was true: The sirens hadn't disturbed them. Sophie was on her back, her hands folded behind her head, like a sunbather at the beach. Ilona lay curled on her side, thumb in mouth. Helen stood there, watching them. Relief welled inside her, an endless surging, though she still hadn't fully returned to herself and was in no hurry to get there. She would hover slightly outside for as long as she could. The last of the sirens faded away. Soon she could hear her own heart, a soft rhythmic rushing in her ears. The stuffed turtle night-light had gone off. She turned it on again, filling the room with purple stars.

CHAPTER THIRTEEN

T here was blood on the cobblestones.

Tom walked down the industrial street, as he had many times before. Warehouses, butchers, meatpacking plants. This time, a steel door opened.

He glided past the bouncer. Inside, he found himself in a vast, dark space where men and women, hundreds of them, were dancing. Or not dancing, really; they were raving, freaking out. In all of his years in New York, he'd never seen a party like this.

A woman appeared at his side. She took him by the hand and led him down a long corridor lined with private rooms. She opened a door, pulled him inside, and turned the lock behind him.

The woman was wearing only a short, sheer robe. She was beautiful; he could see that much, though he couldn't really see *her*. Every time he looked at her face, it slid out of focus, and so he stopped trying. There were other places to look.

She slipped out of her robe and stood before him. Shoulders back, pelvis thrust. He looked down. Between her legs was a network of cogs and wheels and ticking parts. Like the insides of a clock.

"Do you like it?" she asked. "I made it myself."

He was terrified, and turned on.

"I do."

He drifted toward her. He couldn't feel his legs. *I must be drunk,* he thought as she reached out and unzipped his pants. She tugged him closer, taking him in.

Tom woke with a gasp, whirling off the couch as if tossed by an earthquake. His head struck the coffee table, a sharp blow above his right eye that almost knocked him out cold. He landed on his hands and knees, arms flung, legs wide. Drops of blood fell from his forehead to the parquet floor.

He got up slowly. Testing each limb. Noting the variety of aches in his muscles and bones, the throbbing in his back, the pain above his eye. He was soaked with sweat, his skin stretched tight across his face. His heart seemed to be beating everywhere inside him, pinballing around his body.

Jesus.

He looked around him. Velvet couch, beaded pillows. A small desk between bare windows. Potted plants and dozens of framed photographs.

Vanessa. Vanessa's *apartment.* It came back to him with a blinding force, intensifying the headache that was blossoming between his eyes and sending spikes of pain down every nerve.

The lights were on, but the apartment was silent around him. He was alone. He walked the three strides to the kitchen and splashed water on his face, remembering those strong beers, how they'd hit his empty stomach. As he waited for the last wave of dizziness to pass, he noticed the spice rack. There, between the oregano and chili powder, was an economy-sized bottle of Advil.

Thank you, Vanessa.

He swallowed three, then checked out the fridge. It was small but as well stocked as a gourmet minimart, with bottles of coconut water, papaya juice, and acai berry extract. On the top shelf was a giant plastic jug of something green and thick that made his stomach turn. But next to it was something familiar, that miracle cure for toddlers: a bottle of Pedialyte. Was that how Vanessa treated her hangovers? He got a glass and made himself a papaya-Pedialyte mixer.

He returned to the living room, a move that required him only to shift the orientation of his shoulders, then approached the sleeping nook. Though he was sure he had the place to himself, he cautiously pushed aside the Indian print. He was in no mood for more surprises. The bed was covered with a lavender quilt and more of those pillows studded with beads and little mirrors. On the ceiling was a poster of a blue sky dotted with wispy clouds.

A nice place. Even if he wished, too late, that he'd never seen it. It reminded him of his childhood home, the apartment where he and his mother had lived after his father died. Small but tidy, everything in its place, nothing more than a few steps out of reach.

Everything was in its place. But where was Vanessa? He tried to remember how their conversation had ended. Had she told him she was leaving?

He reached for his phone. Finding his pocket empty triggered a low-level, automatic panic response. He checked again. No wallet, no keys, no phone. His messenger bag was by the door and contained only the usual papers. Had he left his phone at work? At Donna's?

Donna. Donna was leaving with Elana, unless he could find a way in the next few days to stop her or convince her not to go. And on Monday, he would learn whether or not he still had a job. He wished he'd either drunk nothing at all or a lot more.

A scrap of paper on the coffee table caught his eye—a note from Vanessa:

Hey Tom—you sure needed that nap!
   Take a break! Check out for a while! You <u>deserve</u> it!!!
   p.s. and if you want to meet up, call me.

She hadn't left a number.

He sank onto the couch. He checked his pockets again, though he knew it was useless. Still, he couldn't understand it, or believe it. Had she taken his phone? Was this her idea of a joke? Of a *favor*?

What time was it, anyway? He didn't have his watch and couldn't even remember if he'd put it on that morning.

He had to get home. Helen was on a deadline.

For one knee-weakening moment, he could picture all of them—Helen and Donna, Sophie and Ilona and Elana—voicing their complaints, commiserating over their mutual grievances. It was a hazy vision of a not-so-distant future. All these women, all of them angry at him.

The Advils weren't kicking in fast enough. His head was

pulsing, splintering; dozens of tiny hammers chipped away at the insides of his skull. He got up, leaned against the wall, and closed his eyes.

When he opened them, he saw her phone. Not a security phone for the front door. An actual phone, an old-fashioned landline. It was attached to the wall and encased in shiny yellow plastic, just like the one in his mom's old kitchen. And it worked.

He had to call Helen. And come up with something to say that wouldn't dig him deeper into the hole he was in.

But first he dialed the newsroom. He got the directory and selected Mark's extension. When the call went to voice mail, he entered the emergency code to reach Mark's cell phone. He wondered if Mark was still speaking to him, after his fuckup that afternoon.

Mark answered with a muffled cough. In the background, explosions from a video game almost drowned out the sirens of a passing fire truck. Tom could hear the same fire truck coming down Second Avenue.

"Futterman."

"Mark," Tom said. "It's me."

From Mark's end of the line came an intense round of digital gunfire.

"If this is Gary, please relay your concerns to my lawyer," Mark said. "During standard business hours."

"Mark, it's Tom." He almost didn't want to know. "Who's Gary?"

Mark sighed.

"My first ex-wife's brother. He calls to deliver her complaints on a monthly basis. Eight years divorced, and she still hasn't gotten rid of our place in the Poconos. Now she wants me to pay for renovations." There was another explosion. "So why are you calling me?"

Tom's face was cold with sweat. He reached for a paper towel. He spoke quickly, getting it all out before Mark could stop him.

"I'm in Vanessa Marlow's apartment. But Vanessa isn't here, and I don't know where she is. And everything I had with me is gone—my wallet, my phone. I don't have any way of getting home."

Mark had stopped his video game. Tom could almost see him settling back on his couch, one foot kicked over his knee as he turned the situation around in his head, enjoying it as much as possible.

"Sorry, but I have to ask," Mark said. "You're not handcuffed to a bed or restrained in some other way that would embarrass both of us, are you?"

"No. Nothing like that."

"So you're free to walk out of there. That's good news. And where is Vanessa's apartment?"

"East Sixties. A few blocks from you." Tom saw the clock blinking over the stove. He'd slept even longer than he'd thought. "Any chance you can spare some cash for food and a train ticket?"

"Let's meet at Ramsey's. You can get a burger or something. I'll bring enough money for the train and all that."

Tom rested his head against the wall.

"Okay. Thanks, Mark. I'll pay you back on Monday. Thanks."

Tom hung up, then took a deep breath and dialed his home number, not knowing exactly what he would say, only that if he thought about it for too long, he wouldn't be able to make the call. To his relief, he got the machine. He could have tried her cell; Helen never heard the house phone when she was downstairs or in her office. But leaving a message would buy him some time. Cover him, for now.

"You're probably doing bedtime stories," he said, though it was hours too late for that. "Things got a little crazy at the office! I'll be there as soon as I can."

Ramsey's had wood-paneled walls, a checkered linoleum floor, and a pool table covered in patchy felt. There was a pair of plywood doors at the back, where the bathroom stalls jutted into the drinking space. Behind the L-shaped bar, a glass tank held pineapple slices suspended in cloudy, low-end vodka. Tom had never seen anyone order a drink from it, though the vodka had been at a different level each of the few times he'd come here with Mark.

He took a seat on the short leg of the bar, where he wouldn't have to see himself in the mirror. Though he'd tried to clean himself up before leaving Vanessa's, there wasn't much he could do about the cut on his forehead. Not that anyone at Ramsey's would notice, or care. The dozen or so customers were well into their drinks, including the woman who was dancing near the jukebox, which wasn't playing any music, and the group of young bankers who were slumming it after a week on the trading floor. The bartender set a beer before Tom, then went back to the bankers, whacking the slab of belly that hung over his belt as he told them, "You see that? That's hard fat. *Old* fat."

Tom wanted to keep an eye on the clock, but the bar didn't

have a clock. Still, if they ate fast, he would be able to catch the 12:57. After that, he was looking at the 1:44 and would have to transfer, which would add another twenty minutes to his trip. And if he missed the last train, he would be spending the night in the station. He didn't know how he could possibly explain that to Helen.

He was starting to lose track of the explanations he owed her. As he stared at the pineapple slices, wondering what might happen to him if he ate one, Mark came in and clapped a hand on his shoulder.

"You want a round?" Mark said, glancing at the vodka tank. "Seems like tonight would be the night to try it."

"No thanks."

"You sure? I might get one myself."

"They probably haven't cleaned that thing since the seventies."

"Even better."

Mark waved to the bartender. He ordered a shot for himself and a round of beers.

"How about some food?" he said to Tom. "You want, what—a burger, fries?"

"Sounds great."

They ordered two with everything. Mark downed his shot, shuddered, and wiped his mouth with the back of his hand.

"Well, it's not so bad if you don't think about it," Mark said. "Which reminds me. How did you wind up in Vanessa Marlow's apartment?"

Tom told him. And before he could stop himself, he told him everything. About Donna and Elana. About Helen, and how he'd never been caught, in all his years of lies. And how at this point, there was no way out without spreading at least some of the hurt around.

Mark listened. Asked a question or two, then told him to start again. By the time he finished, the bartender had cleared their plates. Tom felt as if he'd been released from a fever, having sweated out everything that plagued him.

The feeling didn't last. Mark stared down at his empty glass. When he finally raised his head, he broke into a laugh. It was a huge laugh, enough to draw the attention of everyone in the bar, from the sullen drunks to the slumming bankers. Tom waited, wishing the peeling linoleum beneath him would give way, that he could vanish within the city's guts.

"Sorry!" Mark said. "Really. I'm sorry! But you just made me feel good about myself for the first time in years."

Mark ordered another shot and a beer. Tom had hardly touched his own.

"Sorry, seriously, I don't mean to laugh at your expense," Mark said, though he was still laughing. "It's just...these last few years have been absolute shit for me. The whole decade. Two divorces, three jobs, four apartments. So it's nice to know that I'm not the only one who's been fucking up."

"Glad I could help," Tom said.

"Consider your debt paid. For all the times I've had to deflect Tadpole from your empty desk." Mark studied him in the greenish light of the bar. "So what are you going to do?"

"I don't know." Tom held himself very still. His food sat in his stomach, as unyielding as a clenched fist. "I have to figure that out tonight."

"Well, you're off to a great start!" Mark was quiet for a while, then added, "You should think real hard about being alone.

That's my one piece of advice for you. Whatever you decide, make yourself stop. Wait. And then imagine being alone—truly alone—when you face the consequences."

Tom nodded. He'd imagined that so many times, spent entire nights on the couch staring up at the ceiling or sweating into the sheets while Helen slept beside him. Still, he was surprised.

"That's not what I thought you would say. I thought you'd tell me to come clean."

"Maybe that's what you wanted to hear," Mark said. "That doesn't mean it's what you should do." He pushed his glasses up his nose. "As someone who frequently picks up dinner for one—takeout from Woks, where they no longer even ask me what I want to order—let me caution you about your prospects. Because I think you're going to lose. No matter what you do, you're going to lose something, or someone. All you can really decide is how *much*—and, to be blunt, *who*—you're gonna lose."

Mark's words cut through the din of voices that echoed in Tom's ears. That day, what had for years seemed to him a hopelessly complex maze had been reduced to two paths. One was safe: He could step away and lose only Elana. If he took the other, he risked losing everyone, because he would have to talk to Helen—and Donna might still take Elana away. And yet, even now, he held out hope that he would find a way to move forward without losing anyone he loved.

Mark was studying him again.

"You don't look so good," he said. "Why don't you call Helen and tell her you're crashing at my place tonight? You can put the blame on me, say I took you out and got you loaded. Hell, I can call her if you'd like. Maybe that would be better."

It wasn't a bad idea—getting more time, and some sleep, before facing Helen. Mark's couch would offer him a few hours of escape at least. But he was done with escaping.

"Thanks," Tom said. "But I've got to get home."

"Sure, the train ride should give you plenty of time to solve all your problems. You can hang out for one more, right?" Without waiting for an answer, Mark signaled the bartender. "I figured something was up, with all the long lunches. But I didn't want to ask. You know, at my last job, I used to sneak off and sit on a bench in the park. Sometimes I'd be gone for hours." He shook his head, shrugged. "That was after Carole left."

Mark's second wife. Mark had once shown him a photo of her on his phone. It had been taken right as she and Mark were about to board a sightseeing cruise up the Hudson, and it showed Carole—posture stiff, face frozen in an awkward smile—cringing beneath Mark's outstretched arm. He was leaning toward her, his face pressed into her hair. In his free hand was a takeout cup of coffee, and by the way he was holding it, he seemed about to spill it on his shoes. That was a year or so before their divorce.

Tom thought of the night Helen had accidentally looked at his email. And the joke she'd later made: *Stop worrying. We can't afford to get divorced.*

If he told her everything, the cost of divorce might no longer seem too high. The thought never failed to stop him cold. She would make a decision, and Helen's decisions were final.

Mark reached for his glass.

"Did I ever tell you about the end of my second marriage?" he said. "I'm talking about the real end, when things were so bad I would've cut off my balls to avoid another fight."

"No," Tom said. "I don't think so."

"Carole was unhappy. Of course she was; she was unhappy about everything. But mostly about me. I was a disappointment to her. A drag." Mark's voice cracked, and he coughed, covering his face with his hand. "Back then, I was working the overnight shift at this bureau out in Jersey and sleeping as best as I could during the day. The only time we saw each other was at dinner—when she was exhausted from her day, and meanwhile I was fueling up, trying to energize myself for the night ahead. And it was around this time that she decided to become a vegetarian. A hardcore convert, no exceptions."

Mark had finished his beer and was tracing circles on the bar.

"I was trying to be a good sport, you know?" he said. "So I'd sit there with her and eat fava-bean pancakes while she talked about her day, everyone who'd annoyed her in the office and on the subway, and then I'd hit Happy Taco on my way to work. I was eating junk I hadn't had in years. Fried chicken. Bacon cheeseburgers. One night I went over to that old deli on Fifty-Sixth, ordered the Reuben and actually finished the thing."

The bartender refilled Mark's glass and gave him a shot on the house. Tom watched him drink it. Mark was starting to weave a little in his seat.

"So after a few months of that—me sneaking around, cheating on Carole with food trucks—it was over." Mark gave an unconvincing smile. "I moved into my new apartment. My first night, after the movers had gone, I went out to this fancy supermarket on Third. I wanted to make a real dinner for once. So I cut up all the garlic and peppers, and then I'm dealing with the chicken, washing it, trimming the fat. And when I take it off the cutting board, it slips out of my hands and falls into this box of pots and pans that I'd taken from my old apartment. There I am, in my sad little kitchen, with my one dull knife and paper plates and a clammy chicken breast that I've got to get out of this heaping pile of junk."

Mark raised his head, blinked behind his glasses.

"I spent that whole night feeling sorry for myself," he said. "Thinking that was as low as I could go. As alone as I would ever be. And of course I was wrong."

"Jesus," Tom said. "I had no idea."

"Yeah. Well. It isn't something I usually talk about." Mark looked at him. "But that's what I mean about being alone. Why I think you should be real careful about your choices."

Alone. Tom wondered if Helen had gotten his message. Even at this hour, she might be in her office, working. She would stop to check on Sophie and Ilona, take a moment to watch them sleep. He thought of Elana, sleeping in her bedroom across the park, her window open to let in the cool breeze. And he pictured himself, months from now, living in some studio apartment he couldn't afford, his nights suddenly full of unscheduled hours that would weigh on him because they were empty. Because he couldn't share them with his daughters. Or with Helen. And he would know it was all his fault. He'd made the wrong decisions and would never stop paying for them.

He looked at the faces around him. The crowd at the bar had changed: The bankers were gone, and the woman who'd been dancing was now sitting next to a Vietnam-era vet in a wheelchair. Back by the pool table, a young guy was arguing with the shadowy space around him, throwing angry glances. And two girls who'd been sitting at a booth had somehow gotten the jukebox to work and were now singing along to a Billy Joel song.

Time to settle up. Tom tried to catch the bartender's eye.

"Look," Mark said. "Don't feel too bad about yourself. Nothing good comes from that. I mean, come on—look at me. Sometimes the highlight of my day is getting a withering stare from Rita before she spends the next few hours pretending I don't exist."

"Rita Ravenbush." Tom shook his head. "Whose perfect track record I destroyed in a single afternoon."

"Yeah, forget what I said. You should feel terrible. You should be drowning in despair."

Tom raised his glass. He had nothing to say in his defense.

"I'm crazy about her, you know," Mark said. "Sometimes I think I *love* her."

Tom looked at him.

"Love her? You mean you're fascinated by her."

"Okay," Mark said. "Fascinated. It's a case of unrequited fascination. I could watch her rearrange her pencils all day." He lifted a hand and let it clomp down on the bar. "I'm forty-five years old and I have nothing to show for it. I own *nothing*. Did you know that? Except for the crappy Ikea furniture in my apartment, I have zero assets. Though I guess the benefit of going through two divorces is that my credit's shot, so at least I don't have any debt. I could vanish without a trace. No one even has to go to the trouble of writing me off."

Tom had lost count of how many shots Mark had drunk. And though by now he'd surely missed the 12:57, there was no way he could leave Mark in this sad state, his head hanging over his drink, unaware of anyone around him, unaware even of the bartender, who at that moment was sticking his bare, sweaty arm into the pineapple tank to unclog the nozzle. Tom was sorry Mark was missing that. At any other time, it would have made his night, maybe even his whole weekend.

Mark swirled what was left in his glass.

"You know what I'd like?" he said. "To get married again. It's ridiculous, I know. But I like the idea of it—meeting someone, getting married. Even though I'm not that good at actually *being* married."

"I'm sure it's only a matter of time," Tom said.

Mark smiled.

"It's true. I'm always looking. No matter where I am, what I'm doing, there's a part of me that's looking. I mean, I still have hope, right?"

Mark tilted his head toward the long side of the bar, and Tom, against all of his instincts, gave a quick glance in that direction. A few seats away, a pale, thin girl was drinking double shots of Jäger. She had long black hair and dark eyes, which were lined with inky makeup. With another glance, Tom saw that her eyes were bloodshot, her eyelids fiery and swollen. Not just fiery, but infected. She had one of the worst cases of pink eye he'd ever seen.

Her boyfriend was in the corner seat, on Mark's right. He was a young guy with small, hard features and a buzz cut that revealed his knobby skull. He downed his shot, smacked the glass on the bar, and flicked a finger at the bartender, ordering another round. Then he slung his arm around the girl.

Mark leaned toward Tom.

"You might think I'm crazy," he said. "But that's the hottest girl in the bar."

"Looks like she's taken." Tom kept his voice very low. "You've got to stop staring at her."

"I know," Mark said. "I keep telling myself that. But she's got a great laugh. And sure, right now she looks kind of—I guess I'd say *contagious*—but she's still a beautiful girl."

Nothing would make Tom look in the girl's direction again. Buzz Cut had noticed them; Mark kept veering into his space. He narrowed his eyes at Mark as if Mark were a small animal he wouldn't mind setting on fire.

Mark's face, normally an unhealthy sallow shade, was now an unhealthy red.

"Sorry," he told Tom. "I don't know what's the matter with me."

"Don't worry about it. I'll walk you back to your place before heading to the train."

"You don't have to do that. I can get myself home." Mark raised his glass, saw that it was empty, and put it down again. "Guess I'm just out of practice."

Where was the bartender? Over by the register, eating his dinner out of a Styrofoam container, something that looked like noodles in mop water. Tom didn't want to be here a minute longer. He saw Mark's watch and realized he was cutting it close for the 1:44. If he missed it, he would have to call Helen again. Which he dreaded a whole lot more than spending the rest of the night in Grand Central. (He hoped she'd gotten his message and gone to sleep hours ago. But he suspected he wouldn't be that lucky, not this time.) Maybe what he needed was a few hours of sitting alone in the station. For all he knew, it might be his only chance to get a block of time in which he could sit and think.

Mark was gripping the bar, holding on. Tom stayed on alert, ready to catch him if necessary. He would walk him home even if it cost him the train. He rose from his seat and waved to the bartender. If they waited much longer, Mark would tank out completely. Tom remembered how he'd drifted off at Vanessa's.

And with that, it came to him.

"It's under her couch," Tom said. "Vanessa's couch. My wallet and phone. I took everything out of my pockets and put it there so I could sleep."

Mark laughed.

"Well. At least you know she didn't rob you."

Tom wanted to kick himself. He could call the office, try to connect with Vanessa's cell, see if he could pick up his stuff tonight. But that would mean another delay, and he sensed that seeing Vanessa again, at this time of night, would embarrass both of them. He would have to get everything back on Monday.

Though he couldn't imagine what his life would look like on Monday. It seemed impossibly distant from now.

He motioned again to the bartender. This guy wouldn't see him until he felt like it. Finally the bartender glanced in his direction, but he took his time punching keys at the register. Mark slapped a hand on the bar and with the other fumbled for his wallet.

"Before I forget. So you can get yourself home."

Mark pushed a pile of bills into Tom's hand. He counted out more and put them beside his pint glass.

"Thanks," Tom told him. "Really. You'll have it back on Monday."

Mark shrugged, a movement that caused him to sway precariously.

"You know what? I haven't been out in months. Just *out*, you know? Amongst the people."

Mark raised his arms in an expansive gesture and gave a broad smile to everyone around them, from the bartender to Buzz Cut, who glared back at him. Mark, oblivious, turned his grin toward Pink Eye, who burst out laughing.

"See?" Mark said to Tom. "That's a great laugh."

Her boyfriend kicked a leg, his combat boot thumping against the metal rung of his bar stool. He was still glaring at Mark when Mark lowered his arms and knocked over the guy's shot glass, spilling Jäger into his lap.

Tom's stomach sank, even though Mark was already apologizing.

"Let me buy you another!" Mark called out to the bartender. "Their next round's on me. Next two, make it!"

Mark reached out a hand, trying to clap the guy on the shoulder. Buzz Cut jumped up so fast that he toppled his bar stool.

That got the bartender's attention. He scooped up the money Mark had left and hooked a thumb at the door.

"Out," the bartender said to all of them. "Now."

A last reserve of energy was surging through Tom's veins, though his brain wanted to reject everything he saw: Mark and Buzz Cut heading for the door, both surprisingly steady on their feet, Pink Eye strolling after them with color in her face. Tom was right behind her.

The four of them stood in a loose circle on the sidewalk, staring at each other under the streetlight. Mark shifted his weight from one shoe to the other. Tom wouldn't have been surprised to see him try some footwork, throw some punches in the air.

"Let's go," he told Mark.

With a clarity Tom hadn't felt in months, possibly in years, he knew that he had just a second or two to get Mark out of here before anyone got hurt. Buzz Cut was glaring at Mark, his boots planted on the pavement, but he didn't look like he would make the first move. Beating up a middle-aged drunk guy wasn't worth the hassle.

Tom took Mark's arm and tried to steer him away.

"Come on. I'll get you home."

Mark ignored him. He yanked himself free, causing himself to stagger forward and collide into Buzz Cut, who fell back, tripped over his combat boots, and landed in a pile of trash bags that had been set out by the Chinese restaurant next door.

"Motherfucker," the guy said. "You fucking motherfucking fuck."

A bag had split open beneath him. Slowly he began picking himself up from the garbage, flicking scraps off his skin and clothes, grunting with disgust.

His girlfriend didn't offer any help. Tom couldn't blame her. He'd never smelled anything so bad.

"Oh man," Mark said. "Oh shit."

Tom spoke under his breath.

"Run," he told Mark. "Now. Go!"

Moving faster than Tom would have thought possible, Mark dashed down the street and turned at the corner. Tom tore down the sidewalk, his legs pumping at full speed. When he got to the avenue, he looked around him. Mark was nowhere in sight. There was shouting behind him, and Tom could hear the girl's laugh—it was high and thin, not the deep laugh Mark had admired in the bar. Someone yelled, "Watch where you're going, asshole!" Tom took off, running toward the park. The sounds of the streets faded; he was aware only of the air on his face and in his lungs. He could see the tops of the trees, and he ran toward them, feeling like he would never stop. There was only one word, and it beat in time to his racing heart: *Run, run, run.*

CHAPTER FOURTEEN

HELEN, 1:30 A.M.

A woman answered the phone at the hospital. Helen said she was family, his sister.

They'd taken Karl to Lambert, a much bigger city across the river. Friday nights in Lambert's ER were about accidents and overdoses. The woman put Helen on hold and came back a few minutes later.

"You want to wait for the doctor?"

"I just want to know how he is," Helen said. "Could you give me an update on his condition?"

"You want to leave your name and number?"

She didn't expect a call back. She tried Jackie again, but she wasn't answering her phone. Which to some extent was a relief. Helen had no idea what she would say to Jackie if she reached her.

She sat on her bed in the position in which she'd spent much of the last hour: legs folded, arms wrapped around knees, head blank for as long as she could keep it that way. But without warning, everything would come back to her, and her chest would ache and her eyes would sting.

If she hadn't asked him to stay with her daughters, would he have called the doctor's and gone there right away? How much damage had the delay caused? Enough that he'd wound up getting an ambulance. She didn't want to think about what might have happened if he hadn't managed to make that call.

She checked the clock. It was then that she noticed the light on the answering machine. She played Tom's message: *Things got a little crazy at the office! I'll be there as soon as I can.*

She listened to the message a second time, with a muted awareness of how frustrating it was that she'd missed his call. She tried his cell. Voice mail again.

Then she checked her email. She'd checked several times already, and there was still nothing from Lou. Not even a note letting her know that he'd received the attachment.

She reached for her phone again. A different woman answered at the ER. She was rustling papers and typing hard on a keyboard.

"Look, he's my friend," Helen said. "A close friend. Can't you tell me anything?" She gave it a last try. "Is he going to make it?"

Over the line came the sounds of children crying, a man shouting. The woman kept typing.

"Sorry," the woman said. "Can't help."

When Jackie came home, Helen got her answer.

She went to her bedroom window when she heard a car pull into the driveway. It was a purple convertible with a company name in script on its side. A middle-aged woman with short blond hair got out of the driver's seat and came around the front to open the door for Jackie.

Through her window, Helen could hear the woman comforting Jackie, offering a constant stream of: "It's all right, let's get you rested up, we'll go back in the morning." Jackie looked distraught, and drunk. The friend wrapped an arm around Jackie's back as she steered her toward the door.

Helen went downstairs and stepped out onto the porch. The lights came on in Jackie's house; windows blazed in every room. She thought she would have to wait a while, but a few minutes later the blond woman came out again, heading to her car. She was off before Helen could stop her.

Another car came down the street. It was Monica, holding the wheel with one hand and her phone with the other. She parked in the driveway.

Helen went down the steps to meet her. Monica was wearing her T-shirt from Fat Pete's. Across her chest, neon letters read HOME OF TWO-FER TUESDAYS. She shoved her phone into the back pocket of her jeans.

"How is he?" Helen said. She wondered if Monica knew that the ambulance had come to her house. "I haven't heard anything."

Monica glanced behind her at Karl and Jackie's house. Jackie was switching off the lights in the living room and kitchen, leaving the first floor dark.

"He's all right," Monica said. "Well, like shit, really. But he's out of surgery. They say he's going to pull through."

Helen had to turn away to hide the depth of her relief. It took her a few moments to pull herself together. Not because she was crying. She was warm but shivering, unable to register anything but the dark shapes around her, the shifting of the grass and leaves. She folded her arms over her chest and waited for it to pass.

Monica was studying her. Finally she spoke.

"Was there something going on?"

Helen stared at her. Monica kept her gaze cool. She looked incapable of being shocked or disappointed.

"What?" Helen said. "What are you asking me?"

"I'm asking if there was something going on." Monica rolled her eyes a little, as if she were dealing with a particularly stubborn child. "Between you and Karl."

There was no judgment in Monica's voice, or even a hint of satisfaction. But she was looking at Helen in a different way now, and from a greater distance. Helen could almost see the gap widening between them.

"No," Helen said. "Of course not." Yet she felt her face burn, as if she were lying and had just gotten caught. "You really think that?"

"I never did. But I know Jackie wondered about it sometimes." Monica shrugged. "It seems possible, right? You guys spend so much time together."

The heat rose in Helen's face. Had she overstepped a boundary that was obvious to everyone but her? She remembered listening to Karl's music, thinking it was the best part of her day. And thinking about Karl. How she'd imagined a different life for herself.

"I had no idea," she said. "If I'd known, I would have said something." She looked at Karl and Jackie's house. All the lights were off except the one in their bedroom. "Maybe I should talk to Jackie. After all of this is over."

"Really?" Monica gave her a skeptical look. "In my experience, those I'm-not-fucking-your-husband conversations usually don't go so well."

Helen looked at Monica, who was half her age, and had no trouble believing that she'd already had one of those conversations. She wondered if Monica believed *her*. Even to her own ears, her denial had sounded false. She would talk to Karl about it, she thought, but shook her head as soon as the words crossed her mind. Because that was over, whatever she'd had with Karl. She understood that now.

And that brought a new pain, now that there was room for it. Now that she knew he was going to be all right. But *what* was over? A friendship? It was more than that, even if she couldn't say what it was, exactly. Though she couldn't name it, she could already feel the loss.

In just a few hours, Jackie would know—if she didn't already—that Karl had been at Helen's home while Tom was away. Because Karl was doing her a favor. She could tell Jackie that she hadn't been there, but that might not make things better. Jackie would see all the implications of the delay she'd caused, the cost of that favor. Though she'd never say a word, Jackie would hold her responsible. It would always be there between them, creating distance, until they were no longer friends or even friendly. They would be neighbors, polite and remote. Nothing more.

Helen thought of what she'd known but hadn't wanted to admit to herself earlier that night: Karl wouldn't say no to her if she asked him for a favor. On some level, she'd been testing that, she realized. She needed to know that he cared, that he recognized there was something—some connection—between them. She'd wanted that proof, even if it took the form of what had seemed, at the time, like a small and irrational but harmless favor.

Monica had been giving her space. Now she was studying her again. Helen couldn't meet her eyes, because her usual resources were failing her. She was used to being able to seal herself off, but she'd lost that over the course of this day, leaving her exposed and vulnerable. This girl could see right through her.

Helen let her look. She glanced at the light in Karl and Jackie's bedroom.

"Is there anything I can do?" she said. "How is Jackie?"

"She's a mess. She was out with her girlfriends at Las Margaritas when she got the call. And they were on their third pitcher." A smile passed over Monica's face. "She said the nurses looked as worried about her as they were about Karl. They told her to get some sleep and come back in the morning."

"A friend drove her home. Just before you got here."

"I know. She's trying to find Nick." Monica checked her cell again. "Have you seen him?"

"No," Helen said. Then she remembered. "Yes, I did. But that was a few hours ago. In the parking lot at Wiley's."

No matter what she said, Helen felt like she was hiding something. She wondered how well Monica could see her face in the dim light.

"What was he doing there?" Monica said. "He was supposed to go to Rob's place. Everybody was. But I talked to Rob and he said no one ever showed up." Her voice had turned sharp. "Do you know who he was with?"

"Some friends. A guy and a girl." Helen watched a car approach on Elm. It kept going. "They wanted me to buy them beer. But I didn't."

"What the hell were they thinking? The lady who runs that place knows exactly how old they are. She makes it her business to know everybody." Monica pressed the toes of her sneaker into the grass. It was stained with grease from the restaurant. "Did Nick say where he was going?"

"He was talking about hanging out in a friend's basement. I think he said Rob."

"I'll swing by Tyler's." Monica got out her keys. "They're probably in the garage. Banging on the drums and getting stoned." She shook her head, let out a sigh. "Just like every other Friday night."

Helen stopped her.

"Are you sure Jackie's all right in there? I could check on her in the morning."

"That's okay," Monica said, not bothering to turn as she headed for her car. "I'm sure she'd rather be alone."

Helen looked around her living room. After two years, they still hadn't really made this house their home. There was the stack of unpacked boxes in the corner next to the bookshelf. There was the crack in the wall behind the couch that had appeared mysteriously last summer. And there was the couch itself, left for them by the previous owners. A free couch had struck them as a good idea at the time. The small one from their Queens apartment wouldn't have looked right in this space. Why not use what was already there, at least for now, until they bought their own furniture?

And so they'd wound up with an oversized tapestry-upholstered couch that signaled to Helen, every time she saw it, that the house still wasn't truly theirs.

And, she had to admit, the place was a mess.

It was the kind of disorder you didn't notice if you lived within it, but to an outsider would be instantly apparent. The girls' toys—crayons and stuffed animals and little plastic parts of things—were everywhere. The bookshelves overflowed with their drawings and papers. There were dolls on the windowsills, dollhouse furniture on the floor, stray markers and Duplos under the couch.

You could rake under there, her mother would say. Helen moved closer and saw a collection of objects left by Tom: coins, a pen, a faded receipt. On nights when he was completely exhausted, he sometimes didn't even bother to change out of his work clothes before collapsing. He just kicked off his shoes, emptied his pockets, and sprawled out on the couch. Hours later, he would wake up and stagger upstairs.

Helen picked up the coins and pen and receipt and placed them on his desk.

The first time Tom stayed over at her apartment, they'd closed the local bar, then stumbled back to her block just before sunrise. That afternoon, picking their clothes up off the floor, almost the same items had spilled out of his jeans: coins, a pen, a small notebook. Tom came out of the shower as she was putting the notebook back in his pocket. She tried to explain, knowing it would seem like he'd caught her looking at it, but he laughed, unconcerned. *Don't worry about it,* he said. *It's just a notebook.*

And she was struck then, for the first of what would be many times, at how open he was. She wondered how that felt, that freedom.

Now she allowed herself to consider whether that had changed. Was he no longer as open and honest as she'd always thought he was?

No, not *whether* he'd changed. When.

She went to their bedroom and played his message.

You're probably doing bedtime stories... I'll be there as soon as I can.

She checked the time of the message. Tom knew she wouldn't have been reading bedtime stories at that hour. He also knew she wouldn't hear the landline if she was downstairs or working in her office.

By now, the last train to Devon was on its way from the city.

She looked at the number saved on the answering machine. Tom hadn't called from his cell or his office. And there wasn't any noise in the background. No bar music, no traffic sounds.

So where had he called from?

She dialed the number. And reached voice mail.

"Hi, this is Vanessa. Thanks for calling!" The voice was overly warm and bright, projecting a confidence that Helen didn't trust or believe. "Please leave a message, and I'll get back to you as soon as I can. Hope you have an *amazing* day!"

Helen hung up quickly, but the slight trill at the end gave it away. She thought of the pocket call, that laugh she'd heard in the background. A practiced laugh, forced and self-aware, that had little in common with a natural laugh.

Tom had called from this girl's apartment. Helen stared at the phone, backing away a little, as if the girl—*Vanessa*—could see her. As if by dialing the number, she'd somehow invited Vanessa into her home.

Into her bedroom.

Helen wanted to hear Vanessa's voice again but couldn't

bring herself to dial the number. Vanessa would check her own missed calls, Helen realized. And see *her* phone number. Though Helen didn't think that Vanessa, whoever she was, would call back.

Whoever she was.

Helen left the bedroom and went to her computer. It was just a hunch. She pulled up the newswire's website and searched the staff directory. There was only one Vanessa. (*How many do you need?* she asked herself.) Vanessa Marlow, news assistant. Helen clicked on the name and took a quick breath.

She studied the girl. Though Vanessa wasn't that much of a girl. Helen would bet that she was at least thirty-five. In the harsh light of the building's lobby—the company's logo, in gunmetal, dangled above Vanessa's head—it was easy to see the beginnings of laugh lines and crinkles. But those weren't the details that Helen first noticed or the ones she kept coming back to. What struck her was the girl's mouth, painted a bright, matte retro red; her deep, sparkling eyes; her sculpted and darkened brows.

A pretty girl. One who knew how to smile for the camera. Though Helen could also see how self-consciously she presented herself. In fact, the longer Helen looked at the photograph, the more she was taken by the hints of insecurity, which the girl was trying to channel into confidence. It was just a corporate snapshot, yet it was somehow revealing.

Helen closed the window. She didn't blame the girl.

For twenty minutes she stood in the living room, in front of Tom's desk. His computer.

In all her life, Helen had never glanced at an open diary, checked a friend's medicine cabinet, tested a locked drawer. Even now, despite her great resistance, she could hear her mother's voice: *Anyone who snoops gets exactly what they deserve.* The phrase had come right back to her the day she'd discovered that email.

This is a mistake—we should talk.

It was short, and it was over: That was what he'd told her, and she'd believed him. And forgave him. Though she remembered how she'd told him to come home. *There's no way I'm doing this on my own.* Later, she'd joked about it. *You can stop worrying,* she'd said. *We can't afford to get divorced.*

She knew how to hurt someone when she wanted to. Was that what Donna, Tom's old boss, had meant at that work party?

Tom's one of the good guys. He doesn't have to try. Not like us.

Helen sat down at Tom's computer. Started it up and opened the email. News alerts, sport scores, coupons. Postings from their old neighborhood message group in the city. An occasional note from a friend.

She searched for the name Vanessa. Nothing came up. But that didn't tell her much, except that he might have been careful—for all she knew, he had another email account, maybe several. She searched his bookmarks, his downloads, his recently opened files and visited sites. But all she came up with were news stories and weather forecasts, spreadsheets and bank records.

She knew that *Vanessa* couldn't be the name missing from the email she'd found. That was more than two years ago, before Tom had started working at the newswire.

Which meant that Vanessa was someone new.

A metal taste came to Helen's mouth, and her stomach, already knotted, got even tighter. She rested her hands on the sides of Tom's chair. She was holding on, she realized. As if to stop herself from falling.

She straightened herself in her seat. Pressed her hands to her eyes, to her face. Focused.

She was always at her best when she was working.

She clicked on the icon for his hard drive. Searched, without knowing what she was looking for, open to any clue. She was a determined researcher, and she worked through her exhaustion, as she had so many times on other people's projects. Her eyes so bleary she could hardly see, she went back to Tom's email and checked the oldest folders. Then she turned to his photos. There were hundreds of them, almost all from the years after their daughters were born, and some brought sharp, sudden tears to her eyes in a way they never had before. She worked quickly, resisting the urge to linger over pictures of the girls' first steps, their first trip to the beach, their first day of preschool. She was about to open his spreadsheets when she noticed a folder at the bottom of the list. User Identity. She clicked.

Inside was another folder, Office Data. It had been recently modified and led to Main Data. Then to User Files. MioNet. Documentation. KOR. Backup Files. Work Files. ELA.

And in that last folder were image files, dozens of them. A hundred or more.

She opened one. It was a photo of a baby, wearing what looked like a hand-knitted, crocheted onesie. But that wasn't Sophie or Ilona. Whose baby was that? Did she know anyone who would dress their baby in a crocheted onesie? The photo was fuzzy and out of focus. Yet she was sure she'd seen this baby before.

She opened another photo. This was of a little girl, dressed in a toddler-sized lab coat and holding a beaker, her hair pulled back from her face like Marie Curie. It was a Halloween costume, or a birthday party outfit. Helen could see the play space in the background, its bright mat littered with scraps of wrapping paper.

There was a prickling along her spine. The little girl looked vaguely familiar, and so did the play space—was this photo from a party they'd gone to in the city? There'd been so many little children in their old neighborhood, cycling in and out of the playgrounds. She'd never been able to keep track of their names.

She opened a more recent photo. A little girl, the same one from that last shot. Here she was wearing a Chinese dress, her wild hair styled in low ponytails that fell over her delicate shoulders.

Helen stared at the photo. An uneasy pressure was rising in her chest.

She looked at the list of files, all titled by dates and numbers. She started at the very bottom. A newborn baby, maybe a week old. Home from the hospital, with a little pink-and-blue striped cap on her head.

She kept going. Here was the baby, swaddled in a wrap. In a cotton diaper. In a dress. She clicked through the images, watched the baby learn to crawl, pull herself up on a coffee table, go down a slide, play in the sprinklers. She knew those sprinklers: They were on the Upper West Side, in one of the playgrounds in Riverside Park. She kept clicking. The toddler was now a little girl. A girl who played with Magna-Tiles, who took swimming lessons, who ate sushi.

She knew that little girl.

Her hands were shaking and her body was covered in a sickening sweat. She didn't want to know. She pushed against it, refusing to allow it to come in.

And then that resistance fell away. One thought fired after another. It was like she was caught in a hailstorm, pelted by tiny shards of ice.

She knew. She knew the little girl and why Tom had hidden the photos. What she no longer knew, or even recognized— what had left her, with a force that seemed to knock the air out of her—was her own life as she'd understood it. That had been yanked away, leaving her breathless and stunned.

One of the good guys.

She shoved the laptop off the desk. With a wild sweep of her arm that sent everything in its path to the floor. It was the sort of gesture she would never make, and she didn't care. The laptop landed hard and snapped shut. Which was what she'd wanted. There was nothing more she wanted to see.

CHAPTER FIFTEEN

TOM, 2:00 A.M.

The Uptown 1 train.

Across from Tom, whose sweat was still drying from his crosstown sprint, an old man was unfolding and re-folding dozens of plastic bags that he'd taken out of a tote and spread out on the seats beside him. Farther down the train, a young guy with pumped-up arms and a neck tattoo was cracking his knuckles against the pole. And past that guy was a huge man, wild-eyed and reeking drunk, who was making his way down the length of the subway car.

The drunk man seemed to be heading toward a woman Tom had noticed the moment he got on the train. Middle-aged, frizzy hair, hospital scrubs. Beside her, gripped tight against her legs, was a stroller. Every few moments, the woman peeked beneath the canopy, and the exhaustion in her face would turn into a smile. Tom wondered how the woman had wound up here, at this time of night, with her baby on the subway. He couldn't stop looking at her.

Something about her had caught the drunk man's attention. He stopped beside the woman, his eyes shifting between her and the stroller. Then he took a step closer and leaned down. Tom moved to the edge of his seat, ready to do *something*—what that was, he didn't know—when the woman reached inside the stroller and pulled a fluffy dog onto her lap. She unscrewed a thermos and held out a cup for the dog to drink.

Tom relaxed into his seat. He glanced at the knuckle cracker, who shot a look back, his face instantly hostile. As if to say, *What's your problem?*

No problem here. The doors opened at Ninety-Sixth Street. Tom sprang out of his seat and stepped onto the platform. He climbed the stairwells, pushed through the turnstiles, and was out the door.

There he was. Alone on a traffic island. He looked at the city around him. The streets were empty, the sidewalks clear.

And for just one moment, he let himself imagine—let himself believe—that all of his sad and stupid mistakes were behind him. And that all of his future mistakes were somewhere off in the distance.

A cool breeze washed over him. It seemed to lift him up and let him go.

How many times had he retreated?

When Helen discovered that email. *What is this? How long ago?*

In Donna's office, where he'd sat as mute and unobtrusive as the Plexiglas furniture.

And later, Donna: *This is taking a toll on you. I'm telling you that as a friend.*

In the early months, it took everything he had just to get through the day. He counted the hours; he kept things small. It helped that they were always busy, that there was so much to *do*. The hours were full. But there were times—a free moment or two as he coped with the latest problem at work, tackled the most pressing task at home—when he could see his entire life in these small hours. All his failures and triumphs. All he was and would ever be.

Don't screw up, he would tell himself. *Don't hurt anyone.*

And maybe, if he tried hard enough—if he loved all of his children enough—it would all work out in the end.

Remembering that now, he felt as if his fears and regrets had been concentrated in a cold, hard knot. It was the middle of the night, and he was loitering outside of Donna's apartment building, working up the nerve to make the decision he should have made three years ago.

The doorman had watched him come up Riverside Drive. A college kid, maybe, early twenties, taking a cigarette break on his overnight shift. He was tall and gangly, too slight for his suit. He'd glanced at Tom and gave him a nod. Tom returned the nod and pretended to continue on his way, as if it were the most natural thing in the world to be strolling up this quiet residential avenue at this hour, with a cut on his forehead and no ID and a pocketful of twenties.

He crossed the street and looked back at the building. *A castle,* Elana sometimes called it. He'd always been so proud—too proud—that she lived there, even though he had nothing to do with it, hadn't been asked or allowed to contribute one cent. He pictured Elana, sleeping in her seventh-floor bedroom. She had a very nice life, and it wasn't just the skiing and sushi and exotic travel. She was loved, and there wasn't any reason to upset this life or to take any of it from her. What *he* wanted, even needed, wasn't a reason. That was what Donna would say, and she was right.

Probably.

Without realizing it, he'd wandered back down the street, stopping across from the building. The doorman leaned against its pale façade.

Tom went over to him. The doorman straightened up and reached a hand into his pocket. Not for a weapon; he was taking out his phone. At the first sign of anything crazy, this kid was calling the cops. And getting it all on video.

Tom tried for an easygoing smile.

"Nice night."

"Yeah," the doorman said. "Good night to clear your head." He noticed the bruise above Tom's eyebrow. "What happened to you?"

"I fell off a couch and hit my head on a coffee table."

The doorman's uniform billowed around his narrow frame. He seemed to be arriving at some sort of conclusion. Finally he put his phone away and took out a cigarette pack. He held it out to Tom.

Tom shook his head. The doorman exhaled over his shoulder. Though Tom hadn't smoked since college, he immediately regretted turning down that cigarette.

"So do you live in the neighborhood?" the doorman said.

"A friend of mine lives in this building," Tom said. "I came by to see her."

The doorman's eyebrows went up a notch.

"I know that it's late," Tom went on. "And she isn't expecting me. But if she knew I was here, she would want to see me."

The doorman took another drag, then looked up at the building, as if a great idea had just come to him.

"Why don't you call her?"

"I don't have my phone," Tom said. "But I could give you her cell phone number. And you could call her. Donna Bellini, Seven C. If you call her, she'll let me in."

"Now?" The doorman let out a sigh. "I can't. Come back tomorrow. Or go home and give her a call."

Tom stepped off the sidewalk and crossed the street. He pointed up at Donna's apartment.

"She's up. That's the window in her office."

With a reluctant shrug, the doorman left his post. He joined Tom across the street and craned his neck to look at the building.

"That doesn't mean anything," the doorman said. "Lots of people leave their lights on."

"Keep watching."

They waited. Donna came to the window. She seemed to be looking out at the park, but she was wearing her headset, and Tom knew she was on a call. He could tell by the way her hands rose and fell.

"See?" Tom said. "She's awake." They watched Donna whirl away and come back again. "She'll let me in, if you ask her."

"Sorry, man. Can't do it."

Tom looked at him. He needed one last lucky break.

"Look, I don't mean to cause any trouble for you," he said. "I'm not asking you to buzz her, just to call her on her cell phone. She's up—you can see that. And if she objects, if anything goes wrong, you can blame it all on me. Say I threatened you, say I was trying to force my way into the building. But none of that is going to happen. She'll let me in. It's important."

The doorman ground out his cigarette. He stared up at Donna's window for what felt like a long time.

"I better not lose my job over this," he said.

Donna opened the door, still wearing her headset. She lifted the mouthpiece away from her face.

"Give me a minute," she told Tom. "I'm just ringing off with a friend in Paris. Only time I can reach her."

She gestured in the direction of the couch and walked on to her office. He could hear her in there, laughing. Soon she came back to the living room, looking calm and well rested. She was wrapped in expensive layers, her hair loose around her shoulders, her feet bare. She put her cup of tea on the coffee table. Tom had never seen her drink tea before.

"You *do* know what time it is, right?" she said. "I'm hoping there's a very good reason for this visit." She sat on the other side of the couch, facing him. "I'd offer you a drink but maybe you've had a few already."

"I'm fine, thanks," Tom said. "And sober. Is Alan here?"

"Asleep. In the bedroom. So is Elana, in her room. And Candace is in the guest bedroom. We have an early day tomorrow." Donna glanced at the cut on his forehead. "Do you want a Band-Aid for that? SpongeBob or Hello Kitty, take your pick. Top shelf in the guest bath."

"Maybe before I go."

Donna stretched out her legs, then tucked them beneath her.

"We can talk if that's what you want to do—*talk*," she said.

"But Elana needs her sleep. If you wake her up, you're out the door."

"Don't worry. I won't disturb anyone."

She looked at him as if she could read his entire day in his face. And she *could* read him; it was almost reassuring to see that. It was part of what had gotten them through these last few years.

"So," Donna said. "Why don't you tell me whatever it is you have to say?"

There was that cold knot, a pressure in his lungs.

"I want to be in Elana's life," he said. "I want you to stay. Here, in New York."

Donna kept her back straight, her face neutral.

"You want me to stay," she repeated. A hint of anger flashed on her face, and Tom felt a surge of dread, imagining what she was about to say. She straightened her legs and propped her feet on the coffee table. "Have you thought about what *staying* means for me? It's true that London isn't my first choice. But there's a job. And there's Alan. This isn't just about you." She paused. "You get that, right?"

It was hard to meet Donna's eyes as she stared at him. But he didn't look away.

"Whether or not I go, you can be a part of Elana's life. That hasn't changed," she said. "But it would have to be official, as I've said before. And any agreement has to benefit *her*, more than anyone. She would need to know that she could depend on you. So would I." She waited. "And when Elana starts asking questions, she'll get the truth. In small pieces, as much as she's ready for. When she's old enough, she'll know the whole story."

"I understand that."

He did understand. The idea had been humming in his head these last hours, refusing to be ignored. And though it scared him—the idea of *getting the truth* and all that implied—he was also hopeful.

"You do?" Donna said. "Does that mean you'll talk to Helen?"

Tom wasn't sure what right he had to be hopeful. All day long, he had been telling himself that he was going under, that he was done. And maybe that was true. Maybe he was fooling himself; maybe he'd become completely delusional. But he had—he'd always had—a shred of hope. He held on to that and wouldn't let go.

"Yes," he said. "I will. Tonight. Today, I mean. As soon as I get home."

Donna dropped her feet from the coffee table.

"How do you think Helen will take the news?"

"I don't know."

He didn't, of course. And it pained him to think of her, right now, at home, not knowing what was headed her way. But what he thought, or hoped, was that this might be the start of a new life with Helen. A new openness. A new beginning, in every way. Maybe Helen would accept the mistakes he'd made, the lives they were living. Maybe she would even accept a different kind of family, a complicated family. Maybe they could start again and live as neither of them had for years now. Above the surface.

He thought of all the times he'd waited at night for Helen to come home from one of her runs through Devon. He always watched for her, glancing out the windows at the dark sky. And when she finally came home, stepping through the threshold, kicking off her running shoes before heading to the shower, he would study her face. She had that look he didn't understand, like she was out of reach. Despite all their years together, he had no idea what she was thinking.

He could have asked, but he'd held himself back. He hadn't wanted to intrude. He wondered what she would have said, what he would have learned if he'd stopped her, tried to talk. He could have tried, at least once.

Donna got up from the couch and crossed the room. She stood in front of the fireplace.

"You don't know," she said. "Well, neither do I. But I have a few guesses. What will you do if Helen no longer wants to be married to you?"

She looked at him. Behind her hung the black-and-white portraits of Elana. Maybe she saw something in his face, because her eyes softened.

"I can't give you any advice," she said. "If I'd known any of this would happen—"

"You never would have taken me back to your apartment," Tom said. "I know."

"No. I would have done that anyway. But I would have had a lawyer present." She smiled, then glanced over her shoulder at the photographs of Elana. "Are you kidding? I don't regret a thing. I haven't once, not even for a second. That's selfish, maybe. But I can't help feeling like I got very lucky." Donna pushed her hair over her shoulders. "On that note, I need a drink."

She went to the liquor cabinet and set out two glasses. She raised a bottle.

"This is an excellent Scotch."

"You were right before," Tom said. "I don't need one."

"Well, then." She raised her glass. "Here's to drinking whiskey alone at three in the morning."

He joined her across the room. They stood shoulder to shoulder, gazing at the windows that looked out on the park and river.

"What do you say?" he asked. "If I talk to Helen, if I make everything official? Would you be willing to change your plans?"

Donna was quiet. Tom could see both of their reflections in the window.

"I don't know," she said. "I'm not going to make any promises. But Elana deserves to have you in her life, if you can commit to being there for her. Alan's a good partner for me—for now—but he's not a *father* to her." She gave a slight shake of her head. "As for going to London...I'll have to see. I plan to make trips home. There are arrangements we could make. Don't forget, it's a two-year contract. I haven't made any promises to them, either."

Tom let out a breath he hadn't known he was holding.

"Thanks," he said. "I know it's a lot to ask."

"Don't thank me. I haven't made any decisions. I can't be a factor in whether or not you talk to Helen."

Donna swirled what was left in her glass.

"Where will you stay?" she said. "If Helen kicks you out."

"I don't know." All he knew with any certainty was where he would be spending the last few hours of this night—in Grand Central, waiting for the first train home. "I'm hoping it doesn't come to that."

"You can hope all you like. Do you think she'll leave you?"

He'd been asking himself that question for three years.

"I hope not. That's all I can say."

Donna carried her empty glass to the sink.

"I hope not too," she said. "I mean that. I hope not."

In their silence Tom could hear the quiet sounds of the building, the hiss of the radiators and pipes. Before he left, he had a request.

"Can I see Elana?" he said. "While she's sleeping. I haven't done that since she was a baby."

"All right. But if you wake her up, you're the one getting her back to sleep."

Together they walked down the hall. Donna opened the door to Elana's bedroom.

"Wait," she said. "This will help."

She touched a device on the floor. Constellations began to swirl on the ceiling. Stars flickered over Elana's bed, casting a dim glow on the patterned sheets. It was, Tom realized, a more sophisticated version of the stuffed turtle night-light in Sophie and Ilona's bedroom. But the effect was the same.

He sat down at the side of Elana's bed and heard his bones creak, just like they had that morning, when he'd sat with Sophie and Ilona at the waterfall. On his failed little daybreak adventure.

In just a few hours, there would be another sunrise. A chance to start again. That was what he wanted. What he hoped Helen would give him.

He looked down at Elana. She was clutching her pink corduroy pig, its tail entwined in her fingers even in sleep. Her hair was a dark tangle around her face. He brushed it out of her eyes.

After a few moments, he got up and stood beside Donna. He put his arm around her; she let herself lean against him as they watched Elana sleep. Then Donna led him out of the room, leaving the door open just enough to let in a narrow band of light.

They walked down the hall.

"Where do you go from here?" Donna said.

"Grand Central. Wait for the six thirty-seven. Though if it's all right, I'd like to use your phone first."

"Of course." Donna looked at the cut on his forehead again. "Why don't you take my car? You can bring it back Monday when you come into the city."

Tom let out a soft laugh.

"I can't take your car."

"You can and you should." Donna took her keys from a shelf by the door. "Basement garage, next door. Three-A." She put the keys in his hand. "I think there's something to be said for moving forward. Not losing momentum."

Tom looked at the minimalist, numberless clock that sat on Donna's bookcase. He wondered what difference a few hours would make. It might mean a lot to Helen, he thought. More than he even realized.

"Thanks," he said. "I should clean myself up."

"I'm hungry. Want a quick breakfast before you hit the road?"

"Sure," he said. "Last meal?"

Donna turned on the light in the kitchen.

"Well," she said, and smiled. "Don't say I never warned you."

CHAPTER SIXTEEN

HELEN, 4:30 A.M.

Scared but angry, Sophie stomped her foot. The pigeons scampered back a few inches, flapped and cooed, and advanced again.

This cracked up the teenage girls. They slid off their swings and came over.

"You got the right idea," the skinny one said. "You just got to do it *harder*."

The skinny girl stomped her thick-soled boot at the birds. They backed away, necks jerking.

"See?" she said. "Like that! Tell them to fuck off!"

Helen remembered herself at fifteen, how cautious and polite she'd been. She never would have cursed in front of a grown woman, a mother with little children. Not even as a joke or because she felt like being stupid, for once. Or to show off for her friends.

And now she was letting two teenagers—and not just any teenagers but girls who were smoking, drinking, cutting school—give her daughters a lesson in how to scare off pigeons.

Though that wasn't such a bad lesson, really. How to stand

up for yourself. Defend your territory. She could see that being useful, even at the age of three.

Helen stomped her foot like the skinny girl, driving the birds farther along the path.

"She's right. Do it like you mean it. Don't be scared."

Some of the birds scattered away, only to come back again. The blond girl, who had been waiting a step behind her friend, came forward. Up close, the girl looked a lot harder, more jaded, than Helen had realized. (*Beat tough* was how she looked. Though it was horrible to think about that.) The girl winked at Sophie, and her face relaxed into a smile.

"I'm gonna try," she said. "Think I can do it?"

The blond girl stomped her boot. Glancing over her shoulder at Sophie and Ilona, making sure they were watching, she sang as she chased off the last pigeon: "I'm a mean little foot, I'm a mean little foot..."

Sophie and Ilona loved that. They stomped their feet, even though the birds had gone. Sophie laughed, her tears forgotten.

"All right," Helen said. "Time to say bye. I've got to get you out of the sun."

It could have happened like that. It wouldn't have cost her anything. And with that realization came a deep, piercing sadness that grew sharper with every breath.

Helen opened her eyes and stared up at the ceiling. She'd had several versions of that dream—though it wasn't quite a dream, more like an enhanced state of wishful thinking—as she lay on the couch, listening to the floors creak. She wasn't sure how much time had passed. Though she was in her home, none of it seemed real to her. She could have been anywhere at all.

But she would rather stay in her own wishful dreams than

think about the photos she'd seen on Tom's computer. Or wonder where he was. Or why he still hadn't come home.

Because when she let herself think about *any* of it—about Tom, his lies, his betrayal of her and their daughters—she felt sure she would be consumed by her own fury. There would be nothing left of her.

So it was better not to think, for a while. Her head felt thick, swaddled in heavy layers of wool. This was what was meant by *stoned*.

Which was strange. Because she wasn't high. She was as low as she could go.

Ilona was screaming.

By the time Helen made it upstairs, Ilona was standing at the edge of her toddler bed, gripping the rails. Her eyes were wild with panic, her face streaked with tears. Helen tried to comfort her but knew it was hopeless. Ilona hadn't woken from a nightmare—she was still dreaming, unaware that her mother was even there. Sophie, just a few steps away, slept right through the noise.

Though Helen's heart pounded, her limbs seemed to be turning to water. Tom was the one who usually handled the night terrors. But she was alone, and after spending hours waiting for him, she was now dreading his return, even wishing he would disappear forever. Was this what she wanted? To be alone? She looked at her inconsolable daughter and imagined years of mysterious terrors falling solely on her shoulders. How tempting would it be to break under the pressure?

Suddenly Ilona screamed right into Helen's face, as if seeing her for the first time.

"Want *Daddy*! Not *you*!"

Looking at her daughter's angry eyes, focused squarely on her own, Helen felt a vortex of emotions—frustration and shame, disappointment and fury—spiral inside her.

But then everything stopped. Ilona flopped down on her bed, curled on her side, and put her thumb in her mouth. With her free hand, she played with the ear of her stuffed elephant.

Helen sank to her knees. She brushed her daughter's sweat-soaked hair out of her eyes. Ilona, already drifting, reached for her mother's arm. Helen stayed beside her, bent at an awkward angle, until her arm went numb. Then she carefully freed herself from her daughter's grasp and slipped out the door.

The light was blinking on the answering machine in the bedroom.

"Hey there," Tom said. "I guess you're sleeping..."

A new message. How had she missed another call? And why hadn't he tried her cell? Though she knew the answer to that: If he'd tried her cell, he would have reached her.

After a long pause, the message continued.

"I tried to call earlier," Tom said. "I hope you got my message." There was a hum in the background; he wasn't on a cell. "I'll be home soon. Missed the train—long story. But I'll tell you about it as soon as I get home. I'll explain everything."

He stopped, but it wasn't the pause of indecision she was expecting. Instead there was a confidence in his tone that surprised her, or maybe it was acceptance—of what, she didn't know. She kept listening. The missed connection felt intimate somehow.

"Well," Tom said. "I'll see you soon. Love you. Love to you and the girls. Sleep well, Helen."

A click and then the dial tone. This time he'd called from an unlisted number.

She deleted the message and unplugged the machine. If he wanted to talk to her, he knew where to find her.

———

Each revelation brought a fresh jolt of pain. That day Tom had stood behind her, rocking nervously on his heels while she looked at Donna's pictures on Facebook.

And that time he'd called Ilona "Elana."

And that email. *This is a mistake—we should talk.*

She didn't want to remember but couldn't stop. It was as if every moment of her last three years was reasserting itself, demanding to be reclassified, filed in its correct place.

If she let herself, she would implode.

She could feel it—the desire to seal herself off completely, once and for all. It would be so easy to disappear. A relief to vanish beneath her own skin.

She looked at their empty bed. Listened to the silence of the house around her.

Then she went back to her daughters' room.

Ilona was on her side, her face resting on her hands. It was hard to believe she'd ever had bad dreams. Sophie was stretched out to her full length, arms flung above her head, legs long.

Helen watched them sleep. It was the one thing that had always calmed her. And as she stood there, in the faint light coming through the window, she realized that she didn't want to seal herself off. Or live a life fueled by anger, never free of the threat roiling below the surface.

She didn't know what she would say to Tom or what he would try to say to her. But no matter what happened, or what she decided, she wouldn't live that way.

She'd already lived that life. And she was done.

She stayed a few moments longer, looking at her daughters' long limbs, their fingers and toes reaching. She would stay there all night if she could. Watching them grow.

Helen studied her hand in the light of the kitchen. There was a bruise she hadn't noticed before. A purple mark where she'd pressed her key into her palm. The next time she went to the gym, Joe would give her one of his looks, his eyes asking, *How'd you do that?* He wouldn't expect her to explain, but she didn't want any unspoken questions or concern, even from Joe. Maybe she would stay away from the gym for a few days. Maybe she would spend some time painting instead.

She wished she could talk to Karl, ask how he was, tell him she was sorry. Several times that night, she'd typed out a text, only to erase it, and not because it was too late or because he might not see it for hours, days. Just yesterday, talking to him had felt like the most natural thing in the world.

As she held her phone, it buzzed.

You awake?

Lou. She pressed her hand to her head. Debated it for a moment.

Yes. You want to call?

Her phone rang immediately.

"When do you ever sleep?" Lou said. "So. I got the Mega Crux file. Looks good! But where the hell's the printer? I thought it was right next to the hotel."

She couldn't believe it: For once, she was getting a lucky break. She kept her voice calm, trying to contain her surprise.

"We went with the other place," she said. "It's in the shopping center across the street."

"Good. Okay. I can see it from the window." There was a clinking of ice in the background; she could picture him in his corporate mini-suite. "Well, since I have you here, you wanna talk about that project for Tuesday? Though, like I said, Monday would be ideal."

She took a deep breath.

"I can't do this anymore. I'm sorry, Lou. But I need to take some time off."

It took him a moment to respond.

"How much time are you talking?"

"Well," she said. "How long could you spare me?"

"Two weeks. Any longer, the higher-ups will replace you with a freelancer right out of kindergarten."

"Thanks, Lou. That would help. It would really mean a lot."

"I'll make the calls on Monday, tell everybody they can't bother you. They'll be very disappointed."

"Thanks again, Lou."

A few years ago, when she went to Lou's office and he told her how he'd saved her job by cutting her pay, he'd predicted she would go crazy if she had any free time on her hands. She'd more or less agreed with him. *I'm glad I won't have to find out.*

Well. Now she would find out.

She saw her reflection in the window. Despite everything, for the first time today she didn't look angry.

———

She went out to the porch and sat on the bench. It seemed like she'd spent half her night here, looking out at the street. She looked at the dark lawn in front of Karl and Jackie's house and at the landscaped hedges and precise borders of Butch's house, its small but graceful dimensions illuminated by security lights, and felt like her heart was breaking all over again. As she gazed at the houses, with their tended lawns and curtained windows, the skin prickled on the back of her neck and down her spine. Someone was watching her.

She heard the scuffling footsteps before she saw him, coming along the curve of the street and out of the shadows. Nick's clothes were dirty and torn and his old army bag was in tatters. One eye was swollen shut, and his bottom lip was split. When the lights flickered on in the driveway and she got a better look, she flinched.

"Hey," Nick said. "Didn't mean to scare you."

He made his slow progression up to the porch and lowered himself onto the bench beside her. At first, she could do nothing but stare. Stare and wonder how much of it was her fault.

"Before you ask," Nick said, "it's what it looks like—I got my ass kicked. Finally, you might say. But I'm all right. More or less."

Helen looked at him, taking it in.

"Please tell me you've called Monica. She was trying to find you."

"Oh yeah," he said. "I called her from a pay phone. My phone is probably at the bottom of the creek. She wanted to come pick me up, but for some reason I wanted to come home on my own feet. To prove I could, I guess. Another fucking bad idea."

Helen saw the way he was holding himself, as if even the slightest movement hurt. Like breathing.

"You should go to the hospital," she said. "You might have broken some ribs."

"Yeah. I thought of that. Maybe I'll get checked out in the morning. I didn't want my mom to get two hospital calls in one night. You know?"

Helen couldn't help glancing at Jackie's bedroom window. She didn't want her to get that call either. She closed her eyes for a moment, thinking of what Jackie would see when Nick walked through the door.

"You want to tell me how it happened?" she said.

Nick stretched out his legs. The bottoms of his jeans were caked with mud and giving off the smell of creek water.

"Well, I guess I should've waited longer before showing up at Morey's," he said. "The idiot brothers came in. Ready for a fight." A weak smile appeared on his face. "Somehow, I managed to talk them out of it. We had drinks together. I even paid their tab. Which I now seriously regret."

Nick made an awkward attempt to hook his thumb in his pockets. The chain that was usually jangling from a belt loop was gone.

"They were waiting for me," he said. "I was the first of my

friends to leave. And these guys—these fucking idiot cowards—were waiting for me. Jumped me in the parking lot when I was alone." His eyes darkened. "My car's still there. With the headlights and every window smashed. And no one in the whole fucking bar heard a thing." He glanced at his army bag. "I found that on Osprey. My papers were blowing all over the place."

Helen let that sit for a while. She saw the scrapes and scratches on his arms, the tear in his T-shirt that exposed his ribs.

"I'm sorry, Nick." She put a hand, as lightly as she could, on his narrow shoulder. "I'm so sorry about everything."

Nick let out a soft laugh.

"Yeah, well, don't be. They only did about half of this. I mean, yeah, they jumped me—like, *tackled* me. One of them pinned my arms down before I could fight back. But after a first round, they pulled back, and I managed to pick myself up. I didn't know if they were done or just taking a break. But I ran. I could hear them shouting and one of them coming after me, skidding on the gravel. So I jumped over that fence at the end of the parking lot. And just went flying."

Helen knew the area he was talking about. The parking lot ended at a slope of rock and weeds that led down to a branch of the creek.

"That's how I got cut up so bad," Nick said. "Knocked myself out too. I don't know how long I was down there. All I know is that I woke up with my face about an inch from a puddle. If I'd landed differently, I would've drowned. In a shallow puddle. A fucking shallow puddle."

Helen pictured it. She stared at Nick, beat up, defeated. She thought again of Jackie and felt a shudder of relief.

"Hey," Nick said. "It's not as bad as it looks. All right, it's worse. But it's over."

He gave her his crooked grin.

"You think so?" she said.

"Sure." Nick's hair fell over his swollen eye. He exhaled, blowing it away. "They got their payback."

Helen thought of the car, with its streaks of rust. The guys with their arms hanging out of the windows.

"How can you be so sure?"

"They beat the shit out of me. That's what they wanted." He shrugged, then winced. "So I'll look like crap for a couple of weeks. It's not like it's the first time. Or the last time. Whatever."

He lifted his T-shirt, fanned air onto his chest. A hint of patchouli drifted from his clothes.

"You know, you don't look so good yourself," he said. "Sorry, don't mean that in a bad way. Just saying…you look a little tired or something."

Helen's eyes stung, but she smiled at him.

"I've had better days."

"Yeah," Nick said. "I'm right there with you."

He dug into his pocket and pulled out an Altoids box. There was a bowl in there, already packed.

"Small miracle," he said. "It survived the fall. You want a hit?"

"Thanks. But I'm good."

Nick inhaled but sputtered, unable to hold the smoke in his lungs. He sank lower on the bench and stared at the houses across the street.

"I know you're not looking for advice or anything," he said.

"Especially from me. But if I were you, I'd get out." He glanced at her, then down at his scraped-up knuckles. "Just pack yourselves up and get the hell out."

Helen looked at him. She would miss him one day, this good kid who made bad choices. Who could see the right way to go but decided not to take it.

"Tell me why," she said. "Why do you think we should get the hell out?"

Nick shrugged.

"I mean, it's all my friends talk about. Look at Monica. Sure, she's sticking around till next summer, but she's already gone. You can see it. She's moved on."

Nick took another hit and exhaled, sending a wispy cloud above their heads. He'd probably smoked his whole walk home, Helen realized. Not that she blamed him. She could see the sadness on his face.

"Monica told me today," Helen said. "That she's leaving."

"Yeah. Sucks." Nick shook his head, still gazing across the street. "But why would she want to stick around here? Why would anyone?"

"I plan on sticking around."

Nick raised an eyebrow at her.

"I'm serious," she said. She leaned back on the bench. "I'm not going anywhere. I'm staying."

The idea had been in the back of her mind this last hour, as she'd thought of what she'd learned from Tom's computer, and now that she'd said the words out loud, she was sure. Earlier that day, when she'd come running home from the houses across the creek, she'd thought her time in Devon was over—that this town was done with her, and the feeling was mutual. Moving on seemed like the answer. But she'd done that before. Cut her losses and found a new place, certain that it would make her problems go away. When in fact she'd taken her problems with her and added new ones. She was tired of making the same mistakes. She wouldn't cut and run again.

And Tom was right about one thing: She had been so excited to move here, so happy when they found this house. Sitting out here, looking at her street, she knew she would stay. It was the start of fall, and she would be here for the changing light and colors, the clear, clean mornings. Like now. Right *now*. It reminded her of her own childhood, when time was endless and free. She looked at everything around her, at the darkness fading, and at that moment she thought it was beautiful.

She would stay. Even if it was all so different than she'd expected.

From down the street came a sudden hissing sound. It was Butch's sprinklers, set on a timer to water his front lawn before daybreak. Helen and Nick watched the arc of water rise and fall. Each drop glittered under the security lights, refracting into tiny rainbows.

"I know I'm feeling this weed," Nick said. "But that's amazing."

"You should check out his backyard when the sun hits it in the afternoon."

"I totally will."

They sat for a few minutes, watching.

"Well," Nick said. "I better get in there. Try to clean myself up before my mom sees me."

He rose slowly from the bench, holding one arm close to his

side. He stood under the light, looking at her. Even bruised and ragged, he was working his charms. She was glad to see that.

"Hey," Nick said. "Why are you out here? Shouldn't you be, I don't know, *sleeping* or something?"

"Probably." She smiled. "But I'm not really tired."

"Okay. Enjoy the night. What's left of it."

She watched him go. Over to the east, high above the houses, she could see the first hints of light in the sky. Within the hour, Sophie would stir. She was always the first one up in the morning, often rising before the sun. She would play with her dolls or trains. Later, if she got bored, she might come looking for her mother or father or sister and tell them to *wake up and play!*

Helen looked at the sky. She didn't have much time left before everything started—all of the *busyness* that filled every day. But this day would be different, because something had ended. Whether she liked it or not, she had come to an ending.

And, possibly, a beginning.

A car came down Elm and parked in the shadows at the end of the street. She heard the door slam, the steps on the sidewalk. As Tom got closer, she saw a cut on his forehead and exhaustion on his face. He walked up the path that led to the porch, hesitated, and then sat on the bench. There was something new between them, a shared knowledge, and for a moment she felt crushed by the weight of it. She wasn't ready for this, for whatever he might say. There wasn't room for anything more than what she'd already learned.

Together they looked out at the overgrown grass of their little front lawn. She wanted to stretch out this quiet. Make it last as long as she could.

When she was very young—a few years older than Sophie and

Ilona were now, seven or maybe eight—she would sometimes slip out of her house in the middle of the night and step onto the wide green lawn. In the morning, it would feel like a dream. But for a few minutes, she would stand there and imagine what it would be like if she disappeared completely. How many hours would pass before anyone realized she was gone?

The sky was lightening. She walked down from the porch and onto the lawn. In all their time in Devon, she hadn't once seen the sunrise. She'd thought their life out here would be filled with sunrises, morning walks to watch the sun come up over the river. Though the river wasn't in the right direction, she realized. How had she not thought of that until now?

She sat on the grass. She didn't have to wait long. The sun fell on the siding of the houses around her, the yellows and blues and greens.

She waited until all of the darkness left the sky. Then she went back to the porch, where Tom was standing. Watching her. From the open door came a soft creaking.

Little footsteps. They shared a look then, the first they'd shared in a day.

"I'll start the coffee," Tom said. Helen nodded.

And they went inside and closed the door.

ACKNOWLEDGMENTS

I'm very grateful to Millicent Bennett, who brought her editorial vision, tireless energy, and brilliance to every draft, and to Lisa Grubka, whose advice, insights, and encouragement were indispensable from the very start. Many thanks as well to Dana Spector at Paradigm and to Erin McFadden at Fletcher & Co. And to the many people at Grand Central who have been instrumental in making this book possible: Deb Futter; Jamie Raab; Brian McLendon; Matthew Ballast; Andy Dodds; Nicole Bond; Siri Silleck; Sean Ford; Brian Lemus, who designed the cover; Carrie Andrews, who copyedited the manuscript; Jessica Pierce; and Tracy Dowd and the Hachette sales team.

I'd like to thank Glenn E. Dornfeld, Esq., for his extraordinary patience with legal questions, and Dr. Faraz Alam and Dr. Michael Rosen for their help with medical queries. All errors are my own.

Thanks to Chris Killheffer, for his careful reads of early drafts, and to all the members of the Columbia Fiction Foundry. Special thanks to Richard Hensley, Jon Hull, and Julia Kite for their extensive feedback, and to Ken Jaworowski, Adam Nevill, Heather Bandur, Mark Tannenbaum, Julia Pomeroy, and Lesley McMahon for their help and words of support at various points over the years.

Thank you to my family, especially my parents, Linda and Murray Itzenson. And to John, for everything.

ABOUT THE AUTHOR

Jennifer Kitses grew up in Philadelphia. She graduated from the University of Virginia and Columbia University's Graduate School of Journalism and received an MLitt in Creative Writing from the University of St. Andrews in Scotland. She has worked as a reporter for Bloomberg News, as a writer for Columbia Business School, and as a researcher for magazines. She lives with her family in New York.